# THE RED HEN CONSPIRACY

# THE RED HEN CONSPIRACY

*by*
Kenneth Benton

**Dales Large Print Books**
Long Preston, North Yorkshire,
England.

British Library Cataloguing in Publication Data.

Benton, Kenneth
    The red hen conspiracy.

    A catalogue record for this book is
    available from the British Library

    ISBN 1-85389-986-0 pbk

First published in Great Britain by Macmillan London
Ltd., 1977

Copyright © 1977 by Kenneth Benton

Cover photography © Last Resort Picture Library

The moral right of the author has been asserted

Published in Large Print 1999 by arrangement with Kenneth
Benton.

Dales Large Print is an imprint of
Library Magna Books Ltd.
Printed and bound in Great Britain by
T.J. International Ltd., Cornwall, PL28 8RW.

All the characters, institutions and events in this story are fictional. The *Ejercito Revolucionario del Pueblo* (ERP) was still active at the time of writing, in spite of the death on 19 July 1976 of its legendary leader, Mario Roberto Santucho, and several of his staff officers at the hands of the new military regime in Argentina. At the height of its power the scale of the ERP's military feats and its 'expropriations' were broadly as I have described them.

K.B.

'We deny the snobbish English assumption that the uneducated are the dangerous criminals. We remember the Roman emperors. We remember the great poisoning princes of the Renaissance. We say that the dangerous criminal is the educational criminal. We say that the most dangerous criminal is the entirely lawless modern philosopher.'

*The Man who was Thursday*
G. K. Chesterton

# CHAPTER ONE

James Caudle, Radley and St John's College, Cambridge (Second Class Honours, Eng. Lit.), sat behind his stainless steel, plastic-covered desk in a South London comprehensive school and began to sum up what he had been saying to the Sixth Form Civics Group. He had managed to hold their attention during what he felt had been a colourful exposé of the role of protest in civic duties, illustrated by a film of the student riots in Paris, but there were only ten minutes before break, and they always began to get restive about this time, just when he wanted to ram his points home.

'Now let's just see what we can deduce from all this. We all know the form one kind of protest takes—a bomb. But—'

'Bang!' said a boy at the back of the class, and there was a general titter.

'Exactly,' said Caudle. 'As Roberts, with his usual acumen, has pointed out, a bomb makes a bang. What else does it do?'

'It blows you to bits, sir,' said Roberts, encouraged by his claque, 'specially if it's full of old iron bolts and ball bearings.

11

They have to collect you in a bucket.' One of his friends began to pick up imaginary bits of human remains from around his desk, showing exaggerated disgust. A girl joined in.

The class looked expectantly at Caudle, who usually didn't tolerate this sort of thing for long, but his eyes were on his desk. He was thinking of an afternoon long ago when he had seen, through the wire defences of the compound, a little dark man in jungle-tattered uniform running out of the shelter of the tall rubber trees, with something in his hand. The child had thought it was a ball, and that the man was coming to play with him. It had come over the high fence, and his mother had screamed and rushed forward. Then there was the yellow flash, and the deafening noise, and his day-cot had been covered in blood and strange-looking bits of skin and flesh. There had been a mixture of smells, all horrible and frightening.

The class was silent, watching him curiously. Caudle looked up, and said quietly, 'Yes, Roberts, that's what it's like.' Then he raised his voice. 'But it's more likely to blow *you* to bits, my young friend, if it's you who've made the thing. It's a fact that more people have been killed in Ulster making bombs than have died in bomb attacks. But all right—Roberts makes his bomb, and throws it into a crowded restaurant, because he's protesting about something. What happens? People of your age—for this might happen to any of you—are killed or maimed for life.' At least he had their attention now. 'So what good is that as a protest? Susan.'

A girl in the front row, who had been staring at his face with adoring eyes, blushed and stammered something about bombs being dangerous things.

'Do listen, Susan. I asked you what good was a bomb as a protest?'

'It makes them take you seriously, sir.'

'Yes, that's one reason. It's what motivates a lot of bomb-throwers, I suppose. But doesn't it also rouse up everyone against you? Doesn't it draw down on the protester all the fury of the innocent people who have suffered? And what about police reprisals? We saw in that film how savagely the Paris police and special anti-riot squads reacted when the students' revolt had finally been crushed. Hundreds of people in houses near the scenes of fighting were gassed and beaten up because they just *might* have been among those who had given aid to the students. So we must conclude—Oh what is it, Spencer?'

'May I be excused, sir?'

'You can damn well wait. It's nearly

time for break. What we must conclude is that random attacks that hurt innocent people are counter-productive. But that doesn't mean there aren't other forms of protest—non-violent ones—that *can* be effective.'

'Sir, Spencer's groaning.' Giggles. 'Sir, I think he's ruptured his bladder.'

'Shut up, Marylyn. It's these other forms of protest that are right and indeed essential, if we're going to force the politicians—corrupt and self-seeking as they are—to realise that they must make way for those who are truly representative of the people, that is, the people themselves.'

'But what'll happen to Parliament, sir?'

'Parliament is out-of-date. It cannot cope with the problems and pressures of this era. It is the duty of all of us to protest, to demonstrate against the inequalities and injustices of the Establishment, whether the Government in power is Labour or Conservative. Both Parties are hopelessly out of touch with you and me, and with what we should expect as of right.'

'Coo, sir, you're a revolutionary!'

'Of course I am, Susan, and so ought you all to be.' The bell rang, and there was clatter of desk lids and stamping feet. Caudle roared, 'Wait till I say you can go, you hopeless gang of layabouts! *Sit down!* That's better. All right. Now try and remember enough of what you've seen and heard for your essays. The title is—take it down, Spencer—"The Right to Protest", and I want to have well-written essays from all of you, at least three sides, by next lesson.'

'What'll you do if we don't, sir? Bloodless protest?'

Caudle smiled. Perhaps something might stick, after all.

In the Common Room he slung his gown over the back of a chair, to stake out his claim, and went over to the coffee table. A colleague said, 'There's a telegram for you, Jim.'

Why did they insist on calling him Jim? He went to the message board and took down the envelope, then collected a cup of coffee and a biscuit and went back to his chair. The telegram was short: 'Want to see you urgently. What about Saturday morning eleven. Love. Letty.'

Caudle sighed. He had promised to go shopping with Pat on Saturday, and she'd sulk if he scrubbed it. But Letty's word was law. He telephoned a two-word reply, put money in the box, and wondered if his ancient Morris would make the trip without stalling.

# CHAPTER TWO

St Mary's College lies behind the Cambridge Backs, with its Fellows' Garden running down to Queen's Road, overlooked by the rooms of Doctor Letitia Hennessy, Lecturer in Modern English Literature and known both for her scholarly works of literary criticism and, as 'Harriet Pringle', for a long series of successful crime novels. She was also known, in fact notorious, for the originality and extremism of her political views. She was working on the page-proofs of a new, action-packed thriller when Caudle came in.

There was nothing small about Letty. She was five feet eight, broad with it, and busty, with surprisingly well-turned legs—what you could see of them under the long and shapeless tweed skirt—and small, elegant feet in expensive shoes. She had kept her hair as red as when, forty-five years ago, she had been an unruly, brilliant undergraduate in the first years of St Mary's existence. Her face was commanding, with bushy grey eyebrows and fierce grey eyes, softened now as she looked up at the tall young man in the doorway. He came forward and kissed her affectionately.

How touching he looks, she thought, and really almost handsome. The withdrawn, rather severe look of the long, smooth-skinned face, with its fine bone structure, was tempered by the large brown eyes and sensitive mouth. He ought to have married someone better than that ordinary little Patricia, always whining and using the wrong fork. But he'd conceived it his duty to marry into the plebs. That was his trouble. He was *bon comme le pain*. She patted his shoulder.

'Come out into the garden. It's too bloody hot in here,' she said. 'And anyway, they've probably got this place bugged, and I want to talk secrets.'

Caudle laughed delightedly. 'Not in St Mary's, Letty dear. Even Special Branch couldn't do that.'

'You'd be surprised. There was a girl wandering round, prying, until I showed her off. And she had big feet. Or perhaps you think the President of the New Revolutionary Group isn't worth their attention?'

'Of course you are, Letty, but I hardly think we top their list of dangerous subversives. On the whole, we're very well-behaved.'

'That's just what I want to talk to

17

you about, where no long-eared capitalist lackeys can hear us. Wait a mo'.' She lumbered over to the window. 'There's no one on the bowling-green. I'll take you on.'

'You always invent the rules as you go along. I opt out.'

'No you don't. If you lose you pay a quid into Group funds.'

'And if I beat you?'

The fine grey eyes lit up. 'I'll pay in a lot more than that.'

'How much?'

She took him by the ear and whispered into it, 'What say fifty thousand nicker?'

Caudle laughed. 'I know you make a packet out of thriller royalties and TV scrips, but you aren't worth that much.'

'That's what you think. And what I thought till a couple of days ago. Come on, before someone else bags that damn lawn.'

Caudle followed her along the brick-flanked passage, aseptic, with gleaming oak floor and ugly, functional windows, down the concrete stair and out into the main court, with its spread of cropped turf. The long vac had begun, and there were few undergraduates to be seen. An arched doorway led to a small court and the gate of the Fellows' Garden. There was an irregularly-shaped lawn, surrounded by expanses of flowering shrubs and carefully tended maples and Japanese cherries. Quite unlike the magnificence of the college gardens of St John's, thought Caudle nostalgically, but peaceful and charming in its own way. Bees were busy among the flowers, whose scent came drifting to him through the hot sunshine as he stepped on to the shaven green. He sighed, guiltily, as he thought of the three years he had spent in this town, and how wonderful it had been—a world of friendships, and night-long discussions and lazy pleasures, and crude practical jokes; the atmosphere of ideas, some as old as time, some as new as tomorrow. The guilt came from the fact that, after all, he was a revolutionary Marxist, wasn't he?—and Cambridge was as reactionary as you could get. He opened the wooden chest at the side of the green and lifted out four rather battered woods.

Letty kept her secret well into the game, which was a peculiar one, in that the St Mary's bowling-green was a very odd shape, owing to the intrusion of various flower-beds, and there were special rules laid down by generations of female dons which made things difficult for the uninitiated. She waited until they were close together, near the jack, and then said, 'One of my Premium Bonds has turned up lucky.'

19

'Good for you. How much?'

She took the white jack and sent it rolling away to come to a stop at the very edge of the grass. 'I hit the jackpot, boyo. I told you. Fifty thou.'

'Good grief! You're joking, Letty.'

'I am not.'

Caudle dropped his wood and kissed her. 'But that's simply marvellous. You'll be able to retire and finish your book on Lawrence Stern. I'm—I'm delighted for you.'

'What are you waiting for? It's your go.'

He rolled his wood, which passed the jack and ran off into a flower-bed. 'Look at that,' he said. 'You've got me excited, you old vixen. You did it on purpose. Were you joking about the prize?'

'Not on your Nelly. It's the truth, my lad. And I'll tell you something—let's stop this game, I was going to beat you anyway—I'll tell you something. I don't need the stuff, but the Group does.'

She was walking back across the green towards a wooden bench artfully shielded by a windbreak of Cupressus Lawsonii, and Caudle caught her up and took her arm. 'Don't be a fool, Letty. You're not really well off, not so that you can turn your back on fifty thousand quid, and you've been very generous to the

20

Fund already. That Xerox you gave us is absolutely invaluable. Stash the stuff away for your old age. You'll find uses for it.'

'Nonsense! I can manage perfectly well until I kick the bucket. You don't get the point, James. This fifty thou is money that comes from a misguided scheme for supporting the Government by adding to its revenue. All right, I'm going to use it to help bring the Government down. That's poetic justice for you. I'll get a real kick out of it.' They sat down on the old bench, and she patted his knee. 'The Fund can have the lot.'

'Jesus! The whole lot?' Thoughts raced through Caudle's mind. 'I'll have to call a meeting of the Council.' He was Honorary Secretary of the New Revolutionary Group, as well as acting Treasurer, now that the chartered accountant who had previously lent his services had taken a job abroad.

'No, James, it's too risky. One of those blabbermouths might leak it to the press. Let's first have a good look at this thing, you and I. Now, we've got—what is it?—twelve hundred members?'

'Yes. But only about a thousand pay their subs regularly. So our total income is about two thousand a year.'

'Right. And what would you say our members have achieved this year? What's our greatest success?'

Caudle frowned. 'We backed the Troops Out demo, and had a good turn-out, by and large.'

'And did it have the slightest effect on the Government's determination to keep up the military presence in Ulster?'

'Of course not, Letty. But it did show popular feeling.'

'The feelings of a very small minority, James. It didn't do a blind bit of good, and you know it. We're just too few on the ground.'

'It's not only that,' protested Caudle. 'It's because everyone knows we're pacific, non-violent, law-abiding people, and they don't give a hoot what we say or think.' He kicked out viciously at a pebble lying on the gravel path, and sent it hopping across the lawn. Then he apologised, and went to pick it up and restore it to the path.

'But if we had three times as many members,' she insisted, 'surely we could branch out and be more *active?* Besides which, you'd treble the income and have money to spare for publicity.'

'It'd treble the outgoings, too, Letty,' said Caudle gently. He was very fond of this formidable lady, and enormously admired her qualities, but arithmetic wasn't one of her strong points. 'But I'll work out some figures ...'

'Yes, please do that. But there's something else ...' Abruptly Letty got to her feet. 'Let's go and have some food. Not in Hall. I'll not have you pulled to pieces by those of our High Table harpies who've stayed up, like me. I've booked a table at the "Garden House".'

They walked across Queen's Bridge, around the 'Anchor', and into the pleasant grounds of the hotel. The table was in one of the floor-length windows facing the sun-dappled garden, with the river in the background. People were drinking at the white tables on the lawn, and through the trailing willow branches Letty and Caudle could see swinging punt-poles and the heads of those wielding them as they drifted past.

'It's lucky I got a table,' said Letty, glancing with mild distaste at the foreign tourists filling the dining-room. 'Now for some food.' She had a theory that Caudle, who was as thin as a lath, never got enough to eat at home, so she ordered large steaks and two pints of Guinness, a drink to which she was very partial.

It was when she put down her tankard and began to attack a plate laden with meat, French beans and roast potatoes that she reverted to her plan. 'I get around a lot, you know, what with lectures and the broadcasting spots, and I meet masses of intelligent people who aren't just dons, cock and hen. A lot of them are coming to the conclusion that our so-called democratic system is out-dated and threadbare, and that the people want the facts of life spelled out to them straight and unpolluted, instead of getting them made palatable by these poncey politicians and TUC time-servers and the God-damn media. But they never see *The Banner,* and some haven't even heard of our Group. And yet that's just what we're for—to tell the people what to think and make them get together and find representatives they can trust.'

Caudle nodded enthusiastically. Although neither he nor Letty had any real contact with the masses they were both convinced they knew what 'the people' wanted—or at least what was good for them. In a spirit of euphoria induced by Guinness and right thinking they cleared their plates.

'So,' continued Letty, taking an inspiring pull at her tankard, 'we've got to expand the Group *somehow* and make *The Banner* so full of pep that workers will queue up to buy it when they come off shift. Paid professional organisers, increased recruiting, our own assembly places, wider distribution of the paper, more demon-strations, calls for referenda, mass meetings ... That's what we want, and if the fifty

24

thousand isn't enough there's a way we might get a lot more, as I'll explain later. But first let's think how we can use that fifty thou.'

'What d'you mean—a lot more?'

'Never mind. Concentrate on my windfall for a start.'

'I'll do some thinking and write to you.'

'Don't let's waste time. When we've finished luncheon we'll go back to my rooms and have coffee.' She looked at her watch. 'There's a rather dim first-year child doing the special course, and she's coming in for a tutorial in a quarter of an hour. I shan't keep her long—I've made notes on her essay already. While I deal with her you can be working out a plan. O.K?'

A pretty, frightened girl, wearing the short undergraduate gown, was waiting when they returned to the College. Caudle took a pencil and some paper and went into Letty's bedroom to make his calculations. He could hear through the door the older woman's voice, speaking quietly for the most part, encouraging the girl to explain her ideas, indulging occasionally in mild sarcasm, but with good humour. She even made the girl laugh. Caudle finished his work and stood by the door listening, remembering what it was like to hear Letty analysing an essay with remorseless skill.

She was saying, 'And really, Joanna, you must be careful of these clichés. Steer clear of "hopefully". It's a straight translation from the German and almost always used wrong here. Look at what you wrote—"Hopefully, the day will come—" and so on. *You* may hope, but the day can't; it isn't a person. And why d'you think I scored through "this moment of time"?'

'I suppose it's a cliché, Doctor Hennessy, but people do say it, don't they?'

'They do, but you mustn't *write* it. Still less in an essay, which is a form of literature. *Every* moment is a moment of time, isn't it? It's as bad as saying "this day and age". You're quite intelligent enough, my dear, to choose your phrases for their meaning, and not because you've heard some illiterate politician use them on the telly. All right. That'll do.'

'Thank you, Doctor Hennessy.' Caudle heard the scraping of a chair.

When he went in Letty was lighting a cigar. She looked at him through a cloud of smoke. 'Well, James? Sit down and tell me. I'll make some coffee.'

He waited for the Mouli coffee-grinder to finish. 'You remember what Blackham told us at the AGM?'

'I never listened to Blackham.' She had been delighted when the Honorary

Treasurer, a cautious chartered accountant, had left.

'He pointed out that the Group had no corporate existence, and that some time the Inland Revenue would get wise to us. If we put fifty thousand pounds into the kitty they'd swoop down on us like a flock of vultures.' He paused, looking at her unhappily. 'That's Point One.'

'You're as bad as Blackham. Don't go into details about the other points. What's the verdict?'

'It just isn't enough. The sort of expansion you were talking about before lunch would swallow up the income from your windfall and leave us heavily in the red. But we *could* do something more modest that would raise numbers and attract a bit of attention. I'll explain ...'

'No, you won't. Modesty never did any political movement a blind bit of good. Actually—' Letty tapped the ash from her cigar, thoughtfully, and added, 'I spent a lot of last night trying to do the sums, and I came to the same conclusion. Just wanted you to confirm it. What we need is millions, James, not bloody thousands. Then we'd get somewhere.'

'Listen, Letty. Let's stay as we are. If you'd like to be ready with a few thousand to help me out if I get into trouble with the Revenue or something unforeseen, that's

27

fine, but for Heaven's sake keep the rest for yourself.'

'And leave the Group to carry on in its amiable way, getting nowhere? No, James, I've got a better idea. What d'you know about the ERP in Argentina, the People's Revolutionary Army?'

'That lot? They're Trotskyists, like us, aren't they, but far from peaceable. They carry a lot of weight, I believe.'

'They're the most powerful and best-organised guerrilla movement in Latin America, and that's saying something. Although their numbers are small, not more than a few thousand, I think, they're well-trained and work under strict discipline, like soldiers. They have to surrender their salaries, if they are regularly employed, to the central funds and are given back what they need. It's rather like a sort of lay apostolate. You like Bach, don't you?' She went over to the radiogram, selected a record and put it on the turntable. The sound of a Bach fugue began to issue from the stereo loudspeakers.

Caudle was amused. 'What's that for? To neutralise the hidden mike?'

'We can't be too careful. Now listen. The ERP is extremely rich, even by Argentine guerrilla standards, where the record take is fifty million dollars from a single ransom demand.'

'You're joking!'

'I'm not. It happened in September 1974. Two brothers called Born, snatched by the Montoneros, a rival group. But the ERP has amassed more money in the long run. Unlike the Montoneros they confine their attacks to the military and police forces, and the kidnappings to the very rich industrialists and the foreigners operating in Argentina. They can afford to look forward to the future, and also beyond their own frontiers.'

Caudle felt a quiver of excitement in his stomach. 'What are you getting at, Letty?'

'It's just an idea.' She stubbed out her cigar. 'I told you I came to the same conclusion as you, that fifty thou wouldn't make all that difference to our campaign. But suppose we used it as a means of hiring professionals who could get us the sort of funds we need?'

Caudle was on his feet, stammering protests.

'Sit down, James ... That's better. Now don't speak until I've finished. These ERP people are educated, patriotic, dedicated Marxists who have brought a new dimension to the art of raising political funds without doing harm to anybody who doesn't deserve it. They are interested in forming international relationships, and in fact some of their most successful operations are over the frontier in Uruguay, Chile and Bolivia. Incidentally, they are for the most part drawn from the upper and middle classes, like us.'

Caudle said, 'That's rot. Our members are a cross-section of the nation as a whole.'

'Nonsense! Look at the members' list. We just don't attract the so-called working class, any more than we attract stock-brokers. We're a movement of educated, concerned and intelligent people, and that's how it ought to be. It's our job to point the workers in the right direction, and lead them.'

'And you're proposing to tie us up with a bunch of South American terrorists? At the first whisper of a connection with the ERP half our members would run away like scared rabbits.'

'That's why they mustn't know anything about it.' There was a fighting gleam in Letty's grey eyes. 'This has got to be the best kept secret in England. Only you and I will be in the know.'

'But what d'you expect to get out of the ERP? The loan of some of their thugs?' He looked at Letty in despair. 'Why on earth should they, if they're rolling in money already?'

'I've a hunch they might like the idea. If they don't, *tant pis*, we're back where we started. My proposition is this, that they send over a unit of their trained "soldiers", carry out a few profitable operations, and give us half the take.'

'They'd keep the lot. Why wouldn't they?'

'Because without us they'd draw too much attention to themselves. I've heard about how they carry out their work, and it's impressive. But what they have to depend on is a thorough knowledge of the terrain, the target, the escape routes, the hiding places and so on. Everything, a skilled kidnapper requires to bring off a neat job without risk, even to the victim.'

'Except when they cut off one of his toes to ginger up the reaction,' protested Caudle disgustedly.

'As a rule,' said Letty placatingly, 'they don't have to. It's all a question of planning and expertise. But as I was saying, we could give them all the background information they'd need. It's just the kind of research I do for my suspense stories. And as for targets—I could make out a list without reference to anybody. In fact, I jotted down a few names last night. Where did I put it?' She went to the desk and rummaged through her capacious handbag. 'Here it is. Take Gerald Clements, for a start. Rich as Croesus. He could part with a hundred thousand and not notice it.'

'But he's the Dean of St Luke's and—wait a minute—he's a very influential literary critic. Did he pan your last book?' He looked at her accusingly.

'That's neither here nor there,' said Letitia quickly. 'I chose him because he lives alone except for an old housekeeper in a big house in North Oxford. I've been there half a dozen times and I could draw a sketch of the lay-out, I think.'

Caudle burst out laughing. 'We've got to be serious, Letty. Your crime-writer's imagination is running away with you. Thugs and terrorists are *out.*'

'Put on another record, dear, and let's have a drink. There's some vintage brown port in the cupboard.'

Caudle put a Chopin record on the turntable and found the decanter and glasses. She took a sip and looked across at him. 'D'you like it? You ought to.'

'It's a wonderful port. But don't evade the issue. I say this idea of yours is an amusing pipe-dream but I wouldn't touch it even if you were serious.'

'Why not?'

'Because the ERP operations you describe with such enthusiasm are just another form of capitalism, which we believe is wrong. Secondly, if we did what you suggest, we'd be receiving stolen money—or if not stolen something very similar—and we'd be for it.'

Letty smiled. 'I will dispose of your two objections summarily,' she said, in her debating voice. 'First, it isn't capitalism; it's money levied on the rich for revolutionary ends.'

'That's sheer sophistry, and you know it. What about us being nabbed for an indictable offence, to wit, receiving the proceeds of criminal extortion?'

'Dear boy, you've got it wrong. Any money gained by us would be a free gift from a fraternal movement to our funds.'

'You're thoroughly immoral, Letty, and very persuasive, but I won't play.'

'That's a pity, James,' said Letty mildly, watching him over the rim of her glass. 'You might have liked the trip.'

## CHAPTER THREE

'Trip?' Caudle looked at Letitia's bland face warily.

'I'd have thought you might like to spend, say, a week in Buenos Aires. There's a man who'd show you round.'

'What man?'

'The ERP sent over a man calling himself Juan Santos, but that isn't his real name. He was making a sort of fact-finding tour of Europe. He'd been to Paris to talk to the Fourth International people and afterwards came here and met quite a few revolutionary leaders. Mostly the International Marxists and the Workers' Revolutionary Party, but also some of the International Socialist factions. He called on me early last week, and we had a useful chat.' She smiled. 'He invited me to go to B.A.'

'But surely the IMG and the WRP people are much more up his street. Is he inviting them, too?'

'No. Just me. He thinks the other British Trots are getting too much involved in infiltrating the Labour Party and the unions, and neglecting the direct attack. Whereas, in his view, an independent movement like ours, going straight for the basic faults of society, can do much more for the cause of Marxism worldwide.' Letty drained her port glass, and added thoughtfully, 'He may have been buttering me up, but he seemed to mean it. This policy of entryism—and what a word that is!—is bound to make the Labour and TUC people close their ranks, and all the effort will be wasted.'

'Get back to Santos, Letty,' urged

Caudle. 'What did he suggest, exactly?'

'That I should go over to Argentina and have talks with his principal colleagues, or at least some of them. Of course, at the time I didn't think there was a hope in hell of it coming of—we simply couldn't afford the trip. Then two days ago I got this letter from ERNIE.'

'You might have told me earlier, Letty, all the same. You're getting twisty. O.K, but why me? Why don't you go?'

'I'm too busy with this latest book, and they've got a promotion programme lined up for me. You're the only one I trust. And you'd get on with Santos. He seemed a sensible person, and absolutely on the ball. Very impressive indeed. He'd be your first contact—that is, if you decided to go after all—and he'd make your visit very well worthwhile, I'm sure. He's a well-mannered young man,' added Letty, changing direction. 'He tried to kiss my hand.'

'I see. But I still want to know why you never mentioned this visit of Juan Santos to me or anyone on the Council, as far as I know.'

'I can see you feel hurt about it, James, but it was only sense. I had to check up before going forward with the idea, so I've been having talks with John Parsons, who's one of the Latin-American historians. He's a fellow of Caius. It was he who told me about the ERP being the best disciplined and best-trained of the guerrilla groups. Parsons is a lefty himself, and he admires the ERP wholeheartedly. They do everything in style—beautiful girls, fast cars, their own helicopters, their shadow government ready to take over—it sounded very impressive. You'd better kit yourself out with what you need. I'll write to Santos; I've got his card somewhere.'

'A terrorist with a visiting card,' jeered Caudle.

She was turning out her handbag again. 'Here it is. It just says "Juan Santos, Abogado", with a POB number in Buenos Aires. So he's a lawyer. I believe almost everybody is in South American society. You speak Spanish fluently, don't you?'

'Yes, but it's rusty. School standard and then that year in Peru as a volunteer in a *barriada*.'

'Well, then, you'll be O.K. Your summer holiday starts in the middle of July, doesn't it?'

'The twentieth. But I haven't said I'd go, Letty. Can I take Pat?'

'No, that you can't do. I told you, James, this has got to be a very well-kept secret, or we'll all be in the shit. Patricia mustn't know a thing about what we're doing. The excuse for your visit to B.A is that I'm paying you to do research for a new thriller of mine. And why you? Because you speak Spanish and can do the job in the long vac.' She looked at him triumphantly.

'You've worked it all out, haven't you? Won't it cost the earth?'

'The return trip is about five hundred and sixty quid, I think, and Parsons says the hotels are expensive with the exchange as it is. I'll allot fifteen hundred for the job, chargeable against Income Tax as necessary research, and if you've got anything left over you can keep it.' She saw him beginning to protest. 'Or say three hundred for you as a fee and the rest you can either keep or put into the Fund. You've got to make a profit, or Patricia will get suspicious.' She got up and stretched herself. 'It's always the little mousy ones that worry at a thing with their tiny teeth until they've spilt it all over the floor.' She stopped, realising that she had let a rather vaguely conceived metaphor run away with her.

Caudle was already angry. 'Why do you have to be so damned condescending about Pat? She's completely loyal, both to me and the Group, and she's thinking of giving up her job to help more on the admin side.'

'I'm sorry, James. I didn't mean anything. She's a very nice little thing—'

'There you are again. She's not a *thing;* she's—'

'The woman I love,' put in Letty, tartly. 'Go on, say it.'

'Why not, if it's true.'

'Is it, James?'

'Of course it is. I do wish you wouldn't go on about Pat. I've told you our marriage hasn't turned out quite as we'd both hoped, but that's because we can't have children and still haven't been able to adopt one. But that's all. She's a good wife, and I stick by her.'

'Pity. It'd do you a world of good to have an affair with a girl who'd give you hell.'

Caudle flushed angrily. 'I suppose that's to be the spin-off from the Argentine trip. Well, you can stuff that idea—All right, I'm sorry. But the way you talk about Pat gets on my wick.'

'I'm an old fool, that's my trouble. I apologise, James, and I'll watch my silly tongue when I speak about Pat. And don't forget I'm very fond of her ... And she likes me too, I think. Anyway, she calls me—er—Aunty.'

Caudle smiled, his face lighting up. He kissed her heavily-powdered cheek. 'All right, I'm on for this scheme of yours, so long as there's going to be no commitment to give direct help in snatch jobs. Frankly, I don't think for a moment they'll agree. But it'll do us all good to learn a bit more about fraternal movements. And I don't see why—if your hare-brained scheme comes to nothing—we shouldn't have a useful series of discussions in *The Banner* on foreign revolutionary Marxist movements. Later, we might do the history of the SDS in the States and Germany, and show where they went wrong.'

She looked at him with an enigmatic smile. 'That's a very good idea. Why not, indeed?' Now, let's get down to nuts and bolts. Just in case Santos agrees to your visit—and of course, he might still back out—I'll work out a synopsis of a suspense story based in Argentina and you'll have to study it carefully. I'll give you a list of questions which you can show to anyone who's curious. And of course, you'll have to get answers, and I shall want modern maps and plans, and a few examples of revolutionary journals. You've got to *work* your cover. In the meantime I'll get a letter off to young Santos tonight.'

As Caudle went out through the modern brick arch of the College into West Road his step was buoyant. He smiled as he remembered Letty's vibrant voice expounding her outrageous scheme. She had been one of his tutors ten years ago, when he had come up to Cambridge after a year working as a volunteer in a squatter settlement in Lima. A shy, withdrawn young man, with bitter memories, and one for whom his widowed father had never shown much love, he had found the ebullient society of the University bewildering. Letty had been his first real friend; then there'd been others, but they had drifted away after coming down and finding their own different jobs and different ways of life. Only Letty had remained as his staunch friend and ally, and it was she, of course, who had won his enthusiasm for basic Marxism.

If she wanted him to make this trip, he told himself, he must humour her. But even as he formulated the decision he knew he was being hypocritical. His pulse was already quickening at the thought of a new, strange country to explore, and meeting new, dangerous, unpredictable people.

# CHAPTER FOUR

Caudle parked the old Morris outside the door of his house in Stockwell—there was no garage—and let himself in. There was a smell of cooking, and Pat was in the kitchen, wearing an apron over a smocked shirt and well-worn jeans. She dropped a spoon, which fell clattering to the stone floor, and ran to kiss him. Her face was flushed and perhaps a little shiny.

'I was so afraid the Red Hen would have kept you,' she said her voice muffled by the shoulder of his jacket. 'How is she?'

'In bouncing form, as usual. What are you cooking?'

'It's something I found in the *Woman's Own* Sheila lent me, but it doesn't seem to be coming out right. Never mind, you're home. Go and get yourself a drink. I shan't be long.'

He went into the sitting-room. It was looking unusually tidy, but nothing could make it attractive. The evening sun shone mercilessly on the worn carpet and the bits and pieces of furniture they had bought at sales or acquired as handouts from relatives. But it was home. He washed, and went down into the cellar, switching on the light.

At one end of the low-ceilinged room was the Xerox duplicator on which two thousand copies of *The Banner* were run off every month, and at the other his winery, proudly displaying racks of home-made 'moselle', 'claret' and 'burgundy' and also—a recent innovation—an oak cask in which twelve gallons of an extra-cheap wine made from rice and raisins was still gently seething. This had the great advantage that you could drink it within weeks of manufacture, and was intended for bulk consumption by the Group's voluntary helpers.

This, he felt, was an evening for celebration, because at least there was a chance that something was going to happen. He carefully drew out a three-year-old bottle of wine made from concentrated burgundy grape-juice and took it up to the kitchen to decant. The cork came out with a loud pop, and the wine was frothing as he poured it out. Pat had disappeared.

She came down as he was sipping the wine in his chair by the open window that looked out on to a scrap of sun-baked garden. Pat was wearing a long dress, something vaguely 'ethnic', with a heavy double necklace of wooden beads and her silver ear-rings. And she'd put on eye make-up—as she so often did, he remembered with a smile—when he came from a visit to Cambridge.

'You look smashing,' he said, and meant it. Her small eager face was framed by long straight hair. What colour could you call it? he wondered. Dusty brown with a hint of silver, like the dried seaweed on the Esterel beach where they had once lain all night.

'What's funny?' she asked suspiciously.

'I was thinking your hair looked like seaweed.'

'Thanks a lot, but at least it's natural,' she said pointedly. 'Not like—And what's that you're drinking?'

'A Caudle invention, sparkling burgundy.' He pulled forward a cane chair. 'Sit down and I'll get you a glass. It's the red '73, not too dry—in fact it's a trifle sweet. You'll like it!'

'I thought you were going to leave it for another year. What's so special about tonight?'

'Coming home is always special,' he said lightly.

Her eyes lit up. 'D'you mean that, James?' She put out a small hand towards him, tentatively. He bent and kissed her thin wrist.

'Of course I do. What sort of a day have you had?' It was Saturday, and the school where she taught nature-study to

43

junior forms was closed.

Her eyes—expressive hazel eyes, that were so vulnerable—took light again, giving her little face a sudden flash of beauty. 'I made sandwiches and went to the Zoo. That pair of macaws I told you about are teaching their babies to fly. They're ever so pretty.'

'How much does that bird-watching tour cost, the one that takes in some of the famous sanctuaries?'

'It's a hundred and eighty-two pounds, James.' She had the figures pat. 'That's three hundred and sixty-four the two of us, and there'd be bound to be extras. We can't afford it, love. You said we were overdrawn again.'

'Yes. Yes, it's a lot of money.' He finished his glass. 'Now what about that food.'

Afterwards, when he'd intended to tell her about the Argentine trip, he didn't. After all, it might not come off, he told himself, although he had a strong, excited feeling that it would. They were sitting again by the window, Pat contentedly sewing, when he remembered something that had struck him earlier, what Letty had said about entryism. It was true that the other Trotskyist parties were going the wrong way to achieve revolution. Infiltrating their people into the Labour

44

Party and the TUC might seem like an approach to power, but it would be constitutional power even if they could succeed, and that was not the way of true Marxism.

Caudle went back to his desk, brought back a writing pad and biro to his chair, and began to draft a scathing editorial for *The Banner:* 'ENTRYISM: THE GREAT ILLUSION'.

His pen ran fast over the paper. There was no need to refer to books or periodicals; the Trotskyist infiltrators were well known, and he could flay them with sarcasm without risk of libel. They were betraying the tenets of their professed faith by consorting with the enemy; they could not descend to the level of the political wheeler-dealers without being defiled; they would be corrupted by their first contact with power and influence.

There was something about that last sentence that made him slightly uneasy, and his thoughts flew to Letty and Juan Santos, and Buenos Aires. But he shook his head and re-read the draft, correcting, cutting out unnecessary words and adding bite. He counted. Five hundred and forty-five words. Just right. Now the knock-out blow: 'True Marxism and democracy, in any form, are utterly incompatible; we mix them at our peril.'

Caudle stretched his long legs. Sunday tomorrow. He took his wife to bed and they made love. The earth didn't turn—it never had—but it was very sweet, and they were together against the world.

## CHAPTER FIVE

A month later the Caudles were sitting in the foyer at West Kensington air terminal, waiting for the bus which would take him to Heathrow. It was a hot afternoon. Pat was looking forlorn, but she was determined not to cry until after he had gone. She asked, 'You're sure you've got that summary, or whatever it is, of the story?'

He patted his briefcase. 'I'm going to study it in the plane. There'll be time enough. Nearly twenty hours, for God's sake. Darling Pat, you're going to have a whale of a time on that bird tour.'

She smiled wanly. 'But can we really afford it?'

'I told you. Letty's giving me three hundred quid as a fee for the research and all my expenses, so we'll have enough for your tour and still pay off the overdraft.'

'It's lucky we can both be away at the

same time. I'd hate it otherwise. At least I'll have something to think about, apart from you and all those foreigners.'

He put his arm round her shoulders. 'It isn't just lucky, you goose. I told you I'd chosen Aerolineas rather than BA so as to fit in with your trip. I'll be back in a week, and you'll return the previous day, so it works out perfectly. And we've got *The Banner* off in good time, so there's no need to think of that for another three weeks. You won't be afraid, being in the house alone for a couple of days, will you?' he asked anxiously. He ought to have thought of that before.

'No. Not afraid. But I shall miss you so much. It's the first time you've been away for more than a day or two for those beastly congresses.' She paused for a moment. 'James.'

'Yes, love.'

'There *is* some connection with the Group in all this, isn't there?'

'No, darling. None at all.' He seemed to be lying with accomplished ease. 'I'm just doing this job for Letty so that she can make a success of her next book. She couldn't have done the research herself because she doesn't speak Spanish.' He wished he could tell Pat the truth, but she'd be even more miserable if she knew it.

She turned her face away.

The Tannoy crackled and spoke hoarsely. 'Passengers for Heathrow please go to the departure gate. The coach is waiting.'

Caudle bent down to pick up his hand luggage, then dropped it and hugged his wife. 'I'll send you a cable when I arrive.' He draped his duffle coat over his arm. 'I'll need this, I expect. It'll be winter down there.' He kissed her again, feeling half sad to leave her, half thrilled by the unknown. 'But it'll be summer when I get back and we'll have fun.'

She watched his tall, rather awkward figure, the Tyrolese hat they had bought on a package holiday to Austria set at a jaunty angle as he walked through the gate. She felt herself shivering, which was silly, because it was a very warm day. It hurt her that he had lied about the real reason for his journey. Letty again, thought Pat resentfully.

## CHAPTER SIX

Detective Chief Superintendent Garrard, head of the Ultra Left-Wing Movement Squad in Special Branch, looked out of the window of his office in New Scotland

Yard, frowning. He had finished reading two reports, which now lay on his desk. The first was five weeks old:

*ULM 462/76*
*14.6.76*

*To: Head of ULM Squad*
*From: Det. Sergeant Cobham*

Xavier LOPEZ SUAREZ @
Juan SANTOS

*On receipt of ULM 160/76/7A of 3.6.76 from MI5, based on a report from MI6 representative, Buenos Aires (source Argentine Sec. Service), the a/m Argentine national, suspected of being a staff officer on the High Command of the Ejercito Revulucionario del Pueblo (ERP, People's Revolutionary Army), was put under surveillance during his visit to the UK between 5.6.76 and 12.6.76.*

*Subject stayed at the Hilton Hotel, London, and also visited parts of the country in a hired Rover 2000. The object of his sojourn in London and these trips to the provinces was obviously to make contact, apparently for the first time, with members of extreme Marxist movements, and the visits to Glasgow, Coventry, Manchester and Birmingham were made with WRP, IMG, or IS representatives as guides. He also made a visit to Cambridge on 10th June, when he called on Doctor Letitia*

*Hennessy at St Mary's College. Reports from our sources in the three extremist movements mentioned are at Annexures A—C. They appear to show that subject's visit was for fact-finding purposes, and no special importance appears to have been attached to it by the leaders he met.*

*The visit to Dr Hennessy (known popularly as 'The Red Hen', see file 76/203/6415) may have had the same end in view. As we have no source in the New Revolutionary Group, of which she is President, we cannot know this for certain. However, 4510672 DC Sandford, who carried out the surveillance in Cambridge, reported that subject and Hennessy parted on friendly terms, and she was heard to remark, 'That's a very kind offer, Señor Santos. I might take you up on that.'*

*Apart from this curious remark there is nothing of interest in DC Sandford's report, which is on file ULM 76/203/6415 if required.*

The second report ran:

*ULM 537/76*
*21.7.76*

*To: Head of ULM Squad*
*From: Det. Sergeant Cobham*

Dr Letitia HENNESSY (76/203/6415)
James Mancroft CAUDLE (76/203/6839)
My ULM 462/76 of 14.6.76 refers

On your instructions, following my a/m report, HENNESSY's correspondence was placed under discreet surveillance (external only).

On 16.6.76 subject received a letter from Lytham St Anne's. We made certain enquiries, and discovered that the letter in question informed her that she had won the maximum prize of £50,000 in the Premium Bond draw. (There has been no publicity connecting her with the draw, presumably at subject's request.)

During the subsequent ten days subject received correspondence from the Argentine Embassy, London; Aerolineas Argentinas, London (the main Argentine airline); and also (several letters) from an address in SW4. We suspect that the writer of the last-mentioned correspondence might be James Mancroft CAUDLE (see above for file ref.), the Hon. Sec. and Acting Hon. Treas. of the New Revolutionary Group. His home in Stockwell is in the postal area mentioned.

Further weight was lent to this assumption by the fact that after HENNESSY's movements were put under surveillance on 15.6.76, on three occasions (19.6.76, 26.6.76 and 29.6.76) a man answering the file description of CAUDLE and driving his Morris car was observed to visit HENNESSY, on the first two occasions in College and on the third at her home in Clayhithe outside Cambridge.

51

*The first of CAUDLE's visits to Cambridge appears to have been mainly a social occasion, since the two subjects played bowls together and later lunched at the 'Garden House Hotel'. The later visits were more of a business type, and during the short times when they could be observed they were talking seriously together and (on the second visit) checking points on a memorandum.*

*CAUDLE was also put under surveillance and on two occasions was seen to enter the Consular Department of the Argentine Embassy. He also spent some time in the office of Aerolineas Argentinas in Bond Street. On 12.7.76 he received his visa, and leaves today by AR 131 from Heathrow.*

*SUGGESTION A likely explanation of these occurrences is that HENNESSY was invited by SANTOS to visit his country, presumably for fraternal political discussions. When she came into money she decided—to use her own words (my 462 of 14.6.76, third para)—to take him up on his offer, but perhaps on account of her advanced age—she is well over sixty—to send CAUDLE instead of herself.*

Garrard was amused at the reference to advanced age. His own father could still get round a golf course, and he was nearly eighty. But there was something he didn't like about the information implied in the two reports. He pressed the button on his intercom telephone and asked his PA to summon Sergeant Cobham.

The young man who came into the room a few moments later was in his late twenties, tall and good-looking, in a rather rugged, down-to-earth way. He was Garrard's chief troubleshooter, a man of many trades, quick and intelligent, with a roving eye for the girls.

'Good morning, Sergeant,' said Garrard. 'These reports about the Red Hen and Caudle. What action has been taken apart from surveillance?'

'As soon as we spotted Caudle's intentions we warned Five, and they passed on a summary to SIS for transmission to B.A for the Argentine Security Service, the SSN. They got it in time to have cancelled the visa if they'd wanted to, but they didn't. I imagine because they'll be keeping an eye on Caudle when he gets to B.A.'

'H'm. It's a pity he couldn't have been warned.'

'Sir?' protested the astonished Cobham.

'As I recall, both Caudle and his group, including even their formidable President, are innocuous sort of people. They've never been active in violent picketing or anti-police aggro. I hope he realises what sort of reception he's likely to get in Buenos Aires.'

'You think the SSN will pick him up as soon as he lands, sir? Then why didn't they stop his visa?'

'They want to watch him like a hawk and hope he'll lead them to some ERP hideout, and then pounce. They didn't arrest Lopez Suarez alias Santos when he got back to B.A, did they?'

'No, sir. I checked. They're playing cat and mouse, as you say.'

'Some mouse,' said Garrard. 'It was the ERP—I read somewhere—who attacked a military garrison, captured its second-in-command and later, when the Government wouldn't release two of their members from prison, murdered him in cold blood. I think they're also the people who treat the insides of their gun barrels with potassium cyanide. Is that the sort of thing Caudle wants to learn about? I think our mild, intellectual revolutionaries are playing with fire, and I don't want them burnt, especially in a foreign country. They do no harm in England, and I suppose they sublimate a few batty egg-head ideas.'

'The ERP are stinking rich, sir. Caudle could be going to ask for money.'

Garrard looked up. 'Could be, Robin. They like to say they're philanthropists, taking from the rich and giving to the poor. Find out more about the ERP. You'd better get through to someone in

SIS who can fill you in. I'm thinking of what Caudle's going to do when he gets back to the U.K.' He laughed shortly. 'I rather think he'll be a changed man.'

It was a prophetic remark, that Cobham was to recall in the days to come.

# CHAPTER SEVEN

Neville Bruce, chief SIS representative in Argentina, had his office in the British Embassy building on Calle Reconquista. He had just finished reading through the reports for the London bag when the telephone bell rang, and he picked up the receiver. It was the Ambassador's P.A.

'Is that you, Neville? ... It's Annette. H.E wants to see you right away. He looks a bit miffed, too.'

'O.K.' He was particularly worried as he called in a secretary and handed over the mail for the diplomatic bag. His conscience was clear. But the Ambassador was sometimes unpredictable. When his stomach ulcers were acting up his staff went round with the look of people listening for a bomb to explode.

Sir Roderick Thompson, KCMG, MC, had joined a Sapper regiment at the beginning of the War. He had survived three fierce campaigns in the desert and Italy, and at the end of the fighting decided that further soldiering, as an acting major, in peacetime, would have little to offer, so he had taken the Foreign Service exam and launched out into a second eventful career. Now, he had four more years to go before he was sixty and due to retire. Buenos Aires suited him, since he spoke fluent Spanish, after a first posting in Madrid, and he liked plenty of action. He looked up as Bruce, without knocking, cautiously opened the door and stood inside the room, waiting. 'Come and sit down, Neville. I've just seen a copy in the float of your letter to your Head Office about this man Juan Santos, or Lopez Suarez, which I see is his real name. I don't like the sound of this very much. Do you?'

Bruce began to feel his way, not being certain what his master didn't like. 'We have a useful relationship with the SSN, sir. If they ask us to keep an eye on one of their nationals when he visits the U.K, we can hardly refuse.'

'I'm not talking about that. As a result of that visit a British subject who can hardly be described, from his record, as a security target is coming here on a visit, and his details and ETA have been notified by you to the National Security Service. They will probably pick him up and grill him, and as you know they can be very tough. They'd say that as a potential contact of a suspected member of the ERP they would be amply justified in turning him inside out.' His Excellency pointed the stem of his pipe at the SIS man. 'And you, my lad—what's the word?—in effect, you *fingered* him. Isn't that so?'

'Yes, sir. I suppose so.' It was always, thought Bruce resentfully, like being a junior subaltern and having a strip torn off you by the colonel. This was supposed to be the Diplomatic Service. He said stiffly, 'I don't think they'll do that, sir—I mean grilling him. After all, they knew about it and could have stopped the visa. And with respect, sir, I must point out that Caudle is the secretary of a revolutionary movement. It's not surprising if he has to run risks occasionally.'

'I don't agree. As I said, Caudle's record, if what you've told the Argentines is true, is technically clean. I'm damned if I'm going to have him molested by the SSN. So please make sure they don't.'

Bruce thought for a moment. 'May I say that you are most anxious to avoid any incident which might be reported back to the London press?'

The Ambassador smiled grimly. 'That's the line, my boy. You may also add that if there is any trouble I won't fail to take the matter up with the Minister.' He smiled. 'I can see the spot you're in, Neville, but you've got to get yourself out of it. Put it tactfully, of course, but make it quite clear I mean what I've just told you.'

'Thank you, sir. That'll help.'

'When does he arrive?'

'Ten-fifteen at Ezeiza tomorrow morning.'

'Then I suggest you get one of your snoopers to be at Ezeiza to make sure Caudle isn't arrested on landing, for a start. Will you and Betty be at the Italian's tomorrow night?'

'Yes, sir. I'll be able to report to you then.'

'O.K. That'll do, Neville.'

Back in his office, Bruce rang the SSN headquarters. *'Quiero hablar con el Mayor Urrutia, por favor.'*

There was a pause, then a deep voice. 'Urrutia. *Quein es?'*

'It's Neville, Bernardo. His Excellency is a bit unhappy about this man Caudle.'

*'Por Dios!* Did you have to tell him?'

'Yes, I did, chum. Caudle is a British subject, even if he is a revolutionary, and we don't want any fanciful stories in the press about harmless tourists being victimised by the Argentine police, do we?

His Excellency would plague the life out of your Foreign Minister if that happened.'

'Hey, wait a minute. Who gave you that idea? I never said we'd be picking the guy up.' Urrutia had served in Washington, and spoke English fluently.

'But isn't that what you have in mind?'

'Of course not. Perhaps a friendly chat some time, but that's all. So long as he behaves himself, and sticks to his ostensible reason for his visit, which could scarcely be more innocent.'

'You're telling me something, Bernardo. I haven't a clue what he's supposed to be doing here.'

'Have you heard of Harriet Pringle?'

'She writes thrillers, and very success-fully, that's all I know. I read them. Plenty of blood and action, and very ingenious.'

'She has another name, Letitia Hen-nessy.'

'Good God! I didn't know. She's the President of Caudle's bunch of so-called revolutionaries.'

'Ah, but it's not as Letitia Hennessy that's she's sending him to Argentina. It's as Harriet Pringle. He's coming to do the research for a new story she's writing. He has the synopsis with him. Showed it to our visa officer in London.'

'So that's how you learned all this.' A thought struck him. 'But why did he need a visa? Brit. subs. don't as a rule.'

'Only if they're born in the United Kingdom. Caudle was born in Malaya, where his father was stationed at the time. He was a rubber planter.'

'Interesting. Well, thanks, Bernardo. You've relieved my mind. It's quite a harmless visit after all.'

'You don't fool me, Neville. You don't believe a word of that whodunnit story, any more than I do. But don't worry. If he does something silly I'll let you know before our hooded torturers begin their foul work.'

'Thanks, Bernardo. If I see you in the *Circulo Militar* I'll stand you a drink.'

'A double Chivas Regal is my preferred tipple, if Her Majesty is paying for it. See you, friend.'

The estancia lay forty miles from the centre of Buenos Aires, twenty-five beyond the last sprawling suburbs. The broad grasslands stretched, away, almost treeless, browsed on by fat Friesians and Herefords, with gaucho horsemen in wide-brimmed hats patrolling the electric fences. They rode straight-legged, slouching in the saddle, each man with a knotted handkerchief round his neck and a poncho over the short leather jacket, with baggy trousers gathered into riding-boots and a broad, coin-studded belt. The coiled *boleadora* with its weighted end, which he could swing at the legs of a fleeing animal and bring it down, hung at his saddle bow. It was a peaceful scene, typical of the ranches that spread out towards the distant Andes. But on this estancia there was a difference; concealed under every poncho was a Colt .45 revolver, which its owner could use with deadly accuracy.

The house itself was built in the Palladian style, with a great pillared portico backed by a circular hall, and the sleeping quarters lay in the two low wings that stretched back to enclose the flower garden. There was a stable block for thirty horses, with its clock-tower and cobbled yard—imported cobbles, since there are few stones in the rich loam of the pampa—and a big swimming pool, its changing-rooms and bar set beneath a rose-covered arcade. The private dwellings were surrounded by a high eucalyptus windbreak, which separated them from the ranch and paddocks.

The white Mercedes banged its way across the cattle-grids and followed the drive to the portico, where a mestizo manservant in livery and white gloves was waiting. He opened the car door, and Xavier Lopez Suarez, alias Juan Santos, stepped out. The man's white teeth showed in a welcoming smile. *'Bienvenido,* Don

Xavier!' He signed to a youth in a white shirt, broad cummerbund and flared black trousers, who drove the car into the shade of the stable courtyard. The *mayordomo* led Santos into the house, carrying his overnight bag.

The owner of the estancia was a man of fifty-five, with a face the colour and texture of pale Moroccan leather. This was Don Felipe Ybarra y Urquiza, Chief of Staff to the High Command of the ERP, and feared by many, although not under his real name. The identity of 'Mendoza' was known to very few, and they did not include the Argentine police and Security Service. The ring of security around Mendoza's identity was as taut and well-guarded as his electric fences.

Ybarra and Lopez Suarez were cousins; they embraced each other in the South American fashion, cheeks almost touching, each right arm round the other's shoulder. The chief of staff clapped his hands and ordered drinks. It was chilly, since in Argentina July is a winter month and the icy wind from the snowy Andes cuts across the plain with nothing to stop it. There was a fire of great olive logs in the open hearth of the library, where this meeting took place.

They exchanged family news perfunctorily, and sipped their whisky. Lopez said. 'You've spoken to the *Jefe* about this gringo Caudle?'

'Yes. He agreed that you could have done no less than invite that egregious lady to visit you. It was an act of *politesse de rigueur*. But we were a little surprised that she accepted, in the person of this Caudle. It's an expensive trip, and the English are almost taxed out of existence.'

'She wrote to say he would ostensibly be doing research for a book she is writing,' explained Lopez. 'Some matter of scholarship, I suppose, since she is a professor at Cambridge. In her letter she pointed out, frugally, that she would thus be able to set off the expenses of the journey against Income Tax. She said Caudle would have much to learn from us, which seems odd. I don't think their movement and ours have much in common.'

'I think, my dear cousin, you are mistaken there, in part at least. The New Revolutionary Group are Trotskyists, like us, and like us do not favour close association with other Communist sects. Their hearts are in the right place, I've no doubt, and this forms the basis of what might just possibly be a useful bond.' Lopez waited while the older man was silent for a moment, thinking.

Ybarra continued, 'If Caudle wants to

learn something about how our Army operates you can tell him what is generally known, stressing the purity of our motives and our dislike of unnecessary violence. No contact with any of the cells, of course, unless he is first blindfolded. But really, I should have been inclined to drop the whole idea, if it were not for an idea that struck the Chief while we were talking about it. This is for your ears alone, Xavier. You understand?'

'Of course.' Lopez leaned against the chimney piece and looked down at the reflections of the fire in his glass. He had known there was something important to be imparted to him, or he would never have been invited to the estancia. His cousin was a very busy man, the Chief's most trusted lieutenant, and he had never shown any particular desire for Lopez's company.

Ybarra said, 'The Chief has been thinking about our future. We still hope to achieve what we have always wanted, a complete revolution in our beloved country and the passing of government into people's councils under our control. But the reaction is getting stronger, as you know, and the Government is helping the Fascists in secret. No Triple-A men have been arrested in recent months in spite of their atrocities. It is therefore possible that

64

we may in time suffer the same fate as our Tupamaro colleagues in Uraguay.' Ybarra raised his hand as Lopez started to speak. 'It is unlikely, but we cannot be sure. If that did happen, we might lose *everything*, including the revolutionary funds essential for re-settling our people in other countries. As you know, we have placed substantial balances in a number of banks—'

'Including,' put in Lopez mischievously, 'some that we had previously robbed.'

Ybarra frowned. 'Of course. They are the most reliable banks. But all such balances might be confiscated if the oppression became extreme. Once people saw the Government apparently beginning to defeat us we could not rely on anyone outside our immediate ranks. Those whom we now pay to keep silent—and who rightly fear our anger—would rush to inform on us if they saw a chance of personal gain. Now, we also have holdings in the United States, but there is too much collaboration between the SSN and the FBI for safety, and the powers of the United States Government to control foreign accounts are Draconian.' He paused and finished his whisky. 'The United Kingdom is another matter.'

The young man started. 'You suggest we might explore the possibility of stashing away our currency in London? You mean in *pounds?* But surely there's too much risk of inflation?'

'Not if the accounts are in Deutschmarks or Arab currency. Even in gold. London is still the best place in the world to hide your wealth, far better than Zurich, if you know how to go about it. And I have financial advisers in the City of London who have that knowledge. There is therefore a case, in the Chief's view, for setting up a high-powered mission in England. The members of the mission would not necessarily be idle, while awaiting the unlikely possibility I mentioned. They could keep their hands in by organising some of the MIR operatives who escaped from Chile to England after the *putsch,* and perhaps carrying out a few coups on the lines we have demonstrated so successfully here. This would test the machinery they would be setting up, at the same time, for forming a safe haven for our funds which—just to make you understand, Xavier, the importance of what I am saying—amount to several hundred million dollars.'

'*Cristo Rey!*' muttered Lopez, deeply shaken. '*No es posible!*'

'*Es la verdad,*' declared Ybarra shortly. 'Now do you see our reasoning? If—and only if—you can recommend this young man Caudle as being sensible and close-mouthed, we might impress him suitably with our expertise and later suggest that we should be glad to send a few operatives to England to keep in touch with him. You could suggest that if he were able help us out with background information—our obvious weakness, as far as fund-raising operations are concerned—it might be a profitable business for his Group—or for him personally, if he is venal.

'But on the other hand, if he shows a tendency to indiscretion or weakness of any kind, you will of course drop him at once, if necessary—if absolutely necessary, I mean—by arranging a fatal accident. But the Chief sees an advantage in having a liaison with Caudle and his friends in England, providing they are security-minded and sufficiently tough to stand up to police persecution. They might react well to our appeal to their sense of doctrinal solidarity. According to what I have been able to discover, in addition to your report, they are dedicated, intelligent persons, however divorced they may be from the realities of power, and they will certainly have contacts that could be of use to us. And don't forget, the New Revolutionary Group is a movement without friends and strictly expendable. Maybe,' Ybarra added, with a thin smile, 'we shall end up by converting the gentle NRG into an English branch of our Army, complete with our sophisticated kidnapping techniques, and ready to break into the Bank of England with tactical atomic weapons.'

Lopez laughed politely at the joke. Then he said, 'I told the Professor that I would reserve a room for Caudle at the Reconquista.' It was one of some twenty-three hotels where the ERP had made certain arrangements.

'The SSN hasn't got on to it yet?'

'No. It's only been used a few times, and there's been no sign of surveillance.'

'And you, Xavier?'

'If they suspect me for what I am,' said Lopez impatiently, 'the SSN are cleverer than me.'

'That,' said Ybarra, with a frosty smile, 'is not impossible. Be very careful. You may use my niece Manuela for overt contacts with Caudle. It's time she had more operational experience. But see that she runs no risk whatever.'

# CHAPTER EIGHT

The Boeing 707/230 Intercontinental took nearly twenty hours to reach Buenos Aires, and for much of the time Caudle was thoroughly bored, although he re-read

Letty's synopsis and list of questions, made notes on the flight and occasionally slept fitfully. There were stops at Orly and Madrid, and the great plane finally took off for the transatlantic flight at half-past midnight. For ten hours there was nothing to do but read and try to sleep, and when they landed at Galeão Airport in Rio de Janeiro it was still only five-thirty, because of the five-hour time change, and dawn was still to come.

But he was impressed and fascinated by the far-spreading lights of Rio and the floodlit figure of Christ on top of the Corcovado as the aircraft came circling in. When they took off an hour later and flew out over the sea to gain height before crossing the mountains there was light already in the east, and within half an hour he could see the tips of the skyscrapers of Sao Paulo glittering in the first rays of a brilliant sun. But that was all he did see of the fastest-growing city in the world, because the plane landed at its airport Viracopos, sixty miles away, and there was another boring wait before the final stretch across the great plateau to the Paraguay river and the broad expanse of the River Plate. The airport at Ezeiza, twenty miles from the centre of Buenos Aires, is large and impersonal, but it was a welcome relief to step out into the cold fresh air after the heat and smoke-filled fug of the Boeing. He hurriedly put on his duffle coat, and glanced at his watch. Ten-fifteen, local time.

From the balcony of the first-floor restaurant a tall girl wearing slender jeans and a sheepskin jacket was watching. Her dark hair was held back by a ribbon, framing a pale-ivory face with dark eyebrows, strongly-marked, and deep-brown eyes. Her arched nose and short upper lip were pure Castilian, as indeed her ancestors on both sides had been for generations. At the orders of Ybarra, her uncle, she had twice failed her finals in sociology, and was still an undergraduate at La Plata University. Her father had cut off her allowance and forbidden his wife to have any contact with her, because she had refused to marry the young man of his choice. But this worried Manuela San Martin not at all; the life she was living was too good to give up and although she had to submit to the strict discipline of the People's Revolutionary Army her uncle saw that she was well provided for.

It was useless to try to identify Caudle in the distance, among the long files of passengers walking across the tarmac to the coaches which would take them to the customs and immigration halls. She had to wait half an hour in the visitors' lounge

70

before the Boeing passengers appeared. The diplomats and officials came through the barrier first, followed by the businessmen and Argentine residents, most of whom were at once collected by friends. A tall, lanky young man came through on his own, wearing a duffle coat and carrying a briefcase and a bulky holdall. Behind him appeared a dark-faced man in a blue Dacron suit, without any luggage. He was walking casually—too casually—and catching up the tall Englishman. He would be the SSN man, thought Manuela, correctly. That was interesting, and worth reporting. The man made no approach to Caudle but stayed close behind him and followed him into the airport bus.

What Manuela did not notice, because he was better trained than the SSN surveillance operative and merged easily into the background, was another man, wearing a light overcoat and a snap-brim hat. He watched the coach leave for Buenos Aires, then went into the door marked 'Señores', chose a cubicle and locked the door. Taking a small transceiver from his pocket he spoke into it very quietly, a few words only, for relaying by his control to Neville Bruce.

Blissfully unaware that three pairs of eyes had observed his arrival, Caudle sat back in the coach seat and watched the landscape pass by, stretching into the level distance under the clear winter sunshine.

When he was deposited at the Aerolineas office on Avenida Corrientes Caudle took a taxi to the Hotel Reconquista, just off the Avenida de Mayo. It was the name he had been given in the letter Santos had sent to Letty. It looked all right, but a bit tatty and old-fashioned, like so many buildings in Buenos Aires. The clerk at the reception desk offered his hand. 'We were expecting you, Mr Cowdlay. Room two-four-seven, with private bath. Please sign here and enter your passport details. I've done the rest.'

Caudle filled out the police form and added as the purpose of his visit, 'Literary Research'. He thanked the clerk, and hesitated. 'Er—actually, although it looks different, my name is pronounced Caudle. Perhaps you would let the telephone operator know, or she may not recognise it when it's given to her. I'm expecting someone to give me a ring some time today.' He pushed a hundred peso note under the register.

The clerk smiled. 'Caudle. *Muy bien.* I will see that everyone is informed. Luisito, take this gentleman to his room.' He handed over the key. 'Luncheon will be served from one o'clock onwards, sir. I wish you a pleasant stay in our city.'

He watched the Englishman until he had entered the lift, then went through a door behind the desk, to telephone in private. When he came back a man in a blue Dacron suit was standing at the desk, his eyes on the register.

'Señor,' said the clerk sharply.

*'Nada, nada,'* said the SSN, and walked out of the hotel entrance. The clerk looked after him thoughtfully, and went back to his telephone in the room behind.

Traditionally, all Argentine hotels were built for large Catholic families, and when Caudle dismissed Luisito and looked round his room, which was large and quite agreeably furnished, he saw that there was a communicating door at one end. He tried the handle, but the door was locked on the other side. On his, there was no key. He glanced at his watch. Twelve-fifteen. He knew that lunch would still be available, as in all South American restaurants, for hours to come, so lay down on the bed. If someone was going to telephone, it would be more convenient if he stayed in his room for a bit. And there were things to sort out in his mind.

If the ERP did telephone him, presumably they'd do it from a call-box. But what about physical contact? They would perhaps have some blameless-looking front man who could give him all the information the ERP was willing to impart. He was still wondering what exactly would happen, with a pleasurable thrill of anticipation, when he fell fast asleep. When he awoke it was six o'clock, and dark. Half-amused at himself, half-annoyed at having missed lunch, he took his clothes off, showered luxuriously, shaved, and put on his one good suit, with a St John's tie. In England he scarcely ever wore a tie; this was his concession to a foreign society.

At about this time, in room number two-four-eight, next door, a small white-haired man of military appearance was receiving instructions by telephone. He put down the receiver, took the room key from his pocket and slid it under the handset. He tidied the room and its bathroom, put on his coat and hat, and went out, leaving the door slightly ajar. He walked down the corridor, down the two flights of stairs and out of the front door of the hotel. The reception clerk noted his departure, and knew he would be back in a day or two to settle the bill.

Colonel Isidor Rojas Monterrey, Argentine Army (retired), had earned his fee. Room two-four-eight would remain in his name, but someone else would be occupying it from time to time. Whether that person would wish to wear Colonel Rojas's pyjamas, embroidered I.R.M on

74

the pocket, or his regimental blazer and small, ageing trousers hanging in the wardrobe, or make use of his shaving things in the bathroom, read the array of personal correspondence left with apparent carelessness on the desk, was another matter.

Caudle had arranged the contents of his holdall in the chest of drawers and wardrobe and was concluding a telephoned radiogram to Pat when he heard a quiet knock at the communicating door. He finished the call and as he went across to the door the knock was repeated, louder.

'*Quien es?*' asked Caudle sharply.

'May I come in, Mr Caudle?' came a muffled voice in accentless English.

'The door's locked, I'm afraid. But who are you, anyway?'

The handle turned, and the door opened. A young man in a grey mohair suit, wearing a Yacht Club tie, stood in the doorway, smiling. He stepped forward, holding out his hand. 'Juan Santos,' said Xavier Lopez Suarez. 'At your service.'

Caudle shook hands. 'Well, it's nice of you to call on me so promptly, although—Come in and let me order drinks.'

'I've taken the liberty of doing that already,' said Juan. He went over to the door that opened on to the corridor and shot the bolt. Then he came back and said, 'Come through, please. It isn't my room, as a matter of fact, but the occupant lets me use it. Here we are.'

He stood back and ushered Caudle into the next room. A bottle of Moët et Chandon stood in a bucket of ice on a small table. A pot of Beluga caviar and a shallow bowl of butter lay in a dish of crushed ice and there was a silver cover which Santos lifted, to disclose a laden toast-rack. He drew up an armchair for Caudle and busied himself with the foil and wire of the champagne as he went on talking.

'I gather you have a cover mission for your stay here. Good security! It's literary work, I imagine, since it's for that delightful lady I met in Cambridge?'

Caudle accepted the proffered glass with a feeling of great contentment and buttered a slice of toast. 'Not exactly. Letitia is a very successful writer of crime stories as a side line to her academic work.'

Juan smiled. 'And to her task as President of your Group. She must be a glutton for work. Or is it in fact you who do most of the political work?'

'A good deal of it, yes. But she pulls her weight, you know. Writes many of our campaign articles.' He was hungry, having eaten nothing since a continental breakfast on the plane, and helped himself to a modest quantity of caviar.

'I'm sorry,' said Juan apologetically. He pointed to the caviar, and added, 'Don't you like the stuff?'

'Of course I do, it's delicious, but—'

'Then help yourself properly, my dear fellow,' said Santos, setting him an example. 'We have plenty, through a useful connection with a foreign diplomat. But I don't quite understand. What research are you then engaged on?'

'Doctor Hennessy has given me a list of questions she wants answered as a background for her next thriller,' explained Caudle a little shamefacedly. 'A notional story, in fact. She isn't actually going to write it. She wants things like hotel locations, street maps, descriptions of Buenos Aires and the surrounding country, the police services, and so on. I've got a synopsis of the story.'

Juan was laughing delightedly. He raised an apologetic hand. 'I beg your pardon, but it really is the most magnificent cover. I couldn't have invented anything better myself. And you will of course make a genuine effort to find the answers to the questionnaire?'

'Yes. In fact I must, in case the police become curious. This champagne is excellent, Señor Santos.' His glass was empty, and Santos filled it, and offered more toast. 'Thank you. But of course my main object is to discuss our problems with you, since you so kindly offered advice.' It was too early to broach Letty's extraordinary proposal. Or was it? He liked the look of Juan, who seemed a responsible member of his movement. There was no time like the present, thought Caudle, who was beginning to enjoy himself.

'Doctor Hennessy has in mind a plan which you may feel is quite out of the question. But first, I want to get something clear. She and I assume—I've been doing some reading in the last few weeks—that your organisation goes in for—broadly speaking—three kinds of activity.'

'Go on,' said Santos, smiling.

'The first is political, in the sense that you aim at creating an alternative form of government on Marxist lines. Then I believe you have a military side, with cadres trained to attack military and police targets, and I suppose you plan to use these cadres for a seizure of power when the time is ripe.' He looked up. 'All right so far?'

'More or less. We are engaged in eroding the Government's executive power in all its aspects, as a matter of fact. And our third form of activity?'

'Fund raising.' Caudle saw Juan's lips tighten, and continued hastily, 'I am sure you choose targets which will not only provide the money you need, but which in your view will not harm the people as a whole.'

'That's it,' agreed Santos. 'We aim at making life difficult for the rich foreigners, especially the entrepreneurs, because they have far too much influence on the Government. Once we have forced them to leave the country, as we are already doing to some extent, we shall be better able to achieve the form of rule we want. There is no danger of wrecking the economy for the long term, Mr Caudle. Argentina is a very rich country, still not properly developed.'

'I see. But you agree that there is this third form of action, which is quite essential for the furtherance of your plans?'

'Yes, although at the moment our—er— coffers are full and we are concentrating mainly on military action. The reason why we suffer comparatively few losses is that we spend money wisely on training our members and protecting them. We have only a few thousand active members, as you may know, but there are nearly a hundred thousand sympathisers, and some of these only sympathise loyally if they are well paid.'

'That's one way of describing wholesale bribery,' said Caudle smiling, but seeing

Juan looking slightly offended hurried on, 'And I suppose it is essential for you to have—er—willing helpers everywhere to enable you to plan and carry out your fund-raising operations without danger? These people supply you with background information, assist in surveillance, espionage and counter-espionage and conceal your operatives when they're on the run. Is that it, more or less?'

'Yes, I think you've got some idea of our methods, but why these questions? You mentioned a plan of Doña Letizia's.'

Caudle drained his glass and put it down carefully. 'She wonders if you would not like to consider operating in the United Kingdom, as a sort of side-line and, if you like, a form of insurance should things go badly with your operations here. We could, she feels, provide you with a great deal of essential information for such work, pin-point suitable targets and advise about communications and safe-houses, as I think they're called.' He paused, controlled an incipient gulp, and added, 'We should ask fifty per cent of the take for our part.'

Juan could scarcely believe it. This Englishman was playing straight into his hands. His face was completely expressionless as he said quietly, 'For sheer effrontery that is the most outrageous suggestion I have ever heard. But the *Ejercito* thrives on effrontery. We succeed because we have ideas no one else has thought of. That's why I can't help liking your idea, even though my superiors may take an opposite view.' He glanced at the face of the Englishman, slightly flushed, a little worried, and laughed gently. 'You know, my dear Caudle, you don't really look like someone who is planning to hi-jack the Governor of the Bank of England or empty one of his vaults. And that is what we're talking about, isn't it? Let's get that quite clear.'

'Not the Bank,' said Caudle. 'That's silly. But my President points out that there are quite a number of people, for example in the literary and academic world, who are very rich indeed, and would scarcely notice a large contribution to our funds—yours and ours, that is.'

'What d'you mean by large?'

'Fifty thousand pounds or more. Not so large as to draw down the whole weight of the police force, but such that a few operations would add up.'

Santos looked scornful. 'I'm afraid it simply isn't worth our while to set up an operation for less than a million dollars, or say half a million pounds. It's a question of the overhead expenses, among other things.' He looked at his watch. 'I think we'd better talk this over in greater detail. I'll be delightful to offer you a meal, but we'll have to be careful not to be seen together.'

'Yes, I'd like that very much. But I see your point—I suppose you're under surveillance?'

The Argentine smiled. 'Not me. As a liaison officer I have to be kept very clean. The SSN may suspect me, but they've not the slightest evidence that links me with any ERP operation. We know that through our contacts. They are also wary of molesting me because I have family connections in what I suppose you'd call high places. No. I was thinking of you. It is the other way round. *I* shouldn't strictly be seen with *you*. The SSN have you under surveillance already.' He watched Caudle closely for his reaction, mindful of what Ybarra had said about signs of weakness. If the man showed panic he might prove too dangerous to contact, and there was still time to cut the acquaintance short before any disclosures were made.

But Caudle was merely indignant. 'That's a bloody impertinence! They've got nothing on me, how could they?'

'Card indexes, my dear fellow. And collaboration between intelligence services. Don't forget you're the secretary of a revolutionary movement, however mild and inoffensive it has been to date. I'm not guessing. There was a tail on you from the moment you landed at Ezeiza. He watched you check in here and later took a quick look at the register to discover your room number.'

'How d'you know all this?' asked Caudle sharply. He was becoming angry, in spite of a slight quiver in his stomach.

'Because you were also watched by one of our operatives. A girl, incidentally; you'll be meeting her. Do you remember a dark man in a blue suit, with no luggage, who followed you through the airport checks?'

'There was a man—' Caudle had wondered why the fellow had had no luggage.

'He was the SSN snooper, and a bad one, too. Otherwise Manuela mightn't have spotted him.'

'All right, then. They're following me. So what? They can arrest me and they'll find out nothing. I've got a perfectly good explanation for my visit.' He was still angry. 'If it goes on too obviously I'll complain to the Consul.'

'That's the attitude.' Santos got up. 'Are you ready to go out? Use this bathroom if you wish.'

'Thanks, I will.' When he came back Santos was putting down the telephone. He said, 'There's no sign of SSN surveillance

83

below, but we won't risk going through the foyer. There may be a man outside. If anyone enquires after you the desk will say you went out to find a restaurant some time ago. The door of this room is locked, and we'll go out through yours, if you don't mind.'

They went through the communicating door and Caudle opened the wardrobe and brought out his duffle coat and the Tyrolese hat.

Juan looked horrified. 'You'd better leave those behind; they're a bit distinctive. It's not too cold outside, and we've only a short way to go.' He glanced at his watch. 'Fifteen more seconds. Please open the door. When you get into the corridor check that there's no one there. If there is, come back. If all's clear, turn left. The service lift is half way along on your right. O.K. Go now.'

It was all a bit too dramatic, thought Caudle. Outside the door there was no one to be seen. As he walked down the corridor he heard Santos lock the door behind him. When they reached the lift its door opened and a man in hotel livery beckoned them in. They descended to basement level and went along a tiled passage lit only by open glass hoppers high in the wall, through which came strong smells of cooking and the noise of clattering pans. The man in the lift had disappeared.

The door at the end of the passage led to an ill-lit courtyard, empty except for dustbins, a few cars and a tradesman's van, and beyond was a side-street, where a small Fiat was waiting, its engine running. As he got into the back Caudle could see that the driver was a girl.

Santos got in beside her. Caudle heard him ask quickly in Spanish, 'Any road blocks?' and she shook her head. *'Nada. Donde?'*

'El Ranchito.' Santos turned in his seat. 'This is Manuela.'

*'Encantado,'* said Caudle, and started. 'Oh, it's she who—?'

'Precisely,' said Santos. 'And incidentally, she and I will be the only soldiers of the Army you'll meet, as at present arranged. I'm sorry, but it's a question of restrictive security, you understand.'

'Of course. I'm afraid I don't speak Spanish very fluently, although I can get by.'

'My English is O.K,' said the girl, without turning her head. They were driving down a crowded street, with people just leaving the cafés and bars for their homes. She handled the little car well, unfussily.

Caudle began to feel the thrill of adventure, and almost pleasurable twinges of apprehension. 'That was very smooth,' he said. 'I suppose these aren't your real names—Juan Santos and Manuela?'

'No,' said Santos shortly. 'Just call us Juan and Manuela, and we'll call you James. Or is it Jim?'

'No, not Jim.' Not in this kind of situation, for God's sake. 'Where are we going?'

'To a place outside the city, where we can eat without fear of being disturbed. We have friends there.'

More of those well-paid 'sympathisers', thought Caudle. They were passing through a grid of narrow, drab streets, streets of small tobacconists and bars, lottery agents, grimy shops selling inferior goods, sleazy cinemas with bootblacks crouching outside. All very different from the oppressive grandeur of the great plazas and the broad Avenida de Mayo. Then came a quarter of great houses surrounded by trees and lawns and wrought-iron railings, with smooth half-moon carriage drives reminiscent of the Faubourg Saint Honoré. Later again, they passed through suburbs which with their neat houses and small gardens looked curiously English.

They emerged, finally, into an area of grassland, broken here and there by wide fields of alfalfa and windbreaks of eucalyptus. Manuela accelerated. Some time later she turned the car through an open gate in a patch of woodland. There was no one to be seen, but Caudle caught the flash of a torch directed for an instant at the car's number plate. Then they were running between painted wooden rails, sharply white against the dark trees. The drive must have been fully a mile long, winding through the plantation, until they bumped over a cattle-grid into an open space, lit by iron lanterns hanging from the overhanging branches. A low stucco building bore a sign, 'El Ranchito'.

## CHAPTER NINE

There were a couple of dozen cars parked near the cedar doors, but Manuela swung the Fiat round and stopped facing the drive. Ready for a quick getaway, thought Caudle, half amused. The air was cold and clean after the smog and stale smells of the city, and there was little sound but the rustle of the trees. No moon. Somewhere among the bright stars, he thought, must be the Southern Cross, which he had once seen, low on the horizon, during his year in Peru.

Juan led the way into the restaurant. In

the middle of the lamp-lit dining space T-bone steaks were sizzling over glowing charcoal and great joints of beef turned slowly on a spit. A huge copper canopy hung from the oak-beamed roof. Perspiring cooks in white hats were turning the meat and brushing it with a variety of sauces, and the combined smells of charcoal and roasting meat were immensely appetising.

So—Caudle realised—was Manuela. It was the first time he had been able to see her properly. Her sheepskin jacket had been taken by one of the waiters. She was wearing an embroidered blouse of fine cotton, gathered at the neck and lifting to the swell of her breasts. Her dark hair fell over her shoulders, gleaming in the lamplight. She was looking at him, too, quite boldly and frankly appraising him; it was a little disconcerting. At least, he thought, he had dressed decently; he would have felt shabby in his suede jacket and worn, corduroy slacks.

Caudle turned to Juan, whose mocking bright eyes were missing nothing. 'It's very good of you to take me out like this; I wasn't looking forward to dining in that rather depressing hotel.'

'Sorry about the Reconquista, but you must admit it has its points.'

'Do you always use it for establishing contact with your foreign colleagues?' asked

Caudle, and laughed.

'It's just one of more than twenty we use in rotation for that and other purposes. I hope you're hungry?'

'Very. I had no lunch.'

'Splendid! There aren't so many places now in my country where you can get a traditional *asado*, but they do us well here.' He smiled. 'Us, especially.'

'It smells marvellous.' He glanced at the four-page menu offered him by the waiter. 'I think you'd better choose.'

While Juan was giving his order, having consulted with the girl, she turned to Caudle. 'How was your flight, James?'

'I hate air travel as a rule, and nearly twenty hours is a bit much, but it was quite comfortable. And the food wasn't bad.'

She laughed, and it was a pleasant sound. 'You don't fool me. All that champagne and smoked salmon. I've done the trip a dozen times, and I always feel afterwards as if I'd put on five kilos.'

'Tourist class is not quite the same,' explained Caudle gently.

'Good Heavens!' Her surprise was genuine. 'I'm sorry, I—'

'Good security,' commented Juan quickly, and tactfully. 'Now, I've ordered Chilean wine. It's really better than most French wines with *asado*. But we'll have an apéritif. Vodka martinis? Or do you prefer sherry?'

It was a long and magnificent meal, and Caudle could feel his belt becoming comfortably tight. To begin with, the table was set with dishes of cold *fiambres*, ranging from the delicate flesh tones of Parma ham, the rusty scarlet of paprika sausage and the speckled salamis to the leathery darkness of smoked *lomo* or pemmican. Pale palmito fronds flanked a mountain of fat pink prawns accompanied by a glistening mayonnaise. An earthenware pot of paté and dishes of sliced tomato, fingers of cucumber, and radishes and spring onions filled the last available space on the check tablecloth. And this was the hors d'oeuvres.

Later, they went to the grill and chose steaks, rosy inside their aromatic coating, and great slices of succulent beef were cut off according to Juan's exact instructions and heaped on their plates. The waiter brought bowls of rice, sweet corn, peppers and—to Caudle—strange, hot sauces. The wine was clean, fresh and, as Juan had said, went well with the beef, which was so tender that you could cut it with a fork. It was the best meal Caudle could remember, and at the end of it, as he refused Manuela's demand that he should try the ultra-sweet *dulce de leche*, which looked and tasted like soft fudge, he felt euphoric.

When they reached the coffee and brandy stage Juan said, as he lit a Cuban cigar, 'I want to remind you of what you said earlier, James, about the sort of haul we might expect from operations in Britain. We've acquired our technique over ten years, learning much, of course, from our Tupamaro friends in Uruguay, who were the first real experts. Take for instance an apparently simple task like the kidnapping of an industrialist. It isn't simple at all, but requires very careful planning and a great deal of expense. First, the planners have to study the man's habits, friends, residences and above all his wealth, or his value to the firm for which he works. Then, when the plan, with its fall-back arrangements, has been worked out in full detail and duties allotted, there must be at least one full-scale dress rehearsal, and this means that cars may have to be stolen twice over, once for the rehearsal and again for the attack itself. People's prisons must be set up and furnished with everything required; escape routes prospected; the machinery for the ransom demand and the receipt of the money worked out exactly. The whole thing has to be planned so that no one operative knows more than the absolute minimum. Then, if he's captured before he can use his L-tablet—and thus deprive the police of the pleasure of torturing him—he can give very little away.

'There's also, of course, provision to be made for the wounded, and in fact we have clandestine operating theatres, with nurses and surgeons available in case they're wanted. Unless the whole thing is done properly there are unacceptable risks, and it's careful planning and attention to detail that mark our operations apart from those of other movements. But, as I said, it costs a lot of money. To make this clear, I must repeat what I told you earlier. Apart from training exercises, when snatches may be made just to provide training for the operatives, we find it isn't worth our while to undertake a job unless we can count on a gross profit of a million dollars a time.'

'I think that settles it,' said Caudle, with reluctance tinged with some relief, 'and I'm very glad we've had this talk and you've spoken so frankly. We'd never find that sort of money in the U.K.'

This wasn't what Juan wanted at all. 'I don't say the costs would be the same in England,' he said quickly. 'It might be possible to work out something simpler, and you must remember we should have the element of surprise on our side. As far as kidnapping or bank robbery is concerned, your movement is at present above suspicion; you and selected members of your Group could find excellent excuses to do the ground work. I expect, for example, that you have a few doctors and nurses among them?'

Caudle was enjoying the flavour of his cigar, and it took him a moment to envisage the membership of the N.R.G. 'So we have,' he said, in some surprise. 'Not nurses, unfortunately; we don't seem to attract many of them. But we have a good sprinkling of general practitioners and a few consultants.' And some of them, he added to himself, highly eccentric. But the thought of getting some of his armchair revolutionaries off their bottoms and making them do real work was stimulating.

'Then,' said Juan, 'you'd want experts on different parts of the country, perhaps an estate-agent or two to advise on safe-houses and people's prisons, someone to advise about controls on radio communications and the best frequencies to use, others who can get at facts about target personalities from the press and libraries, and of course talent-spotters of all kinds. That's the kind of thing.'

'I think we could cope with those requirements,' said Caudle airily, partly for Manuela's benefit. (Letty had said only he and she were to be in the know, but never mind.)

'Right, then,' said Juan. 'Let's have

another talk in a few days' time. On Sunday, perhaps. You return to England on Tuesday evening, don't you?'

'Yes, but I could delay my flight if necessary.'

'I don't think it will be necessary,' said Juan. 'You don't need more than a day or two to consolidate your cover, do you?'

'You mean, start gathering information for Letty's story?' It sounded so tame after what he had been hearing. 'No. Three days ought to be enough.'

'I think,' said Juan, 'that Manuela has some ideas about that.'

The girl had been silent throughout much of the meal and while Juan had been laying down the law about the techniques of snatch operations, but Caudle had felt her eyes on him. Now she smiled, put down her cigarette and said, 'I think you'd better tell us what the alleged story is about, James.'

'Oh, that.' It *was* such an anti-climax, just when he was tempted to show off. Her face was slightly flushed, and breathtakingly attractive in the gentle light of the candles that the waiter had brought at her request. 'Well, the hero is an English port salesman.' He saw a look of puzzlement on her face. *'Porto,* the wine, not the other kind. He comes out to Buenos Aires to find clients for his firm. He has

94

a number of names of firms that might be interested, and he also goes to the Commercial Department of the Embassy and gets help there. Within hours of his arrival, however, he meets a glamorous German girl and they begin an affair.'

'Within *hours*,' murmured Manuela. 'He must be a quick worker, your hero.'

'I didn't mean that,' said Caudle. 'He meets the girl very soon after he arrives and it later develops into an affair. Right? It appears there's something mysterious in her background, and he gets an ambiguous warning-off from the Embassy, but that doesn't stop him.'

'Bravo!'

'Don't pull my leg, Manuela. There are some lurid love passages here, which Letty says are essential these days, and some paragraphs about the places in B.A they visit together, restaurants, parks and so on. Like this restaurant, for instance. I'll have to make notes on it tomorrow, but of course give it another name and location. What happens then? The girl disappears, and the hero is frantic. He now learns that she is not only a member of a Neo-Fascist organisation, like your Triple-A, but the daughter of an ex-Gestapo officer who has gone to ground somewhere in Argentina as a result of enquiries made by Simon Wiesenthal, the man who hunts down Nazi war criminals. The hero doesn't get much help from the SSN—'

'That, at least,' put in Juan drily, 'sounds believable.'

'Nor,' continued Caudle, 'from the British Security people, who come out of the whole thing as badly as the SSN.'

'No comment,' murmured Juan, smiling. 'Go on. I'm on edge. What does he do then?'

'Entirely on his own, and through a series of improbable coincidences, he discovers that the girl has been seized by Wiesenthal's agents and transported to Austria. But before they can begin to bargain with her father, or at least force him out of hiding, the hero throws up his job, flies to Austria and succeeds in releasing her. I won't go into that part, but it's cleverly worked out in the synopsis. Letty knows Austria like the back of her hand. It's only the Argentine sequence I'm supposed to research on.'

'But what happens in the end?' asked Manuela. 'Does he marry this Fascist bitch?'

'No. That's the twist. It turns out she's quite as bad as her father, and was simply making use of the hero to get papa into another country. When she learns her father has died from a stroke she tells him the brutal truth. He reproaches her, and she draws a gun. He disarms her, but in the middle of all this the Israelis catch up with them. There is a fight. Girl gets killed,' concluded Caudle, bored with the story by now and speeding up, 'hero is wounded, but is tended by the Israeli agents and returns to England a wiser man.'

Manuela was astonished. 'D'you mean to say people would *pay* to read a story like that?'

'If Letitia wrote it,' declared Caudle loyally, 'of course they would, and there might even be a film. But she isn't going to. It's just a quick mock-up, to give cover to my visit.'

'Every cover story,' said Juan sententiously, 'must be taken seriously. You've got to be prepared to answer questions about it.' He looked up in surprise. The manager with two waiters behind him, was hurrying up to their table. '*Que hay,* Paco?'

The man whispered in his ear, then began to remove coffee cups, brandy glasses and ash-trays and pile them on to a tray held by one of the waiters. The other produced a clean cloth, spread it over the one they had used, which he removed, and began quickly to lay fresh covers. People at other tables were studiously showing unawareness that there was anything odd, not even glancing across the room.

'What's happened?' asked Caudle in a

whisper, as he got to his feet.

'There's a police patrol coming this way, but they're still two miles from the drive. It's a routine check-up, apparently, but I don't want you to be seen here.'

He was leading the way to the door as he spoke. The proprietor was standing there, bowing, but his eyes were shifting from one table to another, assessing whether there were other guests whom he ought to warn. Manuela ran ahead, shrugging herself into her sheepskin coat. She was at the wheel of the little Fiat when they scrambled in, and took off at once, making a slow turn so as not to disturb the gravel, and driving round the side of the restaurant. The place had originally been a ranch-house, and at the rear were stable blocks and bunk-houses, one of which showed lights.

They could dimly see a muddy cart-track leading off into the trees. 'Don't drive into it,' said Juan, urgently, in Spanish. 'The tyre could leave marks they couldn't miss. Find a place where you can get in between the trees and we'll pick up the track later. It leads to a water-tank and there's a windmill; we can hide behind that. Look, there's a gap.'

The earth under the chinaberry trees was thickly carpeted with leaves. The car left the beaten earth of the farmyard and worked its way through the tree trunks, crushing the soggy debris. When it had gone a little way Juan made the girl stop while he took out a torch and ran back to kick leaves over the signs of the car's passage where it had left the open ground.

'*De prisa!*' called Manuela urgently. Looking back, Caudle could see beyond the dark shape of the restaurant the lights of cars approaching. Juan was running back, switching off the torch. The car's parking lights had already been cut and it moved forward. Caudle's eyes were getting used to the starlight, which came bright through the clear air, and he could dimly see the shapes of trees ahead, the mottled trunk of a eucalyptus gleaming like a phantom in the dark. But there was more space now, and the little car was making progress. Then came the drainage ditch.

It was quite shallow, but enough. The front wheel sank into the mud and the rear ones revolved helplessly. 'Switch off,' said Juan curtly, and in the quiet that followed they could hear the crunch of tyres on the gravel of the patio in front of the restaurant, which now lay a hundred and twenty yards behind them, screened from their sight by the trees.

'Give me your jacket,' whispered Juan. 'We've got to cover up anything that shines.' He was stripping off his own as he spoke. Caudle joined him at the rear of the car, and they spread the coats over the bumpers and rear lights, and broke off a leafy branch to cover the windscreen.

'The coats'll fall off,' said Caudle. 'I'll get some pieces of turf.' As they worked their ears were alert for sounds from the restaurant, but they could hear nothing. Caudle whispered, 'I think we're hidden.' Much to his surprise, he was enjoying himself.

'If they bring a car round to the back and turn the headlights on the trees I can't be sure,' said Juan. He opened the rear door, pulled up the cushion on which Caudle had been sitting and brought out a Schmeisser MP40 sub-machine gun. He extended the folding stock and fitted a twenty-eight round magazine. The girl came round the car with a Browning automatic in her hand. Caudle couldn't see her face, but her voice sounded calm enough. 'I'm sorry,' she said to Juan in a low voice. 'I couldn't see that—'

'Leave it till later,' whispered Juan roughly. He tested the turf holding the jackets. 'Keep quiet, both of you, and follow me.'

They trod carefully after him, wincing as the leaves rustled under their feet. He came to three big trees a little way from the car. 'One behind each. Here.' He thrust a small automatic into Caudle's hand. 'I don't suppose you can use it properly, but you might help as a deterrent. Only fire if I do. *Still*, now.'

Caudle felt the smooth weight of the gun butt and pushed forward the safety-catch. What was Juan thinking of doing? Taking on the whole police squad? He stayed behind his tree, waiting. Only a few minutes ago he had been talking about violence and bloodshed, in the phantasy context of Letty's story. Now it was for real, and oddly, he didn't feel afraid.

There was a noise behind him, coming from the grassland beyond the trees. He turned, and at first could discern nothing. Then he heard a rustling in the leaves and a sound of heavy breathing, and a monstrous horned shape appeared, magnified by the darkness. The cow shied away from him, and the bell round its neck jangled loudly. The creature became interested in the car and pushed its nose into the jacket draped over the near part of the bumper. It hooked a fold with its horn, but just at that moment Juan came stealing up behind it and rammed the muzzle of his Schmeisser into its rump. He would have been wiser to have waited, because the startled cow lashed out with its hooves, struck the side of the Fiat a resounding blow, which echoed through the stillness of the night, and rushed forward towards the farmyard with a bellow of rage. There was something trailing from its horn, and Caudle suspected it was his jacket. He raced after it, stumbling through the fallen leaves, and picked it up as it fell. He hurried back and held it over the bumper while Juan fumbled for the turves and put them in place.

'That was a bloody silly thing to do,' whispered Caudle angrily. He was tired of being ordered about by this young man.

'Be quiet. Listen.'

They could see a light moving in the farmyard, and a torch beam flickered through the branches. A voice called, with authority. *'Que pasa,* Pepe?'

*'No es nada, Teniente. Una baca, nada mas.'*

*'Ven acqui, pues. Nos vamos.'*

*'Vengo, Señor.'*

Caudle heard Juan breath a sigh of relief. Still waiting behind their respective trees, they saw the sudden flashes of headlights as three cars started up and turned round in the unseen forecourt of 'El Ranchito'. Then the sounds died away gradually, and shortly afterwards the guests began to emerge from the restaurant and find their cars. The last reflected lights from behind the converted ranch-house became fainter and disappeared.

Juan said, 'Help me to get this thing out of the shit.' He was angry with Manuela, thought Caudle, and it hadn't been the poor girl's fault. The smooth manners of an hour ago seemed to have disappeared. He helped Juan to push the Fiat's front wheels out of the shallow ditch, then Manuela got into the driving seat and with both men bearing down on the rear bumper to stop the spinning the wheels took hold and the car jolted forward. Juan fell on his face, and lay for a moment, cursing.

'I'll go ahead,' said Caudle. 'We don't want to run into another of those ditches. Give me that torch.' The Argentine handed it over as he scrambled to his feet, and Caudle walked forward slowly, finding room between the trees and aiming in the general direction of the farm track they had seen earlier. He flashed the torch only for split seconds. The Fiat followed, its lights still off. They reached the track.

'Can we go back through the restaurant patio?' asked Manuela in a subdued voice.

'Of course not,' said Juan angrily. 'One of the police may have stayed for a drink. We'll take this track to the water-tank and from there I'm pretty sure it continues to the main road. If not we'll just have to wait and freeze until everybody's gone to bed.' He turned to Manuela. 'You can use your parking lights now.'

She made no reply, but turned towards the pampa and drove off. Soon they heard the loud clanking of a windmill, and saw the tall steel pylon looming ahead in the starlight. Below it was the tank and a series of water troughs for cattle. She stopped the car while the two men washed the mud from their shoes and trousers in the ice-cold water and got back, shivering, into the warmth of the Fiat. The track wandered away across the grass towards the line of trees that bordered the road. As they approached they could see the lights of cars passing. Juan still had the Schmeisser cradled in his arms.

Cautiously, Manuela drove through the screen of trees on to the main road. There was no car in sight. She switched on the headlights and set off fast towards the glow of Buenos Aires in the distance.

Juan folded the sub-machine gun and handed it back to Caudle. 'Sorry to trouble you,' he said politely. 'But I'm afraid you'll have to get off the seat for a moment and put this away.'

Caudle's hands lingered for a moment, feeling the cold steel of the weapon and remembering the last time—so long ago—when he had handled one of these things. Then he pushed it under the seat cushion, resumed his seat, and handed the automatic back to Santos, who thanked him and pushed it into the glove compartment.

'Manuela was going to give me advice about gathering material for the story,' said Caudle, to no one in particular. The other two had not spoken to each other since they had reached the main road.

'Your natural course would be to go to your Consulate General and ask to see someone who can help you,' said the girl. 'And you said the Embassy came into it, too, the Commercial Department. I don't know about the British intelligence office, but—'

'I do,' broke in Juan. 'It's run by a man named Neville Bruce, and it's in the Embassy. I doubt whether you'd get to see him because you can't admit you know his name. You'd have a better chance of getting local background stuff if you could make friends in the English Club.'

'I see. Thanks. There's a lot of topographical research, too, like street names and the general lay-out of the city. I can go to the tourist centre for that, I suppose, but I'll also do a good deal of exploring on foot. Then of course I'll have to see Mendoza.' He saw Manuela half turn towards Juan, who said sharply, 'I don't think that will be—Which Mendoza?'

'Where all the oil wells are, but it's also

a centre for the wine trade, according to Letitia.'

'Oh, I see. It's a delightful place.' There was no mistaking the relief in Juan's voice. 'But it's a thousand kilometres away to the west. You'd have to fly there, although the road's good enough if you don't mind making a long trip of it. It's on the slopes of the Andes, at fifteen hundred metres, so it'll be damned cold at this time of year.'

'You may find the air schedules awkward,' said Manuela. 'Why don't you get to know Buenos Aires first, and leave Mendoza till Monday? I'm pretty certain there are planes then. I could take you to see the polo at Hurlingham, if that would come in useful, and there are restaurants with folk-lore dancing and so on.'

'I'd like that very much,' said Caudle, his pulse quickening. 'But how are we going to meet—I mean, officially, so to speak?'

'I'll give you the names of friends of mine in England, and you could say one of them had told you to contact me.' She paused. 'You see, I was at school there.'

'So that explains your really excellent English,' said Caudle.

Juan broke in. 'I'm afraid I don't think this is a good idea,' he said firmly, and Caudle could almost feel the nudge the man gave Manuela. 'For the next two days I think you should get stuck into your cover work on your own. Then, if the SSN is still following you around, they'll get bored by the time we meet on Sunday. Now, this is how I'll get in touch. The man in the room next to yours, where I was when we met tonight, is a Colonel Rojas. I will let you know through him when we can meet. He'll either knock on the communicating door when he's sure you're alone, or push a note under the door. O.K?'

'Thanks. That sounds fine.' He thought for a moment. 'If possible, I'd like very much to see how you train your recruits, and also get a better idea what you might require from us if you should decide to operate in the U.K.' It was what Letty had asked him to find out, even if, after what Juan had told him, the whole scheme looked more impracticable than ever.

Santos laughed. 'I'll see what can be done. You'd have to be blindfolded, of course, if we took you to any of our centres.'

'Of course.' He looked at the time. Nearly midnight. 'Could you drop me at the hotel, please?' The car had reached the central districts of the city and was driving down one of the wide *avenidas*. The streets were brightly lit and looked more animated than in daytime, with the bars and restaurants still full of people.

'No. That'd be a bad thing. We'll drop you, if you don't mind, at a big restaurant on Corrientes. Spend half an hour there over a drink and get to know the place, in case you're questioned where you've been tonight. It's a short walk from the Reconquista.'

As the Fiat entered Avenida Corrientes, Juan turned round in his seat. 'I'm sorry you had this experience tonight, James. It shouldn't have happened. We ought to have been given longer warning. There'll be an inquiry in the morning, and we'll both have to give evidence.'

'You maintain a pretty strict discipline, I suppose.'

'We have to,' said Juan shortly. 'Incidentally, you've forgotten something.' He felt in his pocket. 'Here's your room key.'


## CHAPTER TEN

At about the time Caudle had been tackling his *asado* at 'El Ranchito', Neville Bruce was talking to his Ambassador in a corner of one of the magnificent reception rooms in the Italian Ambassador's residence. The party was in full swing, and the noise was deafening.

'You wanted to know about this man Caudle, sir,' he shouted in Sir Roderick's ear.

'Oh yes, the armchair revolutionary. Did your snoopers pick him up?'

'Yes, sir, and so did the SSN. They had someone at the airport and Caudle was followed to the Reconquista Hotel. No attempt was made to contact him, as far as my man could find out. He didn't appear again in the foyer, so I suppose he went to bed early. He certainly didn't leave the hotel, unless he slunk out by the back door.'

'I see. Oh Lord! There's the German coming across, to talk Common Market, I expect. All right, Neville. Keep an eye on Caudle, the red menace. I don't want trouble.' As the German Ambassador bore down on them Bruce faded into the familiar throng of fellow diplomats.

The next morning Bruce was at his desk early, frowning at a report that had come in during the night: 'Subject returned to the Reconquista Hotel at 0115 hours this morning on foot. I cannot explain how he evaded surveillance earlier. There were two men observing the entrance of the hotel and he did not leave. If he emerged by another door it could only have been with some local help.'

'That's a fine story,' said Bruce angrily to his P.A, a girl named Cynthia Starling, who was the mainstay of the office. 'The bloody fools must have gone round the corner for a quick one.'

'Why did he put up at the Reconquista? It isn't one of the Aerolineas hotels.'

'Why? I don't know. I suppose Lopez Suarez suggested it.'

'Exactly,' said Cynthia, smiling in her superior way. 'You didn't think of that, did you, Neville?'

'Blast you! I think there's something in what you're insinuating. These old hotels have as many entrances as a rabbit warren. Damn! I've slipped up. Tell Jack to make sure they watch all exits in future. And I'd better have a look at this Caudle before he does something silly and makes H.E's bearings run hot. Get a message to all heads of departments, would you, please? Say I'd be glad of a quiet word with them on the blower if Caudle should turn up, as he's almost certain to, in one section or another. I don't mean all departments—just Information, C.G, Commercial—oh yes, and the Council, too. He's researching material for a thriller, ostensibly, and he might try any one of them for help.'

It was the Vice-Consul in charge of the

passport section of the Consulate General who telephoned about an hour later. 'The C.G asked me to let you know if a Mr James Caudle turned up. Well he's here now, filling up his registration form.'

'Thanks, Cecil. Will you see him before he goes?'

'Not necessarily. The seccy'll show him out.'

'Well, do something for me, would you? Find out what he's doing here. Don't let on you know he's gathering background information for a thriller writer, but when he tells you suggest strongly that he goes round to the Information Officer.'

'He's told me what he's doing already. I gave him a few addresses and told him to try the British Council.'

'Change your mind, then. Tell him the I.O might be the better bet.'

'O.K.'

Bruce rang the Information Officer, who was a friend of his. He concluded, 'So that's what I want, Tom. Show such an interest in him that you finish by offering to introduce him in the Club. Say you'll stand him a drink there. I'll pay. And I'll be there from twelve-thirty onwards, to take him off your hands and give him lunch.'

'You don't want much, do you?' grumbled the I.O. 'But since you ask so prettily—' he rang off.

When Caudle was brought into the Information Officer's room he was agreeably surprised at the warmth of his welcome. Tom Bristowe explained that he was a fan of Harriet Pringle's and would be delighted to help her with Argentine material. He told Caudle where to buy a reliable city plan and maps of remoter parts of the country and sent him off to Mackern's English Bookstore for books and guides. But as he took him out through the general office Bristowe paused. 'The question of the wine contacts—I can see that's important. You'd better have a word with Jackson in Commercial Department. Tell you what, there's an old boy named Jasper Rainham who is actually the representative of some of the Portuguese port factors. He's always propping up the bar of the Club about one o'clock. Meet me there, and I'll introduce you to one or two people like Rainham.'

Caudle was delighted. He went to see Jackson and came out with stacks of information about the Argentine wine trade, import permits, remitted profits and ways of coping with a rapidly devaluating peso.

The visit to the English Club was also productive, and Rainham, the wine importer, and another devotee of Letty's lurid stories, invited him to dinner the following night at his home. It would be more useful background, thought Caudle happily. If everyone was so cooperative he could finish up by practically writing the damned book. He had accepted the invitation and was turning away, when Bristowe brought up a man in his early thirties, clean-shaven, with a pleasant, weathered face.

'Here's someone else I wanted you to meet,' began Bristowe. 'He's the chap with the local know-how. Neville Bruce.'

Caudle started slightly. That was the name Juan had mentioned the night before. 'Is that a job in itself?' he asked smiling, as they shook hands.

Bruce spoke with a slight Scottish accent. 'Actually, I'm a First Secretary in Chancery, but what Tom means is that I'm a sort of trouble-shooter, seeing that I know the country pretty well. I was born in these parts. Are you just here on a visit?'

Bristowe explained Caudle's mission.

'Oh well, if there's anything I can do,' said Bruce cheerfully, 'I'll be delighted. Are you lunching here?'

'No. I'd better be getting back, I suppose. I'll get in touch if I'm stuck, then, and thanks.'

'Look here. Why don't you lunch with

me, and we can have a talk about your requirements. I'm going to be very busy in the next few days, and you mightn't be able to find me.'

Caudle hesitated for only a moment. The prospect of lunching alone didn't appeal, after the warm friendliness of the Club. 'That's very kind of you. Thanks very much.'

It was a good lunch, and Caudle began to feel at ease with Bruce, who chatted knowledgeably about the great expanses of the pampas, the ski-ing at Bariloche above the great lakes, and the enormous stretches of Patagonia with its Welsh settlers some of whom, even after four generations, could still speak the language of their origin.

It all sounded idyllic. The man spoke, thought Caudle with a sense of irritation, as if the old capitalist system were still intact. 'But can one travel around in safety?' he asked. 'I thought the whole country was in the throes of revolution. Aren't there regular formations of armed Marxists who keep the military on the run?'

Bruce took a long swallow of lager beer. 'I wouldn't say that exactly,' he said. 'It's true that both the ERP and the Montoneros can and do attack military strongholds, and sometimes successfully. And they've both made themselves very rich from hi-jackings, robberies and so on. But so far neither movement has tried for a final confrontation with the military, and if they did try, they'd lose. That was the mistake of the Tupamaros in Uruguay. They found they could run rings round the police, but when they tried to take on the army they failed. However well-trained and well-armed you are, as guerrillas, you can't sustain a full-scale campaign against professional troops with spotting planes, armoured cars and tanks.

'The real trouble has been the strong feeling throughout the people towards military dictatorship. During Ysabel Peron's time the armed forces held back, for that reason, hoping that the rival armed factions, left and right, would fight each other to a standstill. Peron himself, while he was alive, after his return from exile, never really tried to govern; in fact he called himself *El Conductor,* as if he were conducting a bloody orchestra. Even under the new Government, with full military support, it's going to take a lot of time to get peace. It's a very tragic situation, but in fact it affects the lives of people as a whole less than you'd think. I love this country, Caudle. I think it's one of the most beautiful in the world, and I hate to see it defaced. But that's what's happening.'

'There are still far too many very rich and very poor,' said Caudle doggedly. 'A redistribution of wealth might be just what's needed.'

'I agree, and I think most people think the same. But you don't necessarily get a fairer distribution of wealth by wrecking the economy, which is what both the Trots and the Fascists are doing at present.'

'But don't you see,' cried Caudle. 'That may be the only way. Destroy the whole capitalist system and start again. The very rich, and the foreign exploiters, are already scared for their lives.'

Bruce smiled. 'Take a look around. Do all these foreign exploiters look as scared as that?' He saw the obstinate look on the other man's face. 'Listen, I know that's the Marxist theory, or at least the extreme leftist one, but it's never worked yet, and I assure you it won't in this country, ever. I know the people—the common people if you like. Give them power, and they'll use it to destroy each other.'

'That's the most cynical bit of capitalist dogma I've ever heard.'

'Is it? D'you know what happened when Juan Peron came out of exile to be President in June '73?'

'There was a blood-bath, wasn't there? The soldiers fired on the crowd.'

'Oh for God's sake, Caudle, get your

facts right. All the regulars had been confined to barracks, to keep them away from the jubilant crowds, who lined the route you took from Ezeiza. In millions, literally. It was the paramilitary units of rival Peronist factions who did the shooting, quarrelling about who should be allowed in the grandstand. Those factions called themselves Fascists or Marxists, but they were all supporters of Peron.' Bruce finished his beer. 'Several hundred people were killed, most of them innocent bystanders. You see what I mean.' He called a waiter. 'Cheese or pudding?'

'Just coffee, thanks.'

'Same here. Let's go into the smoking-room.'

When they were sitting in the Club's comfortable armchairs Caudle said, 'I suppose you're on the side of the military?'

'No, I'm not. I don't have any particular political views, but I'll tell you what I don't like, and that's revolutionary terrorism, whether it's left or right.'

'But they *aren't* terrorists; they're revolutionaries who find no alternative to armed insurrection.'

'People who indulge in random slaughter of working-class women and children in a bombed train, and who use assassination, extortion and other acts of frightfulness are terrorists, in my book. I agree the

117

right-wing groups are just as bad as the Marxists, but it doesn't alter the fact that they're wrecking the country, and if it goes on we'll be faced with either civil war or a brutal and oppressive dictatorship.'

'The ERP and the Montoneros have the right ideas,' said Caudle defiantly, 'but it takes time to get rid of the trappings of capitalism. Once that's done they'll give the people the government they want.'

'My dear chap, you're talking out of the back of your head. The Marxists have no real support from the people at all, who were brought up by Peron to want a sort of moderate Fascist state—which is a contradiction of terms, of course. The last thing they want is Communism. They've shown that again and again.'

'You're saying that to provoke me,' said Caudle angrily.

'No, I'm not. I'm saying it with a purpose. I just want to warn you to be very careful not to get involved with the ERP. They're dangerous people, and you might get yourself into serious trouble.'

'Why d'you think I'm interested in the ERP?'

'You're Secretary of the New Revolutionary Group, aren't you?'

'You know a lot, don't you? I heard you were—'

'We hear things. I told you; one of my

jobs is to prevent trouble with the local authorities. So now you've been warned. And incidentally, who told you I was something? And what?'

'A friend. You're the SIS representative.' He had to score off this man somehow, and shake his blasted self-confidence.

But Bruce laughed. 'If I denied it, you wouldn't believe me, would you? I've told you what my job is, and what I want to make clear is that if you get into a jam, tell me at once. I may be able to help.'

'You're going to a lot of trouble for a casual acquaintance. Although I don't imagine this meeting was all that casual. You worked it somehow, didn't you?'

'You flatter yourself. Her Majesty's Embassy is not concerned in the least with you or your personal safety, unless you get involved in political issues. If you get robbed or go bust in the casino I couldn't care less; the Consul General will cope. But if you play around with the ERP or otherwise attract the attention of the security people I will help you to get out of this country fast. In fact,' added Bruce smiling. 'I will make bloody sure you do.'

'I see. Well, I'd better be going. Er—thanks for the lunch.'

'It was my pleasure. Where are you going now?'

'It's really none of your business, you know. But there's nothing to hide. I'm going to explore the city a bit more and go and see the British Consul. Then Thomas Cook's. I've got to be able to give a description of Mendoza.'

'Who?' said Bruce, startled. Caudle remembered Juan's similar reaction to the name.

'Not who, but what. The town in the Cordillera. Where all the wine's made.'

'Oh of course. It's a delightful town.'

'Come on, Bruce. Why did you jump when I mentioned Mendoza? It's the second time it's happened to me.'

'Mendoza is the pseudonym of the Chief of Staff of the ERP,' said Bruce, and he was very serious now. 'No one seems to know his real name, but he's a very clever and powerful man, and completely ruthless.'

Most of the shops and offices seemed to be closed between noon and four o'clock, and Caudle spent an hour exploring the older part of the city around the Plaza de Mayo, and admiring the few great colonial buildings like the Casa Rosada, the pink headquarters of the President, and the impressive Cabildo, where the movement to break away from Spanish rule was born in 1810 and the Viceroy was deposed. The rest of the inner town he found impersonal and rather shabby, but the parks were beautiful, and in a rose garden surrounded by high trees, in the Parque Lezama, he found a bench, and sat there for nearly an hour, making notes and putting down answers to Letty's questionnaire.

This was a welcome development for the SSN spy who was trailing Caudle, because his shoes were hurting him. When the Englishman finally got to his feet and wandered back into the streets the man sighed and began to follow, keeping well behind as his target went first to Cook's, where he booked a return passage by air to Mendoza for Monday, and then to the British Council, on Marcelo T. de Alvear. It was dark and nearly seven o'clock when, thankfully, he saw Caudle re-enter the Hotel Reconquista. He turned into a doorway to make his report by radio, and then found a seat in a café opposite the lighted windows of the hotel foyer from which he could watch the entrance until his relief arrived.

Caudle found his bed had been turned down and the room looked tidy, apart from some tourist literature he had brought back earlier. Then his eye was caught by a sheet of writing paper which he didn't remember leaving on the beside table. He read it with interest:

'Dear Mr Caudle,

I promised Letty Hennessy I would write to a friend of mine in Buenos Aires, and she has just replied. Her name is Manuela Belgrano, and she'll be delighted to meet you and help you to get the information Letitia wants for her book. I've given her your hotel address, and she'll be getting in touch. Please give her my love.

I do hope you enjoy your trip.

Yours sincerely,

Susan Radcliffe.'

There was a Chelsea address as heading, and the letter was written in a round, bold hand, of the kind Caudle associated with girls' boarding schools in England. He smiled. It must have been written by Manuela; she'd said something about having a notional friend in England who could notionally write an introduction for her, and this was it. All very efficient. Folded and a little rumpled, as if he had been carrying it in his pocket. But who had put it on his desk?

As if to answer his question, there was a quiet knock on the communicating door. He opened it.

On the threshold was a small white-haired man with a carefully tended bristly moustache. He was standing at attention and bowing formally. '*Coronel* Isidor Rojas

Monterrey,' he introduced himself, holding out his hand, and continued in Spanish, 'I am glad to make your acquaintance, Mr Caudle. Would you care to join me in a glass of sherry?'

Caudle thanked him. He locked the door of his own room and slid the bolt. In the next room was a bottle of sherry and some *tapas*—olives and shellfish—ready on the small table at which Juan had entertained him the day before. They sat down, and Rojas filled the glasses.

'Did you put a certain piece of paper in the room next door?' asked Caudle, smiling.

The little Colonel looked guilty. 'I must beg your pardon for the intrusion, but my friend Santos was anxious that you should have it. I gather you have already met the enchanting young lady in question.' His stiff manner slipped for a moment, and he permitted himself a small, lecherous smile. Raising his glass, he said, *'Olé las mujeres castizas!'*

'I will certainly drink to that,' said Caudle, and did so. It was a genuine Spanish fino, probably extremely expensive in South America. He looked at the little man speculatively. 'I am delighted to find in you, *mi Coronel,* evidence that proper revolutionary thoughts are found even in the armed services of Argentina.'

The brown, wrinkled face of the Colonel became blank. He put down his glass and said carefully, 'I'm afraid I don't get your meaning, Señor. I am now on the Reserve, owing to my age, but I am still a loyal officer of the General Staff and have no truck whatever with what you call revolutionary thoughts.'

'But you work for Juan Santos,' protested Caudle.

'I do not *work* for him, Señor. I see you are referring to his occasional use of my room at this hotel. But that is just an act of friendship. When Santos wants to meet a young lady of society in—er—strict privacy I am always glad to vacate my room for a few hours while youthful desires find their natural expression.' He gave again that slightly leering smile, and added, 'Just as I shall be delighted to offer you the same service if you should wish to enjoy the company of a young lady, and you may rely on my complete discretion.' He made a deprecating gesture. 'There is a small fee, since I am a poor man, a retired soldier. Ten dollars. You would have to pay much more in a *maison de rendezvous.*'

Caudle was half shocked, half amused. So that was *his* cover story. Suddenly, he began to feel impatient with this labyrinth of lies and deception. 'Have you any instructions for me?' he asked bluntly.

124

The little man was obviously offended. Caudle had shown a lack of *puntillo*. He said, 'I gather that Señorita Belgrano will call for you on Sunday morning and take you to see places of interest. She invites you to lunch, and it may be evening before you complete your tour. She will be in the foyer at half past ten.' He set down his glass, touched his moustache with the back of his index finger, and looked at Caudle fiercely.

'Thank you, I shall look forward to it. And thanks for this excellent sherry, *mi Coronel*. I had better get back to my room now. There is much work for me to do. Goodnight, Señor.'

The Colonel took him to the door, bowed rather stiffly and wished him a pleasant evening. Caudle heard the key turn in the lock behind him.

He spent some time in writing up his notes, went downstairs as soon as the dining-room opened at nine o'clock and retired to bed early.

Saturday was a pleasant day for Caudle. A young man in the British Council office, with whom he had struck up a friendship the previous day, drove him out to the Country Club at Hurlingham, which they both agreed was a stronghold of capitalist privilege and arrogance, and Caudle gave

125

him lunch at a wayside restaurant. The evening spent at the Rainham's was thoroughly enjoyable, and for once, Caudle had the sense not to talk politics, for fear of shocking his host and Mrs Rainham, a gentle white-haired woman who insisted in telling him all about her married daughters and their troubles. After a final talk with the old man, who plied him with vintage port, Caudle returned to the hotel in a roseate glow.

Bruce's man had been recalled earlier, when they reported that Caudle was under constant watch by SSN snoopers. These wretched men, however, kept up their cold watch throughout the night, relieving each other at intervals and—as Juan had predicted—becoming increasingly bored.

## CHAPTER ELEVEN

When Caudle entered the foyer of the hotel the following morning there was a man in a grey suit sitting by a potted palm, reading *La Prensa*. For a moment Caudle saw a pair of sharp eyes watching; then they were hastily lowered to the newspaper. He went to the desk, handed in his key and bought a copy of the English language

*Buenos Aires Herald.* Then he glanced at his watch. Ten twenty-eight. He stood at the counter, reading the headlines with an eye on the revolving doors. It was a cold day, and he was wearing his duffle coat, but not the Tyrolese hat. As Juan had said, it *was* a bit distinctive.

When Manuela came in he did not recognise her. Her dark hair was piled up on top of her head and she wore enormous sunglasses. She was wrapped in a long fur coat, and looked extremely expensive ... But her voice was unmistakable.

She spoke to the desk-clerk. 'Would you ring Mr Caudle's room, please.'

The man smiled. 'Mr Caudle's here, Madam.' He pointed to the Englishman standing next to her.

She turned with a start, and spoke in English. 'How d'you do, Mr Caudle. Susan Radcliffe wrote about me, I think?'

'Señorita Belgrano?' He held out his hand, smiling. 'It's very kind of you to take charge of me today.'

'I shall enjoy it,' she said coolly. 'Are you ready to come with me now? The car isn't supposed to wait outside the hotel, so we'd better be quick.'

'Of course.' They moved towards the doors. Out of the corner of his eye Caudle saw the man in the grey suit put down his paper and pick up an overcoat.

Outside, a man in a chauffeur's uniform was standing by a pale grey Mercedes. He opened the car door, quickly closed it after them and got into the driving seat.

The SSN man was close behind, struggling into his coat. As he stood on the pavement, signalling to the driver of his own car, parked twenty yards away, a large man in a coat with an astrakhan collar came up to him and asked the way to the Banco de Londres y America del Sur.

'It's on the corner of this street and Bartolome Mitre,' said the man in the grey suit hurriedly. 'Excuse me, Señor.' His car was sliding up alongside.

The big man held his arm. 'But where is that, Señor?' he persisted. 'I don't *know* the city. Which way?' His hand tightened as the other tried to break away.

The SSN man lost his head. 'Let me go!' he shouted. 'Ask someone else, *por Dios!*'

The big man had somehow got between him and the car. 'Such manners!' he admonished. 'So that is how you Porteños treat a provincial.' He released his grip just as the driver of the car opened the door, ready to jump out. 'I will ask someone else,' he said with dignity.

The man in the grey suit hesitated for a moment. Had the incident been staged? But his priority was clear. He shook his head angrily and got into the passenger seat, telling the driver to get moving.

The Mercedes had disappeared. 'Which way did it go?' asked the agent anxiously.

'*Hombre,* I don't know,' said the driver reproachfully. 'I was trying to help you.'

The SSN man swore. '*Animal!*' he cried. 'Did you forget to look for the number, too?'

'No, Señor.' The driver gave it, and with a sigh of relief the agent reached for his pocket radio and switched on the transmitter.

'There was a man following us from the hotel,' warned Caudle.

'Yes, I saw him. It's O.K I'd made arrangements, and he's lost us.'

'But he'll have your registration number,' cried Caudle. 'Every prowl car will be looking for us.'

'Not for long, James. You'll see.'

They had turned from the Avenida Corrientes into the smaller streets of the old town, which Caudle had explored earlier. Several turnings later the Mercedes drew alongside a parked blue Porsche. Manuela already had her door open, with a set of car keys in her hand, and sprang out, calling on Caudle to follow. She ensconced herself behind the wheel of the Porsche and opened the door on Caudle's side. The Mercedes was already purring away, and vanished around the next corner.

'What'll happen to him?' asked Caudle, fascinated by this practicable example of ERP expertise.

'He'll get his plates changed a few hundred metres from here.'

'Then why couldn't you have gone there, changed the Merc's plates and saved trouble?' He started. 'I see. So that I shouldn't see where it was done. Is that it?'

'You're catching on, James. For the same reason why I wouldn't want the chauffeur to see where I'm taking you. It's all a question of need-to-know. Now you can sit back and enjoy a nice long drive.' She turned a flashing smile at his thoughtful face. 'D'you like watching birds—the feathered kind?'

'My wife does. She paints them. She's on a bird-watching tour now, while I'm away.' So very far away, he thought. Among strange, unpredictable, devious people. Manuela's proximity was disturbing.

'That's very clever of her to paint them,' said Manuela. 'Is she good at it?'

'Very,' he said loyally. It wasn't really true. 'If genius is a supreme capacity for taking pains, then Pat's a genius.'

'Is that her name, then, Patricia? It's a pretty name.'

'Like her. She's pretty, all right.'

'But?'

'What d'you mean—but?'

'Oh, it's what people say, isn't it?' said Manuela casually. 'She's pretty, all right, but she can't cook. Or spell. Or she's got bad breath, or something.'

'Just let's stop talking about my wife, shall we?'

Manuela sighed contentedly. 'That's the attitude I like men to take, when they're with me. Now, where was I? Oh yes, the birds. You'll see what I mean when we get clear of the suburbs.'

Caudle glanced sideways at the girl's cool, serene face, the lips slightly parted and delicious, as she drove smoothly and quickly through the crowded streets. 'Juan said there would be an enquiry on Friday, after what'd happened at "El Ranchito". What was the result?'

'Someone got disciplined,' she said briefly, discouraging further comment.

The bright sun was behind the car, which meant, in this topsy-turvy southern hemisphere, that they were heading roughly southwards. The suburbs fell back and they were out on the pampa, stretching dead flat and green to the horizon, with endless wire fences held by *quebracho* wood posts, which will blunt an axe. The splendid cattle grazed on the lush grass. Mile after mile, there seemed to be no streams at all,

131

but spidery windmills dotted the landscape. Shielded by screens of eucalyptus trees the estancias lay at some distance from the highway. Some of the approach roads bore English names, but Manuela said most of the former landowners had left.

They came to a stretch of marshy ground, with pools of standing water. 'Now you'll see the birds,' said the girl. 'Look!'

A pink and white cloud of flamingoes rose from a reedy little lake, circled round, and returned to the water's edge as the car passed. Other birds were flying about officiously, screaming at each other. Then they, too, went back to the pool.

'The frogs must be having a bad time,' commented Caudle. 'What are those other birds? They look like herons.'

'They're egrets.' Manuela pointed out the enormous nests which topped every telephone post. 'Those are oven birds, what we call *horneros*. I suppose they do look a bit like those tall domed bread ovens, made of straw and clay, that the country people use. The birds make them almost as strong, and they're far too big for their families, but they somehow stay balanced on top of the poles in spite of all the high winds we have here.'

'It's fantastic. I've never seen so many birds outside a conservation area.' All over the pampa birds were rising, their wings wheeling and flashing in the sunlight, and planing down again to the reeds.

'I'm afraid that's all you're going to see,' said Manuela. 'Feel in the glove pocket. There's an eye-mask. Put it on, and no cheating, James, please.'

He found the mask, similar to those given out to passengers on the aircraft to help them to sleep. The black nylon patches, held by an elastic string that passed round the head, fitted closely over his eyes and made a most effective blindfold. Then he felt the girl put something into his hand. It was the pair of jumbo-size sunglasses she had been wearing. 'Put them on over the mask,' she ordered. 'Then if a car passes it won't look odd.'

He did as he was told. It was clever, he thought grudgingly. You could hardly have a passenger wearing a blindfold on a public road, but the eye-mask was hidden behind the large sunglasses. He felt the car accelerating, smoothly and noiselessly, and it went at high speed for what seemed a long time. He found it was difficult to maintain a conversation when one couldn't see. Then the Porsche slowed down, turned on to a dirt road, to judge by the feel of it, and proceeded at a modest speed for what seemed a mile or more. Then came the bumping rattle of a cattlegrid.

'When we arrive,' explained Manuela's voice, 'you must please keep the mask on until I tell you to take it off. You'll then be in a room with closed shutters, and that's where most of the talking will take place. Juan will be there, too, and he and I will not be wearing masks, of course. But the man you'll be meeting will. I'm sorry, but that's the rule.'

'Who is he? May I at least know that?'

'He's called Mendoza, and he's our Chief of Staff.'

## CHAPTER TWELVE

When Caudle was told to remove his mask and sunglasses he found himself blinking in a brightly-lit room. The light came from a crystal chandelier hanging from the cedar-wood ceiling and, as Manuela had said, the high windows were covered by heavy wooden shutters. A wood fire was burning in the open hearth. The room was large and elegantly proportioned, but converted into an office, with desks, a conference table, map-cabinets and card-indexes. There were darker patches on the pale blue walls where pictures had once hung. Nothing remained that gave the room individuality or connected it with any family or person. Some armchairs had been arranged around the fireplace, and a table was set with drinks and glasses, but these were the only concessions to comfort.

After a very brief glance around him Caudle's eyes were fixed on a man who stood with his back to the fire. He was tall and strongly-built, dressed incongruously in a hacking coat and breeches, with polished riding-boots, and he wore a stock. Below a black hood, which concealed his hair, the face was moulded in smooth black leather, with only a thin line of lips and a glint of dark eyes to be seen through slits in the mask. The holes pierced for the nostrils added a chilling suggestion of an animal, rather than a man.

Mendoza spoke Spanish, in the harsh Argentine idiom, as he held out a hand from which the signet ring had been carefully removed. 'Welcome, Señor Caudle. I apologise for this charade, but I'm afraid there's no alternative. I gather you understand Castilian?'

'Adequately, I think.'

'Good. If you don't follow what I say Santos will interpret. But first let me offer you a drink after your long drive. Juan.'

Santos filled slender glasses with Tio Pepe, well chilled, and Manuela offered them around. Her fur coat had vanished, and she appeared in a black sweater and slacks. She chose a high-backed chair a little outside the ring of armchairs where the three men took their seats, and sat attentive, her legs demurely crossed at the ankles.

The masked man said, 'I am called Mendoza, Señor, but that is not my name. My duties on the staff of the *Ejercito* include both our military and civil operations, and I gather it is about the latter you wish to be informed. Is that so?'

'Yes, Señor. On behalf of the President of my movement I am instructed to consult you about fund-raising operations.'

There was a twitch in the smooth black surface of the mask, as if the man behind it had frowned—or smiled. 'That is not a term we use ourselves. The civilian tasks have three objectives: to discourage foreign exploitation of my country's wealth, to show up the weaknesses of the Government in power and thirdly, as you put it, to raise the necessary funds.'

'I see. It is the last objective, however, which concerns us. We do not believe in violence—'

The masked face jerked up. 'My dear sir,

that is surely a remarkable statement for a so-called revolutionary to make. Would you explain?'

'Certainly.' For once Caudle felt himself on firm ground, and his once-fluent Spanish was coming back to him. 'There are other Marxist movements in the United Kingdom which are doing their best to discourage foreign investment and to make the Government unable to govern. We fear however that these activities will prove counter-productive. They will provoke repressive action by the Government, the further restriction of civil liberties, and in the end, a resentment of revolutionary activities by the people as a whole.' He saw Mendoza about to speak, and held up his hand. 'Permit me, Señor. I think you were about to suggest that quite the contrary result might be achieved, that as life became unbearable for the people they would become embittered with the Government—indeed with any system of constitutional government—and demand sweeping changes in the whole of the system of rule. In fact, that is exactly what other revolutionary parties—I exclude the Soviet-dominated Communist Party—regard as the end in view. They are seeking what the Brazilian Carlos Marighela called a climate of collapse, in which the revolutionaries would be

137

seen as the only viable alternative to the constitutional government.'

'And what is wrong with that theory, Señor?' asked Mendoza sharply.

'I will be frank, Señor Mendoza. The people of the United Kingdom are conservative, and I am speaking of members of all three main political parties. They would turn against the revolutionaries, not against their elected Government. And with good reason. Because they know that in the final struggle the armed forces, which are almost—I regret to say this—wholly loyal to the regime in power, would be called in and would crush the guerrilleros and the paramilitary forces of the revolutionaries. Is not this what happened in Uruguay?' He remembered what Bruce had said, and added, 'Could it not happen here?'

There was a moment of thunderstruck silence. Caudle pressed on. 'If I am right, the Tupamaros in Uruguay were able to produce a state of near-collapse, because they showed that they were more than equal to the forces of the police. But once the armed services were called in they could not continue the fight. They were out-numbered—and out-classed.'

Mendoza's mask turned towards Juan Santos. 'Our friend does not mince his words, does he? You really think, Señor

Caudle, that the same thing might occur here?'

'I cannot possibly judge, Señor. All I am certain of is that it would happen in my country. Everyone would suffer, we might be given a government with dictatorial powers, but the people as a whole would not go into the streets. They are not ready for revolution.'

'Then what precisely, Señor, do you see as the proper line for a revolutionary party in Britain to follow?'

'What we are doing. Our aim is to educate the people so that they will learn the true meaning of the theories of Marx and Engels, from which Lenin deviated all too tragically. But it will take a very long time and a great deal of money. We should like to be able to launch newspapers with wide circulation and persuade—even hire—men in positions of political power. If the British trade unions can use their large funds to sponsor Members of Parliament so could we, if we had the money. We need men in the highest places to propagate our views.'

Mendoza said slowly, 'The German revolutionary Rudi Dutschke concluded that the alternative to violent revolution was what he called the long march through the institutions. Is that what you have in mind?'

Caudle sighed. The man had missed the point entirely. 'No, Señor. That again is what the other Marxist parties, including the Communists, are trying to do. It is what we call entryism. They hope to gain ultimate control of the unions and in the Labour Party by infiltration, but they are already provoking a tightening of the ranks of the so-called moderates. What we believe is that nothing less than a real revolution in the thinking of all the people is necessary before there can be any attempt to take power in their name. Our campaign, to make it quite clear, is one of enlightenment only, and is non-violent. But in the long-term it will be decisive.'

'I am not surprised,' burst out Santos, 'that your movement is headed by a woman.'

Mendoza turned on him quickly. 'Let us not forget,' he said in a tone of sharp reproof, 'that Señor Caudle is our guest. His views may seem strange to us, perhaps impracticable, though I find them interesting. But,' he added, turning to Caudle, 'you must surely realise, Señor, that if you wish to raise very large funds by the methods we have developed here you cannot exclude the element of violence. Even if we were prepared to provide skilled operatives we should still need a great deal of what I might call lay assistance, and don't forget that if your part in such operations were discovered you would be equally liable at law.'

Caudle was still smarting from Juan's remark. Made in the hearing of Manuela it had an added sting. He began to depart from his carefully planned brief. 'Of course. In fact, we might wish to take part in the actual operations, if you were agreeable. We have no objections to using arms,' he added, wondering what Letty would say if she knew what he was offering, 'but as deterrents wherever possible.'

Before Juan could again interrupt Mendoza said suavely, 'That is exactly what we also aim to do. Bloodshed is unnecessary in kidnapping operations, provided the plans are laid with care. And I should explain that we do in fact depend very largely on kidnapping and ransom demands, rather than bank raids, which are riskier and more likely to lead to the bloodshed we deplore. For the same reason we eschew hijack operations completely; they inevitably cause suffering to innocent people.'

The bloody hypocrite, thought Caudle. What about—But before he could speak, and perhaps it was just as well, he saw Mendoza getting to his feet. The black mask turned towards him. 'You said you had no objection to firearms, Señor Caudle.

Perhaps at this point you would like to see the weapons we normally use?' There was a hint of mockery in the courteous voice.

'Thank you,' said Caudle.

'I'm afraid you will have to be blind-folded again. Juan, take charge of Mr Caudle. *Hasta la vista,* Señor. I have some work to do, but shall look forward to another chat before luncheon.'

As they went down a flight of stone steps Caudle heard an electric bell ringing, and guessed it was a signal for other members of the staff to keep out of the way. He smiled, remembering a visit with Pat to see the frescoes in the convent of Santa Cecilia in Rome, and the little nun who went in front, ringing a bell with a similar warning. He could see nothing and had to feel his way, but Manuela had joined them, and her hand was on his arm. The warm air gave way to a chilly atmosphere tainted with damp and, vaguely, the smell of wine casks. Then a door was closed behind him and the girl removed his mask, standing very close, so that he could smell the scent she was wearing.

Juan and Manuela were standing beside him at the end of a long, low-ceilinged room, lined with brick. It had buttress walls projecting into the central space from the sides, and there was a system of

142

overhead wires connected with hand-grips dangling in a corner at the near end of the cavern. The other end was unlit, but Caudle judged it must be at least twenty yards away.

On a counter lay an impressive collection of small-arms, sub-machine guns, fuses, booby-trap devices, grenades and more sophisticated bombs. There were some curious weapons that Caudle did not recognise. Santos picked what looked like a powerful air-pistol. 'This fires an anaesthetic dart,' he explained, 'which we use for short-range work when silence is essential.' He pointed to some metal cylinders. 'Those are silencers for automatics and rifles.'

'But if your target is wearing thick clothes,' asked Caudle, 'will that dart penetrate?'

Santos smiled. 'Accurate shooting is most important for all our operatives, as you'll see in a minute. You must aim at the neck or hand.' He smiled. 'I suppose you were too young for national service?'

'Yes,' said Caudle, shortly.

'That's a disadvantage. Fortunately, we still have obligatory military service here, so that our recruits come with at least some experience.' He moved on and selected a sub-machine gun. 'This is the JCR-1, of which you may have heard.' Juan smiled.

'Although I don't think it's likely.'

Caudle picked it up and examined it. 'I have an idea,' he said gently, 'that this is the weapon you developed yourselves. There was a clandestine factory for making them, near La Plata, I think, but it got raided early in 1975.'

'It did,' said Santos, a little surprised. 'You're well informed, I see. But luckily we had already made a large number of the guns, and they're very effective. I should explain it wasn't exclusively our factory. It was when we'd established a Revolutionary Coordination Command, jointly with the Tupamaros, the Chilean MIR and the Bolivian Army of National Liberation, and I'm afraid security suffered. Most of the operatives captured were Uruguayan, incidentally.'

'And women,' said Caudle, getting a bit of his own back. 'I remember it was said at the time that even the ERP depended greatly on girls for its most effective guerrilleros.'

Before Juan could retort Manuela intervened. She always felt that a little animosity between young men in her company was natural, but she liked to control the situation. 'Of course we have a lot of women soldiers, like me. But that wasn't why the RCC base was captured. It always happens when you link up with

144

other movements.'

'That's quite true,' said Juan, still smouldering. 'Would you like to try out one of these weapons, Caudle? Just to get yourself into the swing, so to speak?'

Manuela protested. 'Why waste time, Juan? He's said he's had no experience. You show him. I'll work the levers.'

'All right.' Juan picked up the Browning P-35 and looked it over carefully. There was a fully loaded magazine beside it on the counter and he slipped it into the butt, pulled back the breach to slide a round into position and pushed forward the safety-catch. He went round the counter and stood in a crouching position facing the dark end of the range.

The girl explained. 'This is supposed to imitate the situation of a man going down a street with enemies ready to jump out at him from every doorway. When I pull the handles the targets appear from behind those little walls at the sides.' She went over to the corner and turned a switch. Hidden lights came on down the length of the firing-range. *'Pronto?'*

*'Pronto,'* acknowledged Juan, tersely. He took a cautious step forwards.

Manuela pulled one of the dangling handles and the cardboard figure of a man with a gun sprang out from behind the first buttress.

145

In a split second Juan's two hands came up together and he fired twice before the figure, suspended from a wire, had whisked across the narrow space and disappeared behind the opposite wall. He continued his crouching walk. From the left another figure appeared, and he fired, again twice, the shots ringing out almost like one.

'One more,' said Manuela quickly, and pulled another handle. Juan was taken by surprise, but his reaction was swift. Again the double crack rang out.

Caudle and the girl joined Santos, who was looking ruefully at the last target. There was a hole in the cardboard near the neck of the painted gunman. The other shot had missed.

'I didn't expect you to show another before I'd started moving,' protested Juan wrathfully.

'Then it was a good test,' said Manuela blandly.

'You drilled the other two nicely,' said Caudle, but added with a touch of malice, 'You'd have had them to your credit before the third man got you in his sights.'

'Suppose you have a go,' said Juan. 'There're three more traps. Take the gun and go on from here.'

Caudle felt the girl's eyes on him. He took the automatic, went back to the counter to change the magazine, and took up his stance, holding the gun at the full extent of his arm, pointing downwards. 'When you like,' he said quietly.

Santos and Manuela went back to the controls. He pushed her away and reached for the handles. *'Pronto?'*

'I'm ready.' Caudle began to move forward in a way quite different from that adopted by Santos. His legs were wide apart, and he shuffled forward, the gun still pointing downwards, the other arm balancing.

A figure sprang out from the left. Caudle's arm came up in a smooth sweep, extended, with his forefinger pointing along the short barrel. The other arm swung backwards slightly, adjusting the balance, as he fired a single shot. Then he continued his jerky, straddling walk.

'Fire twice,' shouted Juan from behind him, and at the same time pulled the next handle. The gunman target slipped into view on the right, and Caudle fired another single shot. He braced himself for the next test, guessing that Juan, sore at the trick Manuela had played on him, would try something on. He was right.

'Last one coming up,' called Juan. 'Hang on, I'm just going to—' The cardboard figure was slipping out of its hiding place as he spoke. It was on the same side as the last one, whereas the previous targets had appeared on alternate sides. But from the position of Caudle's extended arm it was equally easy to swing in either direction, and he caught the figure just as it disappeared.

He heard Manuela cry furiously to Juan, *'Sin verguenza!'* and called back, 'Nonsense! It was a fair test.' He was walking back towards Juan and the girl when they stopped him.

'Don't you want to see if you hit one?' asked Manuela.

Juan laughed, restored to good humour. 'You're a defeatist, James. Come on, let's have a look. You might have touched one.'

Caudle said casually, 'I think I did. Middle body the first two, gun arm the third.'

There was a moment of astounded silence, then Juan ran forward and pulled out the targets one by one. He turned. 'Just as you said. Very good shooting.' His voice was shaking slightly.

'Why didn't you fire twice at each target, as Juan said? It's our rule.' Manuela was staring at him wide-eyed, hoping he would make the classic reply and rub Juan's aristocratic nose even more firmly in the mud.

'No point in wasting ammunition,' said Caudle.

'How right you are,' said Manuela softly. 'Can you use a sub-machine gun, too?'

'You had a Sterling on the counter. D'you want me to try it?'

'We'll take it for granted,' said Juan, but Manuela ran back to the controls in the corner by the counter. Caudle picked up the Sterling, fitted the curved magazine and worked the slide. 'Where do I stand?'

'On that white spot.' They were both ignoring Juan.

'I want a sighting shot first. I've got to know how it fires.'

'O.K.' She let the third target appear and held it in position.

Caudle had the gun in his hands, pointing away. He swung it and squeezed the trigger, releasing it immediately. A hole appeared on the edge of the cardboard figure, low and to the right. He called 'Ready', and as the furthest three targets appeared in succession fired short bursts. When they examined the targets there was no doubt about the lethal scatter of holes.

'Very impressive, James,' said Juan in a strangled voice. 'We have nothing to teach you in one respect, anyway.' His face bore a fixed smile, but when Caudle met the man's eyes he knew he had made an enemy.

Before they left the cellar Manuela rang the warning bell and made Caudle put on the eye-mask. 'What's the point of this?' he asked. 'There's no one else around, is there?'

'There are plenty. But the other reason is so that you can't recognise this house. Juan and I aren't allowed to see most of the people who work here, nor they us. Hence the bell. We can go up now.'

She guided him up the steps and they returned to the room where Mendoza was waiting. When Caudle could see he found that a table had been laid for a cold lunch, with plates of sliced beef and *fiambres*, a great wooden bowl of salad, and a cheese board with drinks and wine on a side table.

Mendoza was speaking to Manuela in a low voice. He turned to Caudle, and when he spoke there was an edge to his voice. 'What's this I hear? You appear to be a remarkable marksman for a pacifist. I hope you haven't been deceiving me, Señor Caudle. That would be very unwise, I assure you.'

'My father taught me,' explained Caudle. 'We had a rubber plantation in Malaya. I was brought up there in the Emergency, when I wasn't at school in England. I started to use a Sterling when I was ten. The C.T's were extremely clever, and attacked without warning. Quickness with firearms was simply a question of survival. We were ten miles from the nearest town, and the C.T's were in the jungle between.'

'The C.T's?'

'Communist terrorists. The Chinese.'

Mendoza waited until Manuela had served sherry. 'It seems strange to me that you were fighting on the side of the capitalist rulers against the men whose views you now appear to share.' There was clearly suspicion in his tones.

Caudle said, 'I can see that it must seem odd, but we didn't see it that way at the time, and of course I was still a boy. The Chinese had killed my mother and a dozen of our Tamil rubber tappers, with their wives.' He spoke quite unemotionally. These were the building-bricks of personally experienced history, and all sentiment had been leached out of them by time. 'Some of the Tamils were tied to trees and tortured before they were killed, as an example to others. The C.T's hated the Tamils as fanatically as they hated us. So we had to protect them, too, and it meant constant readiness and ability to use guns.' He smiled. 'My nursery was heavily sandbagged.'

Mendoza said slowly, 'Your *nursery?*' He made a helpless gesture with his hand.

'How old were you when the insurrection began?'

'That was in 1948, when I was two, and it lasted twelve years. But even after 1960, when the last Chinese units were being rounded up, my father kept up our state of readiness, and during school holidays my brother and I had to practise with guns every day. He also kept his old Ford V8 protected with steel sheet and retained the barbed wire around the tappers' quarters. My father, you see, never forgot how the whole thing started with men rushing out of the jungle to kill and burn without anyone having known they were there. That's how they killed my mother while he was away from home.'

'But the insurgents got what they wanted, didn't they?' asked Mendoza sharply. 'They fought against imperialism and won.'

'No, Señor. There had never been any doubt that Malaya would get independence, but the war went on long after Merdeka. It was started from outside by the Russians—then still allies of Mao Tse-tung—who used some of the best jungle fighters, whom we had taught to fight the Japanese, as the nucleus of the insurgent forces. The Malays and Tamils never wanted a war of liberation; it was forced on them by the Chinese, and when they collaborated it was through fear.

That's why in the end the C.T's were defeated. Mao's theory that the country people would rise against capitalist rulers the moment someone gave them arms was disproved—as it's been disproved everywhere else, except in China.'

Mendoza drank the last of his Tio Pepe and set down the glass. 'It's a little surprising,' he commented severely, 'to hear a Marxist-Lenninist—as I must assume you are—scoffing at Chairman Mao's theories.'

'I don't say they can't work, Señor, but they haven't yet, not in any of the countries where they've been tried out. Che Guevara was a very brave man, but his insurrection was doomed before it got off the ground. That is why—I'm sorry, I seem to be repeating myself, but I do want to make our position clear—my movement believes that in Britain, at least, the only hope of a truly socialist revolution lies in a process of enlightenment and education. Until all the people really understand and want Marxism no revolutionary movement can succeed.'

'A very lofty and proper concept, I'm sure,' said Mendoza coldly. 'In Argentina we see a shorter road to victory.' He looked at his watch. 'I think we should now take luncheon.'

Afterwards Mendoza, who had seemed to experience no difficulty in eating and drinking through the mouth slit in his mask, drew Caudle to the chairs in front of the fire. 'In a little Santos will be showing you the plans, and the research involved, for some of our successful kidnapping operations and bank raids, and will also—in a general way only, you understand—explain our system of command and the cell structure. Also, the arrangements we have made for forgery of documents and vehicle number plates, arms storage and distribution, hospitalisation of casualties, safe houses, people's prisons and so on. I want to be clear now about what you feel you could offer if we should agree to collaborate in Britain. How many members have you?'

'Twelve hundred only at present, but once we have funds we shall launch an intensive recruiting campaign. Our existing members include several very distinguished Marxist scholars.'

'More to the point, perhaps,' said Mendoza drily, 'do they also include young and active men and women who might be willing to be trained for support activities?'

'There are some, both men and women.'

'We have no objection to women; they attract less attention than men and we

154

have found them equally discreet, even under pressure. I take it you would have no objection to revealing the names and details of such potential recruits?'

'I don't see why not,' said Caudle. But what Letty would say was another matter.

'Good. You also have some ideas about targets?'

'I have discussed this problem at length with my President. There aren't as many excessively rich persons, on a percentage basis, as in this country. Ransoms like that paid for the Born brothers—fifty million dollars, I think—are out of the question. But there are large numbers of those in the second grade, for whom a ransom of several hundred thousand pounds might be paid. There are also leading figures in the industrial world whose firms might pay up handsomely.'

'I see. It is then, in your view, a question of staging a number of smaller operations, which we dislike doing. Each one requires many months of work and the more we spread our effort the greater the risk of detection. If we came into the British scene, Señor Caudle, we might decide to fall back on commercial operations.'

'You mean banks, and so on?'

'Or trains. We all admire the great train robbers, and in fact I've had the pleasure of meeting one of them. Three million pounds. Nearly six million dollars. It was a good haul, quite in our tradition, although not as high as in some of our operations. I imagine the same thing could be done again.'

'We shouldn't be able to help you, I'm afraid. You'd need agents inside the post office and the railways.'

'There is nothing one can't do in the way of getting reliable informants if one has money to spend. But I agree banks are more likely to be fruitful of large returns, and probably easier to attack. Again, however, there is the need for expert background information, and if we should decide to come in with you we shouldn't be able to spare more than, say, half a dozen operatives. You'd have to recruit—or at least point out to us—a large number of smaller people, many of them "unconscious", that is, unaware of exactly why they were being used.'

'Doctor Hennessy has an idea about that.' He hesitated. It would sound so crazy.

'Proceed, Señor.'

'As you know, she is a writer of crime novels. She is very well known as such and has many acquaintances not only in the profession—she was formerly Chairman of the Crime Writers Association—but among police officers, lawyers, business men. She has a whole network of informants who help to provide material for her stories, and she is a prolific writer.' Caudle could sense the amused, contemptuous smile behind the black leather mask. He hurried on. 'Her idea is that she has an excellent excuse for obtaining information about local police forces, escape routes, and so on. Her search for story material would be a perfect cover, even if she found it necessary to visit the place in question.'

The mask moved. Mendoza was laughing silently. 'And do you not anticipate, Señor, that after a successful operation the police might connect the occurrence with the recent visit of someone as well known as Doña Letizia—both for writing stories and for revolutionary thinking?'

'Whatever might be suspected, nothing could be proved if she kept completely clear of the actual attack. And surely, you would not give a revolutionary explanation for your United Kingdom operations?'

'No. That is perfectly true. We should give no explanation at all. If the police concluded we were common criminals, let them do so. But I still think it would be dangerous. However, that is your concern, Juan, I will leave Señor Caudle in your care for the time being.'

Some two and a half hours later Caudle thanked Mendoza for his hospitality and for the extremely interesting insight he had been given into the techniques of kidnapping, armed robbery and the complicated security procedures which made them possible.

The tall figure with the dark, blank face bowed slightly. 'I feel, Señor Caudle, that we have both given each other a good deal to think about. Santos has given you a means of secret communications between us, and if all goes well will himself be visiting your country very shortly. He will bring with him the decision of my High Command, to whom I shall be reporting.' He added piously, *'Vava Usted con Dios,* Señor,' and stood waiting while Manuela slipped the eye-mask over Caudle's head and handed him the sunglasses. Then he shook hands and accompanied Caudle to the door.

When the girl had helped the Englishman into the Porsche and driven off in a splutter of gravel Felipe Ybarra reached up and took off the silk hood and the leather mask. He was laughing as he led his cousin up the steps and into the library of the estancia. 'What did you think of him?' He clapped his hands and ordered his butler to serve maté tea. It was too early for serious drinking.

'*Es loco,*' said Santos, with conviction.

'Yes, he's as mad as his extraordinary Letizia, according to your account. But remember, cousin, that it was mad Englishmen who conquered India, and who were still running this country until not so long ago. Our own Spanish ancestors produced a rich strain of equally mad adventurers. No sane man could have conquered either Mexico or Peru with a mere handful of horsemen.'

'Hernán Cortés and Francisco Pizarro believed they were directed by God.'

'Perhaps this Englishman thinks he's equally inspired, but by the shade of Karl Marx. We shouldn't underestimate him, Xavier; in some ways I found him impressive. But any idea of practical collaboration in the field is too risky. I'll talk to the *Jefe,* but I'm sure he'll agree that you should go to England in a week or two on an exploratory mission. Change your pseudonym and avoid all the other Trotskyist movements, but you might take a closer look at Caudle's group. It's just conceivable that some of their ideas are worth following up by an operational team—but working alone, without any amateur activists. Your main task, as I told you earlier, will be to find safe havens in England for our surplus funds—and for ourselves, if the worst should happen. Our young friend was quite perceptive in that respect, wasn't he?'

'He was guessing,' said Santos contemptuously.

'I don't think so. He seemed to be remarkably well-informed. I wonder whether he's spoken to anyone in the British Embassy.' Ybarra put down his cup. 'Now, as to your visit, I want you to take Manuela with you, not—let me make it plain—for your own convenience or pleasure, but simply to get her out of the country during a period which I expect to prove increasingly difficult for us. She can make herself useful, but remember Xavier, she is my sister's only daughter and while her father retains his present attitude I feel I must act *in loco parentis*. And although I appreciate your many good qualities I do not wish to have you as a close relative.'

## CHAPTER THIRTEEN

When they had driven for several miles down the main road Manuela stopped the car. Caudle could feel the soft brush of the fur coat as she turned towards him. 'Don't bother,' he said, 'I can take these things off by myself.'

'In a moment.' Her hands were framing his face, turning it, and he felt her lips against his mouth. They lingered for a tiny space, lightly, and were withdrawn. 'Now you can take off the mask,' she said composedly.

He removed the glasses and the eye-mask, blinking at her as she sat back in her seat and slowly reached for the controls. 'What was that for?' He could still feel the soft touch of her mouth.

'Just for letting some of the wind out of Juan,' she said. 'He's so conceited.'

'If you want to know,' said Caudle, 'I don't feel proud of myself. Both Juan and I ought to have known better than to get ourselves into a *machismo* competition, egged on by you.'

'I did nothing of the kind,' she protested indignantly. 'It was—'

'It was you being there that made us act like fighting cocks; I saw he was trying to make me look a fool in front of you, and I led him on.'

'And now you're blaming me. How typical of a man!' She glanced sideways at him, his serious face lit by the lights of an oncoming car. What was the matter with the man? Any Argentine would have taken that kiss of hers as an open invitation, and grabbed her. It was what she'd expected him to do, and it'd have been fun. Of

161

course she would have told him he'd misunderstood that gesture of hers, but she might have been persuaded to let him take a few liberties ... Anyway, it would have enlivened the boring drive back to the city. A thought struck her. It *surely* couldn't be that he was thinking of his wife. She was six thousand miles away, *por Dios,* and no man could be faithful at that distance. Then it occurred to her that Caudle mightn't find her attractive. Her small mouth tightened. That could *not* be tolerated, in him or any man.

'When will you be returning to London?' she asked.

'Day after tomorrow, as arranged. I've got a provisional booking with Aerolineas for the five o'clock plane.'

'We'll have another meeting before that, so that we can test that secret ink and developer Juan gave you.'

'He told me exactly how to use them,' protested Caudle, rather weakly.

'Everything must be tested and checked properly,' said Manuela didactically. 'I'm busy most of tomorrow, but what about the evening, after dinner?'

'That'd be fine,' said Caudle, 'but—'

'I know what we'll do. I'll get the hotel to serve dinner in Colonel Rojas's room, for just the two of us. We can do the tests afterwards. Rojas usually plays cards

162

at the Military Club till midnight, but to make sure I'll give him a ring.'

'Thank you. I'll look forward to it.' His head turned slightly, and his eye lingered on the profile presented to him. 'Where are you going to drop me? At the hotel?'

'It's better not. We can pass the entrance to the courtyard at the back, so I'll put you down there, and you'll only have to walk round the corner.'

'Thanks.' He had an idea that she might have expected an invitation to dine, which would have been the obvious polite return for so much hospitality. If so, she was going to be disappointed. She had already—well, indirectly, at least—made him offer far more than he and Letty had planned. There had never been any intention of bringing in other members of their group, still less as active participants in crime. All right, perhaps it was Juan who had needled him, but the girl was altogether too disturbing. It was time he thought about Pat, and whether there could be a letter from her already. But Pat was far away, and his thoughts kept turning to the girl at his side, and that fleeting kiss.

During the rest of the drive they made desultory conversation. Manuela told him about her schooldays in England, and asked him what he did for a living.

When he replied, rather curtly, that he was a teacher she said she wasn't surprised. After that, idle chat languished.

It was nearly six, and the light had gone, when they came into the centre of the city.

They turned into a narrow, empty street, and Caudle saw ahead the entrance to the service courtyard of the Reconquista. As Manuela stopped the car, for Caudle to get out, they heard shouting, and a strange metallic clamour. The next moment Colonel Rojas appeared, running very fast on his short legs through the cluttered space, and pushing over dustbins as he passed. They were clanging and rolling over the stones, scattering kitchen refuse in the path of a tall man, dimly seen in the light of a street lamp. He was slipping and stumbling through the rolling bins, shouting at the little man to stop.

Caudle felt an automatic pushed into his hand. 'Open the door and get him in,' ordered Manuela briefly.

Just opening the door would have been useless, as Rojas was running for the corner of the entrance and wouldn't see it. Caudle jumped out into the street, jerked open the door and shouted to Rojas, *'Por acqui, hombre!'* The little man swerved, whisked past him and dived into the car like a ferret into a hole.

The pursuer stopped fifteen yards away and pulled a gun from under his jacket. He could see Caudle was armed, and hesitated.

'*Get in,*' screamed Manuela. But the Englishman knew what would happen if he did. The car would be riddled with bullets. He pushed forward the safety-catch, backing towards the open door, keeping the muzzle of the gun down.

Suddenly, the man raised the automatic and fired. At that range, and in the dim light, it was a lucky shot or very well aimed, for at least it hit Caudle, who felt as if his left arm had been hit by a flying brick. Instinctively, his right arm came up and he fired. The man was already aiming for a second shot, and the little bullet from Manuela's pistol seemed to have had no effect. But his gun remained silent, and he crumpled and fell. Caudle stood stock still for a moment, hearing the noise of approaching footsteps and people shouting. Then he jumped back into the passenger seat and pulled the door shut with his gun hand. The tyres squealed as the car took off, scattering the running pedestrians.

From the back seat, between gasps, the little colonel spoke. 'Señor,' he said, with much feeling, '*es Usted un caballero.* Such a sense of honour! You let him shoot first, although he was a rat of a secret

165

policeman.' He paused to take breath. The car was speeding through the streets, turning corner after corner. 'You could have shot him at any time but no, you stood your ground and let him compose himself for the duel.'

'I'm afraid that's nonsense, *mi Coronel*,' muttered Caudle, 'but it's kind of you to say so. What happened?' They had left the busier streets. Manuela had said no word, intent on her driving.

'I had just returned to my room on Don Juan's orders, telephoned to me at the Club, when I saw the door of your room was open, with the key on my side.' He took another deep breath. 'Like a flash I turned towards the other door, but this man came running from your room and saw me. I threw a chair in his way and heard him fall as I ran out into the corridor. I raced for the service stairs,' continued the Colonel, becoming almost lyrical at the memory of that desperate chase, 'and threw myself down them. His footsteps were following close behind me, I could hear them only a flight above. In the basement corridor there was a trolley laden with dirty plates. With one jerk of my hand I twirled it into his path. Then,' he added, the excitement fading as he began to think of his predicament, 'I came out into the courtyard. The dustbins helped, but God brought you to save me in time. What will happen, Señorita?'

'We shall change cars in a moment. You will walk to a safe house, whose address I'll give you.' (But not in my hearing, thought Caudle, with a twisted smile.) His arm was still numb, but pain was beginning to stab through it. He found the hole in the sleeve of his duffle coat, and tried the other side. No hole there. He began to feel slightly sick.

They had turned back towards the centre, and came to the place where they had changed cars in the morning, but this time there was a new number plate on the grey Mercedes, and no chauffeur. Manuela stopped the Porsche and got out quickly, calling Rojas to follow. She took him to one side and spoke to him out of Caudle's hearing. He came back to the car, thanked the Englishman effusively, and walked away. Manuela locked the car, took another key from her handbag, and opened the door of the Mercedes, signing to Caudle to get in beside her. She drove off fast.

'You're rather quiet,' she said suddenly. 'You aren't hurt, are you? That man missed, surely?'

'No, he got me in the arm. It's only just begun to hurt, but I'm afraid the bullet's still inside.'

'*Madre de Dios!*' She stopped the car, looked quickly round, and switched on the roof light. 'Show me your arm.' There was a small red patch on the sleeve of the coat, but no blood was running down to his wrist. She looked worried. 'There's only the one hole. I'm afraid it's taken in a lot of wool and plugged the wound. If it had gone clean through you'd be bleeding like a pig, but the wound would be cleaner. You need a doctor. I'll take you to my flat.' She started the Mercedes and drove more quietly through the broad streets of the main shopping area.

'Isn't that dangerous?'

'Why? So far as I know the SSN and police don't have any reason to suspect me, and Rojas can't tell them as long as they don't catch and torture him. Even then, I think he'd keep mum for a long time. He's a gutsy little man. He'll be in the safe flat by now; there's someone there who'll let him in. No, with me you'll be all right, and all I have to lose is my reputation. The garage is in the basement, so with luck, you won't be seen. It's some way from here, but I'll go as fast as I can without bumping you. You won't faint, will you?'

'No. It's hurting like hell now, but I shan't faint.'

The apartment block was in a fashionable

168

part of the city and luxuriously modern. The entrance to the underground garage was lined with lights and curled down into an enormous cavern, equally well lit, with ample space for the gleaming cars. She stopped near a lift entrance.

An attendant came up, saluting. *'A sus ordenes, Doña Manuela.'*

She gave him the keys and went round to Caudle's side, where he was extricating himself awkwardly. His left arm was now quite useless. The attendant was already driving the car away as they got into the lift. She pressed the button for the eleventh floor. 'He'll find a parking place and leave the keys with the concierge, so he won't bother us.'

There were four flats on each floor and Manuela's was small compared with the others, but furnished expensively and with taste. But Caudle had little time to see it as he was led through a bedroom and told to sit on a bathroom stool while she eased off the duffle coat. The sleeve of his jacket had stuck to the wound, so she made him rest his arm over the basin and hold a sponge of warm water against the dried blood. Then she left him, and he could hear her voice in the other room, but not the words.

When she came back she said, 'The doctor's coming and I've arranged the disposal of the Porsche.' Caudle wondered how. Were they going to dump the car in the docks? She had removed her fur coat and put on a striped apron over her black sweater and slacks. She carried a pair of surgical scissors, a bowl and a bottle of Larios gin. 'You get a shot of this internally,' she explained cheerfully, 'and then I tidy up your arm a bit so that I can at least get you into bed.'

'There's no need for that,' said Caudle. 'The doctor can get the thing out as I sit here.'

'And risk you falling off the stool? No. He's told me what to do, and he'll be along himself soon.' She poured gin and a little water into two tooth glasses, took one herself, and set to work. The jacket sleeve came away without much trouble, and she cut round the part of the shirt that was still firmly attached and cleaned the surrounding skin with gin. Caudle was able to see, fascinated, that part of the shirt material had indeed gone into the wound and was held there by dried blood. Then she led him into the bedroom and despite his protests removed his string vest and trousers, and made him lie down with his arm on a folded bath towel. Shortly afterwards the doorbell rang.

When Manuela came back into the room she was followed by a man wearing a

170

white hood over his face, with holes for eyes, nose and mouth. Caudle wondered where all these masks were kept. Did every professional 'sympathiser' of the ERP keep his personal mask carefully folded and concealed somewhere in his clothing? She introduced him as Doctor Almagro.

The doctor was brisk and efficient. He spoke good English with an American accent, and his medical jargon made Caudle speculate that he had studied or practised in the United States. He examined the plugged wound, pressed around it gently with rubber-gloved fingers, causing a good deal of pain, and then produced a syringe. 'You're lucky,' he said. 'The tough wool of the two coat sleeves made a sort of cocoon of the bullet, and it came to rest quite quickly, or so I think. No real harm done, but it'll be a few weeks before the internal clots are absorbed and your muscles tie up with each other. I'm going to put you under completely for a few minutes, so that I can dig around and get all the extraneous matter out and clean you up without you going through the roof. Manolita, get me a bucket of warm water and two more towels.'

He was laying out sharp instruments on the bedside table as he spoke, and then picked up a syringe and a glass phial. The needle went in. Caudle began to answer

171

the fatuous remarks doctors make on these occasions—and stopped in the middle of a word.

When he awoke his arm was bandaged and in a sling; he could vaguely feel a throbbing pain through a haze of sleep. There was a smell of cooking. Someone had attached a dressing-gown cord round his waist, secured so that he could not roll off the bed. He heard talking, somewhere in the flat. The only light came from a bedside lamp. He closed his eyes and slept.

Much later, or so it seemed, he awoke to find a hand on his forehead. It was Manuela, wearing a neck-to-toes nightdress and smelling delectable. She shook her head at him, frowning and picked up a glass. He objected. 'I've had enough liquid, and I'll have to get up anyway.'

'Stay where you are. I'll bring you a potty.'

'You'll do no such thing. Just untie this cord, will you?' Reluctantly, she helped him out of bed and he walked unsteadily, with an attempt at dignity, to the bathroom. When he came back she was lying on the other side of the wide bed. He stared. 'Where do I sleep?'

'Here, of course. But drink up what's in that glass first. I don't want any nonsense in the night. There's only one bed.'

172

'Don't be silly, Manuela. But are you sure?'

'Of course. You're not much of a wolf, are you?'

He said nothing, but drank the sleeping draught and got back into the bed. 'Shall I put out the light?'

'Yes, please,' she said sleepily. 'And don't worry about tomorrow, James. We've decided what to do, and you'll be all right. *Buenas noches!*'

'*Buenas noches!*' He woke once during the night, and found Manuela's arm was round his chest, and her warm body very close. There was no doubt, thought Caudle, he liked it. It was very thoughtful of her to make sure he didn't slip off the bed and burst the stitches. If that was it. He smiled, and fell asleep.

The next time he awoke it was broad daylight, and he heard the sound of splashing in the bathroom. His arm hurt, but not savagely, and he felt extraordinarily hungry. Except that it wasn't extraordinary, seeing that he had eaten nothing since lunch-time the day before. He looked at the bathroom door, speculatively, remembering the consciousness of Manuela's body, that had been with him all night. Few men, he thought virtuously, would have passed up a chance like that, arm or no arm. Then he sat up, frowning. 'You're not much of

173

a wolf, are you?' That had been a bloody stupid remark. What did she think he was, a plaster statue?

The sounds of water ceased, and a short time later she appeared, wearing nothing but a large towel. Her dark hair was falling over her shoulders. He pretended to be half asleep and, bending down, she put a cool hand on his forehead.

Caudle curved his good arm round her neck and brought her face down, giving her a brotherly kiss on the cheek. She started back, and somehow the towel slipped. 'That was to thank you for being so kind,' he explained, trying to keep his eyes from straying, and stammering a little.

'If it was,' she said severely, adjusting the towel, 'you could have kissed me properly.'

All pretence at virtue left Caudle. He even forgot how hungry he was. 'Show me, then,' he whispered.

She threw off the towel and climbed into the bed.

Later, as they lay in each other's arms—one of his, two of hers—she told him how magnificently he had fought it out with the gunman the night before. 'It was just like the sheriff and the baddie in a Western,' she said dreamily. 'You stood four-square to him, and let him draw first.'

Caudle groaned. 'You're as bad as Rojas,' he protested. *I didn't mean to shoot.* It was just a reflex action. What worries me is that I must have got him in the chest. I hope to God he's not badly hurt.'

'But he's a cop, Jaimito. It doesn't matter.' She twisted her head so that she could look at him. 'In some ways, my English friend, I find you very attractive. And I don't just mean the way you fire a gun.' She bent forward and kissed him, and he held her tight. Then she struggled free. 'This will have to stop, James, although it shouldn't. It's getting late, and people will be coming. Are you hungry?'

'Ravenous.'

'I'll cook you a proper breakfast, then. In the meantime you'd better shave. What's more,' she added, wrinkling her nose, 'you could do with a shower, but me first. You'll find your trousers in the other bedroom.'

'You little devil! You told me there was only one.'

'I had to be sure you'd be all right during the night. I didn't think this would happen.'

'Oh didn't you?'

'Of course not. Who started it, then?'

'I did. It won't happen again. Damn it,

175

Manuela, I'm married. I'd better get up.'

'No. You wait until I'm ready.' She walked stark naked to the bathroom door, trailing the towel over her shoulders. When she had closed the door she showered and then looked ruefully at her reflection in the mirror, noting the tell-tale marks left by Caudle's unshaven cheeks. She was smiling as she dabbed the sore places with cream from a gold-topped jar, then applied solid make-up.

By the time Caudle was ready, and dressed in his string vest and trousers, with a silk dressing-gown she had lent him on top, she had cooked a breakfast of eggs and toast, with a large pot of coffee. He made short work of it, while Manuela ate one brioche, dipped into her coffee.

She said, 'There'll be a number of people coming to see you, and you'll have to stay here tonight. I shall tell Juan you slept in the guest room, of course, and that's where you'll be tonight.'

'Of course, Manuela. But what's the plan?'

She smiled. 'You'll see our escape organisation operating, which will be a useful lesson for you. Of the experts who'll be coming here, only Juan will be without a mask, but you've got used to that, and you know why, don't you?'

He nodded. 'But what's the plan?' he repeated.

'You'll see.'

The bell rang. Manuela said hurriedly, 'Go into the guest room and wait there.' He did so, and noted that the bed had been artistically messed about, so that it looked as if he had tossed on it all night. He sat in the armchair, waiting.

Juan came in and greeted Caudle coolly, without any reference to last night's occurrences. He had a large parcel under his arm, and produced from it a suit, three shirts and some underclothes. 'I think the suit'll fit. I took measurements from your clothes yesterday evening. But try them on, please.'

Caudle took off his trousers and put on the shirt and the suit. They fitted well enough on his lanky frame. He said urgently, 'Juan, what happened to the man I shot?'

'He was an SSN agent, and he's dead.'

'Christ! *Dead?* Are you sure?'

'It was on the news. There's been no mention of your name, as yet—at least, publicly—but we can't risk your appearing anywhere as James Caudle. So we're going to disguise you, provide you with false papers and send you back to England by the same flight you are booked on in your real name. You must do exactly as we say, is that understood?'

'Of course, and I'm more grateful than I can say, Juan.'

'It's in our interests, too,' replied Juan coldly. 'You agree to give us complete obedience, then?'

'Of course he does,' said Manuela.

'I'm in your hands,' said Caudle heavily, thinking of the man he had killed. He had *killed* a man. It was sickening, outrageous. He, James, had ended a man's life.

The bell rang, and a few moments later Manuela returned with a woman wearing a white overall, with a hood over her face. She said no word of greeting, but went about her work quickly and competently.

From a large plastic shopping-bag she produced a notebook and pencil, then a number of other things that she laid out methodically on the bedside table. Coming up to him as he sat by the bed she took his head in her hands, turning it from side to side so that she could examine it more closely. After making some notes in her book she seized the hair at the back of his neck, which he wore rather long, and twisted it together, tying it back with a piece of tape so that from the front it couldn't be seen.

Then she pulled up a chair to face Caudle and studied his features intently. From the table she took a toothbrush and a tube of paste, squeezed out a little on to the brush, rubbed it well into the bristles and carefully stroked a silvery sheen into the dark hair of his side-whiskers and above his temples and forehead. It was some time before she was satisfied, and she then chose a greyish moustache from those she had arrayed on the table and with some kind of adhesive attached it under his nose. Finally, she went to work with a box of grease-paint, powdered the skin lightly, and gave him two thin pads to insert into his cheeks.

'*Muy bien, Señora!*' exclaimed Manuela, who was leaning over the woman's shoulder, studying the effect. She brought a hand-mirror so that Caudle could see for himself. It was almost unbelievable. The face that stared back at him unhappily was that of a man at least ten years older, and dissipated, at that. Serve me damn' well right, he thought.

The woman took Manuela aside and spoke to her briefly. Money changed hands. Then she packed up the tools of her trade and left, without a word to Caudle from start to finish.

He tried to reach into his mouth to extract the ridiculous pads, but Juan stopped him. 'This is just for the passport photograph,' he explained. 'Before you leave on Tuesday she'll come again,

179

cut your hair, attach a more permanent moustache and make you up properly for the journey. You'll be able to wash everything off, but you'll have to think up an explanation for cutting your hair.' He looked at his watch. 'Good timing. The photographer's due any minute now. Just sit quietly.'

Caudle had no wish to do anything else. There were too many things to think of, and his conscience was still troubling him.

The bell rang again, and a man—masked, of course—came in with a camera and flash equipment, positioned himself directly in front of Caudle and took three shots. Then he bowed, murmured *'Mucho gusto,'* and went out.

Someone else rang, and after a whispered discussion in the hall Juan came in with a used, rather smart suitcase and a soft leather holdall, which he opened to bring out shaving and teeth-cleaning gear, a hairbrush and comb, face lotion and some socks and handkerchiefs. 'I want you to think carefully,' he said. 'These things replace items you must have left in your room at the Reconquista, besides your spare clothes, shirts and underwear. What else did you leave there?'

'Not much. Books, maps, all my notes on what I'd learned the day before, tourist information about Buenos Aires, Mendoza and other places, the synopsis of Letty's story and—oh my God!—that letter from Manuela.'

'No, you didn't,' said the girl. 'We found that in your pocket. With the gun, too. It's lucky you didn't drop that in the street.'

'Good. I think that's the lot, except for my hat.' That was a pity; he'd been fond of that rather dashing piece of headgear. 'There is one thing, though. I must have left fingerprints in the room next door, so that connects me with Rojas.' He looked up, frowning. 'But what happens when I get back to England? If the Argentine police think I've shot their agent, won't they ask for my extradition?'

'They have no proof. They'll see you've left the hotel, but that doesn't connect you with the shooting, does it?'

'But if it's found I've disappeared, and then I turn up in England, someone is going to put two and two together. If I'm to use a false passport, how am I—me, Caudle—supposed to have left the country? Damn it, Juan, you've got to think the whole thing out.'

Santos put on an air of insufferable superiority. 'My dear fellow, that is exactly what I have done. Relax, don't worry. It's all been planned very carefully. I may add that I spent half the night working at it while you were fast asleep—I hope,' he added suddenly, throwing a glance of suspicion at Manuela. But she was not a girl who blushed easily, and she returned his gaze with complete serenity.

'I'm very grateful,' said Caudle warmly. 'I think you've arranged everything very quickly and effectively. Well, if you've thought out the British end, that's O.K, although how you've planned it I can't think. What passports do I travel with?'

'A British one, of course, in the name of Frederic Mason. You'd better practise making the signature. I'm sorry we can't change your booking to first class, but I'm sure you'll understand that in the tourist class you'll attract less attention.'

'It's how I came out, anyway,' said Caudle, smiling. 'It'd look odd if I returned first.'

'As Caudle, you mean,' said Juan, with the same superior smile. 'But you must remember you won't be James Caudle, you'll be Frederic Mason, a schoolteacher from Southampton, who's been visiting his married sister in Cordoba. But I shouldn't get talking to other passengers, if I were you; it takes time and training to keep up a fictitious character for long.'

'I see. And what about my arm?'

'The doctor will be seeing you again this afternoon. I hope he'll agree that you can just keep your hand in your pocket, and you'll have pain-killers.'

'I don't even know what he found.' Caudle turned to Manuela.

'He found the bullet, which he said had done little damage to the humerus because it was pushing a pad of wool in front of it, but it had made a large hole and cut some muscle tissue. He put in five stitches and you'll have to have those taken out.' She looked at his pale face anxiously. 'You're not frightened about having them out?'

'No, it isn't that. It's the thought that keeps on coming back, that I've killed someone.'

Juan laughed shortly. 'He probably deserved it. What did you expect?'

'I didn't mean to, for God's sake. Can't you realise that?'

Juan sneered. 'From what you told us about your childhood I thought you used to kill a dozen Chinese before breakfast.'

'We never saw one during the last seven years. We just had to be ready if they came.'

'*Por Dios!*' exclaimed Juan contemptuously. 'And I thought you were such a hero. You can use a gun, but you don't like blood, is that it?'

'Yes it is. But you wouldn't understand.' He was trembling, but he met Juan's eyes and held them. 'And now we'll drop this subject.'

'Some people have *cojones*,' said Juan insultingly, 'and some—' But Manuela interrupted. The two men were facing each other, and Caudle's face was slowly flushing.

'Stop this, Juan,' she cried quickly, in Spanish. 'You two have got to work together. Explain, James. It was something that happened in Malaya, wasn't it?'

'All right. I was three years old, lying in a day-cot in the garden, when a man ran out of the trees and tossed a grenade over the fence. He was aiming at me, I think, because it fell near. My mother ran forward to protect me, and threw herself on the thing. I was drenched with her blood and bits of—bits of her body smacked into my face.'

There was a long silence. Then Manuela put her arm around Caudle's shoulders. 'Poor child!' she said softly. 'Poor Jaimito.' She turned imperiously on Juan. *'Pide perdona.'*

His eyes flashed jealously. 'It was a very long time ago—' She stamped her foot. 'All right,' he said, 'I'm sorry, James. It was a terrible experience. We must be friends.' He held out his hand.

The trembling had gone. Caudle smiled, and shook hands. 'As I said, let's change

184

the subject. Have you had any message from Mendoza?'

'We shall be sending a mission to England in ten days' time. I shall be in charge.' He did not mention Manuela, and she looked at him curiously. He continued quickly, 'We still have a lot to discuss—your cover story and the escape plan, means of communicating in England—'

'And the choice of targets,' said Caudle.

'That, too. It has been decided,' continued Juan carefully, 'that I should keep an open mind, until I have properly examined the terrain, as to whether the main thrust should be in kidnapping, bank-raids, or other forms of profit-taking, and also the extent to which we may ask you to participate.'


## CHAPTER FOURTEEN

About the time this conversation was taking place in Manuela's flat, Neville Bruce was making a report to his Ambassador, who was listening impatiently, tapping a pencil on his great mahogany desk. He interrupted.

'You still haven't made it clear why

this is worth reporting to me, Neville. I've hoisted in the fact that Caudle has disappeared, but it's only since last night, so he may be swanning around somewhere in the red light district for all we know. Now you say that an agent of the SSN was killed last night outside the back courtyard to Caudle's hotel while he was pursuing a suspected ERP man, who got away in a car. The SSN had another agent there, sitting in a car in the courtyard, but he was unsighted when the first agent was shot. There was a man with the getaway car and either he or—what was his name? Rojas—shot the secret policeman. Some passers-by ran up when they heard the shooting, but none of them will talk, probably too scared of ERP reprisals. Nothing in all this implicates Caudle, except the fact that it was his room, apparently, that was being searched when the man Rojas arrived and was given chase. There. Have I got it right?'

'Admirably, sir. I'm sorry I took so much longer. But it was vital for you to understand the background before I came to the last bit.'

'Which is?'

'As you know, sir, I had an agent watching the hotel where Caudle was staying. This man suspected that on the previous night he had left the hotel by the rear entrance, so he put an assistant to cover the yard behind the hotel. This agent was in the street outside the courtyard when Rojas came running out of the hotel basement, followed some way behind by a man whom the agent recognised as an SSN operative. At this moment a blue Porsche car drew in the street and a man sprang out. The agent swears it was Caudle. He called to Rojas and covered his pursuer with a hand-gun, probably an automatic. The SSN agent shot at Caudle, who returned his fire and killed him.'

'At what range?' asked the Ambassador, reverting for a moment to his earlier military career.

'About fifteen yards, as far as I can make out, and by bad light.'

'Pretty good shooting,' said His Excellency approvingly. 'But I thought you said Caudle was a harmless sort of chap. You've got him into a real balls-up now.'

'*I* have, sir?'

'Well, I suppose you felt in honour bound to tell your bosom friend in the SSN what your agent thinks he saw Caudle do?'

'No, sir. I thought I'd have a word with you first.'

'Ah,' said Sir Roderick, 'now you're talking. That was very sensible of you, my boy. Let me get this right. Caudle is alleged to have fired at an SSN agent, but in self-defence?'

'You could put it that way, sir. The other certainly fired first.'

'Did he hit Caudle?'

'Not as far as my man could see. He got back into the car.'

'And how did your agent know, or think he knew, it was Caudle?'

'From the photograph and description he'd been given. He hadn't actually seen him before.'

'Then he might have been mistaken, don't you think?'

'Of course, sir,' said Bruce, seeing the light. 'He couldn't have seen the man clearly, and it might have been anyone about Caudle's height and with similar features. And as you say, there may be some other explanation for Caudle's disappearance.'

'Then—when does Caudle leave?'

'Tomorrow evening by Aerolineas, if the SSN let him go, but as far as I can see they've got no charge to hold him on if I don't tell Urrutia what my agent saw. And I'm not particularly anxious to admit to him that I've been duplicating his surveillance.'

'Then keep mum, Neville. This man is a pain in my neck. He's obviously been hobnobbing with the ERP, and I suppose he could have absorbed some of their ideas about the sanctity of human life. But I'd be surprised if the secretary of such a high-minded movement were so handy with a gun. Anyway, that's for Special Branch to sort out when and if he gets home. I don't want trouble here, but you will of course see that the Branch is fully informed?'

'Of course, sir.'

'Good. But for the SSN, silence, I beg.' His Excellency clasped his hands behind his bald grey head and looked up at the painted ceiling, adding dreamily, 'Silence! What a golden word it is! It has rotundity; it embalms the spirit.' His head came forward and he levelled his sharp eyes at Neville Bruce. 'If he does get picked up by the SSN let me know at once, and I'll pull strings. I don't want him made a martyr; the whole of the New Left press in the U.K would be clamouring for vengeance. Thank you, Neville.' He nodded his dismissal.

If Manuela had not succeeded in convincing Juan that her interest in Caudle was professional and strictly platonic he would never have allowed the man to spend two nights in her flat. But she could be very persuasive, and it was obviously far better security to leave him where he was until he could leave for the plane.

Juan was showing himself to be a conscientious and meticulous organiser. The disguise expert was to return the following morning, so Caudle was allowed to clean up his face and hair. They packed the suitcase with the newly-bought clothes, except those he would need for the flight and the suit. Caudle's own shoes, socks and tie were all fit to wear, but he pointed out that he would need a new overcoat and hat, and after some telephoning these were purchased and brought to the flat. Nothing whatever of his own was to go into the suitcase and the trousers of his ruined suit, which were still presentable, were packed in the holdall.

The forged British passport was brought in, and Juan exhibited it with pardonable pride. He explained that it was a false real passport, that is, a genuine British passport with the ink entries in the 'window' of the cover and on the title and description pages carefully expunged and re-written. His photograph had been affixed on page 3 and stamped with an embossed seal which looked identical with that used by Her Majesty's Passport Office. The rest of the passport was genuine, except for the Argentine entry stamp, dated a week earlier, which had been cleverly forged. The previous owner, whoever he was, had only apparently travelled to Israel.

'That's how we got it, of course,' explained Juan. 'You have to have a separate passport for Israel if you plan to visit an Arab country, and some of them come on the black market. Here is your currency form, showing that you entered Argentine with twenty pounds in cash, but no traveller's cheques, and in the last page of the passport you'll see that you've notionally changed fifteen pounds at the Banco de Argentina. You didn't need more money because you were visiting your sister and staying at her home in Cordoba. Read the description.'

Caudle looked at the back of the first page: schoolmaster, born Weybridge, 5.7.36, residence U.K, height 5ft 11 inches. 'It's perfect,' he said warmly.

'Is there anything else you would have carried in your passport?'

Caudle took his own out and looked through it. 'Only the vaccination and innoculation certificates. They've been stapled in.'

'Those don't matter. They won't be asked for. Anything else?'

'No. It's a splendid job, Juan.'

'It should be. It's cost a lot of money. Now we'd better go over your "Mason" story again, and after that I'll tell you exactly what you must do, at the airport, in the plane, and when you arrived in London.'

Manuela grilled steaks and made a salad for lunch, which Juan ate with them. By this time Caudle's arm was beginning to play up, and he was sent to bed, in the guest room, for a siesta, with a couple of Panadol tablets to ease the pain.

In the afternoon the doctor came again, and frowned when he looked at the wound. 'I told you,' he said through the slit in the mask, 'to give your arm a complete rest. What have you been doing with it?'

'It's difficult,' mumbled Caudle, remembering.

'I'm afraid it was trying on those clothes,' explained Manuela, never short of an explanation. 'We had to buy him new ones.'

'All right. But it's slightly inflamed. You'd better see your doctor as soon as you get home and let him decide when to take the stitches out. Good luck!' He shook hands and departed, and Juan left with him.

'It's time for your secret writing lesson,' said Manuela.

Caudle had rather expected she might react differently to the chance of being alone together, but she made no reference to what had happened between them earlier. Just as well, he told himself.

Caudle had kept the fountain pen Juan had given him at the estancia in his jacket during the drive to Buenos Aires and had transferred it with his other possessions to the new suit. He pulled it out.

It certainly looked like a 'Parker' pen, but when the two halves were unscrewed they were seen to contain narrow glass cylinders, firmly stoppered. They were labelled, one with a 'T' for *tinta* and the other 'R' for *revelar*, and when opened disgorged tiny white and red pills. Manuela took a white one and crushed it with the hard plastic end of the 'pen' in the bottom of a wine glass, fetched from the kitchen.

'Now,' she said, handing him a teaspoon. 'One spoonful of water only. Then stir it with the pen until it's completely dissolved.'

He did as he was told, while she took some writing paper from a drawer in her rosewood desk, switched on a lamp and sat down facing the light, with a sheet of paper in front of her. 'You've got to be able to see what you're writing,' she explained, 'although the ink is just like water. So you keep the light reflected in the wet letters, and you do it like this'—she turned the paper sideways—'so that you can write the cover letter in the normal way.'

'I don't quite see that. Show me.'

She thought for a moment, and smiled impishly. 'All right, but stand away. It's *secret.*'

She dipped the nib of the 'Parker' into the solution in the glass, adjusted the lamp, and keeping the light reflected in the letters as she formed them wrote a few lines. From where Caudle stood, a yard away, the paper appeared to remain completely blank. She waved it about to evaporate the last traces of damp—the air in the centrally-heated room was warm and dry—and put it down again. Taking another sheet of paper she made it into a small pad and gently rubbed the whole surface of the letter.

'That's to make the fibres lie down and remove any extra bit of ink that might show up under an ultra-violet light. Now watch.'

She turned the paper right way up, drew out a fountain pen from her handbag and wrote, in her rounded, schoolgirl hand: 'Dear Mr Caudle, I fear I must ask you to refrain from forcing your unwelcome attentions on a defenceless woman. *Goodbye.* Yours sincerely, Manuela Belgrano.'

'Now Manuela—' began Caudle, then stopped. 'What did you write first?'

'That's for you to find out. Take another glass from the kitchen cupboard and dissolve one of the "R" pills in a teaspoonful of warm water. I'll show you how to use it.'

When he came back with the developer she had prepared a cocktail stick with a little ball of cotton-wool on its end. 'Dip that in and squeeze it out almost dry. Otherwise you'd make the real ink run. Just pass it gently over the paper from top to bottom until you've covered it all.' As he sat down she whispered into his ear, 'Then you'll read the secret message.'

Caudle smiled fondly. What a child she was, he thought—mistakenly. He took the little swab, dipped it into the 'R' solution, squeezed out the surplus moisture with his fingers and began to stroke the paper with it, covering the surface carefully.

For a moment nothing happened, then bright green letters appeared, forming words at right-angles to the cover letter. He twisted his head to read them: 'Darling Jaimito, Next time I'll be more careful with your poor arm, but *please* make it soon. Your Manuela.'

Caudle turned to look up at the girl. Her face was slightly flushed, and her eyes enormous. His self-imposed vow of abstinence was forgotten and jumping to his feet he reached out his one good arm. Then they heard the front door open and Juan's steps in the hall.

'*Mierda!*' whispered Manuela furiously,

and snatching up the letter bounded into the bathroom like a startled deer.

Hastily, Caudle sat down again and picked up another sheet of paper. His back was turned as Juan came in.

'Where's Manuela?'

'In the bathroom, I fancy.' He hoped she was pulling the plug on that damned piece of paper. 'She was just showing me the technique.'

'Good,' said Juan. 'Now, you understand I'll be using the same ink when I write to Doctor Hennessy on my arrival in England. So give her the developer and show her how to use it. I don't want to write *en clair* because by the time you get back to London both you and Doña Letizia will be of some interest to Special Branch, and they might keep a watch on your mail. But this is a secure ink, and short of really sophisticated treatment I don't think they'd spot it. When you leave here, of course, you'll only have the "R" tube in the pen. The ink pills you have there were just for testing.' In fact, Juan had only just made that decision.

Caudle protested. 'But that means we can't write to you.'

'It won't be necessary, and the composition of the ink is extremely secret, more so than the developer. We can't risk it falling into the wrong hands.'

'You don't seem to trust our discretion much.'

'I don't,' said Juan drily. 'You can't expect to lose your amateur status, my dear James, on a couple of lessons.' He came up to the desk. 'Let me see you through the whole exercise.'

Which of the two glasses held the ink, wondered Caudle, desperately. The girl had driven everything else out of his mind. It must be the one further away. He picked up the 'Parker', dipped it into the colourless fluid, and turning the paper at right-angles began: 'Your message received and understood. I shall look forward to our meeting.' It was a little difficult at first to get the light reflected properly, and by the time he had written the first line it was already disappearing, but he thought it would do. He waved the paper in the air, examined it closely, rubbed the surface with the pad, and turned it round. Taking Manuela's pen he wrote, 'Dear Señor Santos, Thank you for your letter. Unfortunately, I shall be unable to see you during your visit to England this time, since I have to go abroad on a lecture tour. With kindest regards, Yours sincerely, Letty Hennessy.'

Manuela had come into the room and was standing by his shoulder. 'Now let's see if my pupil has done his homework,' she said, and reached for the swab. The ink was dry already, and she applied the developer.

'That's very good for a first attempt,' said Juan condescendingly. The green message stood out clearly. Caudle felt Manuela's fingers pressing into his shoulder. His heart thumped.

Caudle was again made to rehearse his 'Mason' cover story and the rest of the plan. Juan tried to find gaps, but failed. He said, 'I think it's going to be O.K. Now, when you get back to London you'd better write to the Reconquista, explaining why you left your luggage behind, in the way we've agreed, and ask them for the bill. When you've paid it they'll send your suitcase on by sea.' He seemed slightly embarrassed. 'In the normal way we should have settled the account ourselves, of course, but at the moment the hotel is under suspicion, owing to the fact that the key of the communicating door was found in the lock, owing to a stupid slip by Rojas, and this links you with him. So I'm afraid you'll have to do it this way. I'm sorry.'

'That's quite understood,' said Caudle. 'I should have insisted on paying the bill in any case. Have you heard what the SSN are doing?'

'They are looking for you intensively, but there's no warrant out for your arrest, and I don't think they can have any firm evidence against you. If anyone in the street saw what happened he's been wise enough to refrain from coming forward.'

Manuela said, 'Does James have to stay here another night? Can't we take him to another flat?' Caudle could hardly believe his ears.

'No. It'd be too risky. Why? I hope he's behaved himself.' Juan shot a suspicious glance at Caudle.

'Good Heavens yes. Like a perfect gentleman,' she replied laughing, with a touch of well-contrived contempt in her voice. 'But I have a date.' She was now speaking in Spanish.

'Who with?' asked Juan sharply.

'That's no concern of yours, my dear Juan. A very attractive man whom you don't know.'

'Then you'll have to ditch him, Manolita. The Army comes first, you ought to know that. No, Caudle must stay here. I've got to go out shortly. Have you enough food in the flat?'

'Plenty. But it's annoying about my boy-friend. I'll just have to put him off.'

'Do that. I don't want you thinking of other things until our guest is safely on that plane.'

Caudle's struggle with his conscience had

ended in complete rout, and as soon as they heard, with both heads pressed against the flat door, the sounds of the lift descending, he brought her face close and kissed her soft mouth. She threw her arms round his neck. 'He's gone to his girl-friend, I bet. He won't be back—but just in case ...' She fastened the chain on the door. Then she ran to her bedroom, telling him to wait until she called. 'Don't undress,' she cried, over her shoulder. 'I want to do it.'

Much later they shared a bottle of chilled champagne and she prepared a sketchy but adequate dinner while Caudle opened a bottle of red wine. Afterwards they sat for a time over coffee and brandy, talking about everything except the ERP, Patricia and what might happen the following day. They both knew Caudle would be running a risk in spite of all the careful planning. The news of Colonel Rojas, was, however reassuring; he was still ensconced in his safe flat and hadn't shown his nose outside. Apparently, he would be disguised, equipped with false papers, and sent into Uruguay, where a job had been found for him. (The ERP had excellent reasons for protecting its own.) But no one could tell how much the SSN knew, and the risk of Caudle's discovery at the airport was there in their minds, ominous with all the latent threat of the unknown. It lent added spice and urgency to their love-making.

Manuela was aware, as Caudle was not, that she would be accompanying Juan to England, but she kept that knowledge to herself for the time being. Caudle argued that if this was to be their last night together it must be a long one, and so it turned out.

She pushed him gently out of her bed at eight o'clock the next morning and told him to finish his sleep in the guest room. When Juan arrived an hour later, looking rather overhung, she was busy cleaning the flat, with an apron over her jeans. 'Don't wake James,' she said. 'He's still fast asleep. I had to give him a sedative.'

Juan opened the door of the second bedroom and verified her statement. Caudle lay flat on his back, with his left arm lying on the counterpane. He was snoring gently—and quite genuinely. He had arrears of sleep to make up.

When he awoke there was still much to be done, and the morning passed quickly. No news had come in during the night, according to Juan, and the newspapers had relegated the story to the inside pages.

The disguise session took nearly two

hours before the masked woman was satisfied, and Caudle was made to eat lunch with the pads in his cheeks and get used to his hairy upper lip. His hair had been tinted with a washable dye and cut shorter, and his neck shaved. He was wearing a thin, inflated rubber cushion under his shirt. It filled out his lean figure so that the suit buttons dragged at the cloth most realistically. He felt utterly ridiculous and was furious when Manuela had to stifle giggles.

After lunch he packed his holdall, checked his papers and wallet, made sure that it was the 'Mason' passport in the left-hand pocket of the overcoat, and that the Caudle one was in the holdall, clipped the 'Parker' pen alongside the Biro and pencil inside his jacket, and put on the large plain spectacles that had been provided. It was just ten to three.

He donned the sober overcoat and hat, shook hands with Juan and Manuela, avoiding her eyes, waited while unseen agents down below lured away the concierge and another signalled by radio that the coast was clear. Then he picked up his bags. Juan held a little transceiver in his hands. He spoke into it, then listened. 'O.K, he said. Manuela said 'Good luck' in a cheerful casual voice, as if he were going to play a game of tennis. He walked rather stiffly to the lift and pressed the button. He was on his own now.

## CHAPTER FIFTEEN

The taxi Juan had called, which in fact belonged to the ERP and had been waiting in a near-by street for the radio signal, was standing at the front door. There was no one else to be seen in the foyer.

The long drive to Ezeiza passed without incident, and at the airport he could see no sign of special controls. He presented his 'Mason' ticket and passport at the Aerolineas counter, checked in his suitcase and went through into the departure lounge. With his last pesos he bought scent for Pat, a box of cigars for Letty and a litre bottle of whisky for himself at the duty-free store, and was looking for paperbacks to read when he heard his name called on the Tannoy system: 'Mr James Caudle, please. Will Mr James Caudle, passenger on Flight AR 130 to London, please go to the ticket counter. Mr James Caudle, please go to the ticket counter of Aerolineas Argentinas. Thank you.'

Fortunately, two men who were covertly studying the passengers for Flight AR 130 were both in the outer hall, near the reception counters. Otherwise, Caudle's reaction might well have been noticed. Automatically, he had looked up, lifted his holdall and was moving towards the inside barriers when he remembered that he wasn't Caudle any more.

He turned away towards the men's lavatory and once inside looked at himself in the long mirror, half expecting to see drops of perspiration bubbling through the make-up. But the plump, bespectacled face that looked out at him was unchanged. He pulled his hat more firmly over his eyes and went back into the departure area, just in time to hear another call for the missing James Caudle. There was urgency now in the message, and five minutes later it was repeated. 'Mr James Caudle, please go to the Aerolineas counter immediately, as your flight is about to leave.' A little later the instruction for AR 130 passengers to present themselves at the departure gate was heard. He went with the crowd and took his place in the coach for the short trip to the aircraft.

The hostess at the foot of the tourist-class steps checked his false name and embarkation card against her list and he went up and into the big Boeing 707. He had chosen a place on the aisle, and found two passengers already seated on his left. They were both Argentines, and showed no interest in him beyond casual nods of greeting.

It was five o'clock when the plane took off, and Caudle gave a sigh of satisfaction as they flew north, following the shore of what looked like an inland sea, but was in fact the estuary of the River Plate. Then, as the sun sank beyond the endless stretches of flat grassland they turned to pursue the line of the Paraná, with Uruguay on their right. Two hours after leaving Ezeiza the plane was well inside Brazil and approaching Viracopos.

The flight was just like the outward trip in reverse; the same half-hour's stop at Viracopos, the longer pause among the lights of Rio, and the breath-taking view as they rose into the air and flew past the Sugar Loaf towards Madrid, ten hours away. But the time-change worked the other way, so that although the Rio departure was at half-past nine in the evening they arrived in Madrid after noon the following day.

When he had finished dinner Caudle put aside his book and tried to clear his thoughts about what had happened. The main thing was that he was safe, and he had to thank Juan and his organisation for that. But then the Manuela situation had to be faced. That relationship, he pointed out to himself, was now irrevocably ended, and there would only be memories—pleasurable, yes, for damn it, she was a very attractive and passionate girl. Pictures and sensations recalled themselves to his mind, and his nerve-ends tingled. He pushed these thoughts away. It had only been an *affair*. It was true he hadn't had one since he married Pat, but lots of other people did. Just an affair. Whereas Pat was his wife.

Of course, he would have to tell Pat everything, and it would make her miserable however hard he tried to make up for his—his what? Hell! His lapse, he supposed. But how else could he explain that he'd left his clothes behind, and how he'd acquired new ones, and shorter hair, and a bullet hole in his arm? Well, that was all true, but he didn't have to mention Manuela, did he? In fact, coming to think of it, mightn't it be better to invent a story that would cover everything, and keep her in ignorance? Then their lives could go on just as before. A little tame, admittedly, but their own. How shocked she would be if she knew he had been consorting with what she'd regard as a gang of upper-class cut throats! And of course, it would be a breach of faith with Letty, who had been so insistent that Pat must be kept out of the whole thing. Yet, in spite of this, he must try to tell Pat as much of the truth as was possible.

As the ceiling lights dimmed, and the Argentine by his side, who had dined well, began to snore, Caudle slowly and tortuously worked out what he would tell his wife, and the truth gradually dissolved in an acid brew of lies.

As regards Letty, he would have to tell her exactly what he'd discovered about the ERP, and achieved in negotiation, including his maniac offer of practical help in snatch operations. With wishful hopefulness, he thought she might be so horrified at what he had done that she'd drop the whole idea of collaboration with the ERP. Then, thought Caudle, they could get back to their task of enlightening the British people about the sins of capitalism and all British political parties, and the virtues of Marx and Engels, if not Lenin. In a way, Caudle had to admit to himself, it was a pity. It had been extraordinarily stimulating to see a real red-blooded revolutionary movement in action, if only in its own defence, with its absolute control over its members and its ability to spend money like water. There was something very attractive, he concluded, about great wealth, and the power and people it could buy.

On these thoughts, strange for a man of Caudle's long-held beliefs, he fell asleep.

There was an hour's stop in Barajas and again in Orly Sud, but the cities these airports served were hidden under a haze of heat and smog. The whole of Western Europe was still suffering from the drought, and Caudle realised that he would look ridiculous arriving in Heathrow still wearing his heavy overcoat. At three o'clock the Boeing left Orly on the short run to Heathrow, where Pat had said she would meet him with the Morris. This was the testing time; this was when the elaborate plan, intended to baffle both Argentine and British security forces, had to succeed.

He waited until he could see the Channel below the clouds, put on his overcoat and hat, took his holdall and went into the men's lavatory. Using the sponge and the bottle of spirit the masked disguise expert had given him he cleaned the make-up from his face and removed the moustache; then he washed his face and hair, and saw the pale make-up base streaming down into the basin. Finally, ignoring a loud knock on the door, he used his battery razor and with two spots of gum from a small tube replaced the moustache so that from then on a single tug would detach it. Hastily, he stripped off the inflated rubber cushion, which had kept his stomach far too hot all night, let the air out and stuffed it into the holdall, together with the 'Mason' passport, which he exchanged for his own. Then he returned to his seat, urged on by an indignant hostess, with his overcoat—which concealed his loss of embonpoint—still on, and his hat pulled down above the large spectacles. The hostess fussed over his seat-belt and he doubted if she even looked at his face, which after all was still pushed out of shape by the cheek pads, even if it had become much younger-looking.

When the Boeing landed at Heathrow and the passengers could descend he was blowing his nose vigorously as he nodded his thanks to the girls in uniform at the top of the steps. At a point along the long glazed walkway he turned towards the windows for a moment and secreted the moustache and the cheek pads in his handkerchief. Later, before presenting his Caudle document at the 'British Passport Only' control, he removed his glasses and put them in his pocket. He had slung the overcoat over his shoulder; the heatwave seemed to be over, but it was still too warm for that garment.

The immigration officer glanced at the passport photograph then at the man in front of him. 'Did you have a good flight, Mr Caudle?' He raised his voice slightly as he pronounced the name.

'Yes, thanks.' Caudle went past the baggage conveyors and through the 'Nothing to Declare' channel without trouble. He hurried on, swinging the holdall, eager to meet Pat and get over the first piece of deception.

The Special Branch man who had stood beside the immigration officer was in his office, telephoning. 'Put me through to the Yard, please, miss ... This is D.C Baker, Heathrow, Janet. Get me Sergeant Cobham, quick please ... This is Baker, Sarge, Heathrow. This man Caudle. First we were told he'd be on the B.A flight, then you said he wasn't. Well, he was, Sarge.' He listened for a moment, and scratched his head. 'Well, I don't get it, Sarge. There can't be a mistake. The face, the passport pic and our description all tally. His hair looks a bit shorter than in the description, but that's nothing. If you ask me the Argentines have been playing silly buggers with us. Do you want me to pick him up? ... O.K, then, I'll just see him through customs and note if anyone meets him.'

Baker took his time, because he knew the registered baggage would take a long time to come out on to the conveyors, but when he joined the impatient ring of passengers waiting to seize their bags as they passed he could see no sign of Caudle anywhere. He tried the customs officers, unobtrusively showing each the photograph he took from his pocket. 'Anyone seen this bloke?'

A man on the 'Nothing to Declare' channel said, 'Sure. He passed through twenty minutes ago. Said he hadn't any heavy luggage. He just had a leather holdall.'

'That's a bit odd, isn't it?'

'Some of 'em travel very light, these days.'

The S.B man ran out into the exit hall, but by this time Caudle was already being driven in his ancient Morris down the motorway, with an adoring Pat at the wheel, full of questions. What had happened to his suitcase? Was there something wrong with his arm? Where had he got those new clothes? Above all, *why* had he cut his hair?

But curiosity changed to dismay, and she was nearly in tears as she heard the dreadful story, which she accepted, naturally, as Gospel truth because it was James, her James, who told it. But what a country!

'You'll never go back there again, will you, darling? It simply isn't safe, with people like that on the streets. How kind of that doctor to help you! I must write and thank him. Oh James, it's so marvellous to have you back!' Affectionately, he patted her knee with his good right hand.

When all the Aerolineas passengers had collected their luggage there was still one suitcase making the round on the conveyor belt. No one claimed it, and in the end it was taken to the airline office. Someone telexed Ezeiza to check the baggage ticket, and it appeared that it belonged to Frederic Mason, the one all the fuss was about. The Argentines said he'd caught the plane; British immigration at Heathrow said he hadn't.

## CHAPTER SIXTEEN

At the Yard Cobham was speaking to Detective Chief Superintendent Garrard. He finished, 'I think they made a muddle of it at Ezeiza, sir. He may have been delayed, couldn't collect his luggage and got on the plane at the last moment. Obviously, he *must* have checked in, or he wouldn't have had an embarkation card.'

'I suppose that's the most likely explanation. But there is this curious story about

Caudle gunning a man down in the street. It doesn't sound like him, I admit, but I think you'd better have a word with him. In the meantime, let SIS liaison know, so that they can tell their rep in B.A to stop worrying. The man's on our plate now.'

Caudle's school was still on holiday, and the following morning, when Cobham called, he was doing small jobs around the house. Pat was out shopping. He glanced through the window, saw a face he did not recognise, and hurriedly put down his screwdriver and struggled into a cardigan. In his T-shirt the stitches were all too visible.

Cobham showed his identity card. 'I'd just like a few words, sir, if I may.'

'I don't see what right the police have to pry into my affairs.'

'It's just routine, sir. May I come in?'

'Oh all right.' Caudle led the way into the sitting-room. 'Sit down if you want to.'

'Thank you, sir. I gather you've just returned from a trip to Argentina. May I ask the purpose of the visit?'

'I'm afraid it's none of your business, but if you must know, I was hired to undertake research work for Doctor Letitia Hennessy, in connection with a book she is writing.'

213

'I see, sir. A work of scholarship, I suppose?'

'No. She writes thrillers, as well as books on English literature, and it was for one of that series.'

'Very nice job, sir, if I may say so. Why did she choose you, then?'

'Because I speak Spanish.'

'And I suppose you took the opportunity of meeting some of your fellow-Marxists, did you, sir? I believe they're much in evidence in Argentina.'

'They may be,' said Caudle firmly, 'but no. I made no contact with them.'

'Not even with Mr Juan Santos, sir? I thought he was a friend of Doctor Hennessy. I mean, it seems a bit odd if you didn't even look him up. A man like him might have been very helpful in suggesting sources for your—er—researches.'

'You're trying it on, Sergeant. I didn't meet anyone of that name.' He got up. 'Is that all?'

'Yes, sir. Except—you didn't get into a spot of bother while you were there?'

'I did not. And now, if you'll excuse me—' He heard the key turn in the front door lock. 'That'll be my wife. That's all I have to say, Sergeant.'

Cobham stood up slowly and saw Pat come in with a bag full of groceries. Pretty as a picture, he thought, and a nice cuddly shape, too. Caudle tried to shoo him out, but he stood his ground. 'How d'you do, Mrs Caudle. My name's Robin Cobham.'

'He's a cop, love,' said Caudle hastily, 'and on his way out.'

'Yes,' said Cobham, 'I must be on my way. I was just asking your husband about Buenos Aires, Mrs Caudle. It sounds a fascinating place.'

Her eyes flashed. 'If you ask me, it's a jungle. Did James tell you about how he was mugged?'

'He's not interested, Pat,' said Caudle sharply.

'Well,' she said indignantly, 'he ought to be. I mean, if English people can't be protected when they're abroad, what's the Foreign Office for?'

'I've often wondered,' said Cobham. 'But I'm very sorry to hear this, sir. You didn't tell me. How did it happen?'

Caudle ground his teeth, but the fall-back story he had already told Pat was ready on his tongue. 'If you must know, I was exploring part of the old city, getting information for Doctor Hennessy's questionnaire, when two men came at me. One of them struck at me with a knife and got me in the arm. The other was trying to kick my head in when a car came up and they scarpered.'

215

'Good Heavens!' said Cobham. 'Did you get the arm attended to?'

'Yes, that was lucky. The man driving the car happened to be a doctor, named Claudio Guzman, and he picked me up. I'd passed out, but he got me into his car and took me home, where he applied first aid and put me to bed.'

If ever, thought Cobham, a story was learned by heart, this was it. He appeared very concerned. 'Then he took you back to your hotel, I suppose?'

'I told you I'd passed out. In fact I was quite badly concussed, and lost my memory temporarily. I couldn't even remember the name of my hotel. But he was a good chap, and didn't seem to mind. I slept at his house and it was well into the following day that I recalled I was due to catch the plane that afternoon. My ticket confirmed that there was no time to lose. It was too late to collect my bag from the hotel or even pay the bill, and he just put me into a taxi and sent me off to the airport. And now, Sergeant, I'm afraid we must get on with our work.' For a moment he met Cobham's eyes, and read sheer disbelief in them.

'I wish I could meet that Doctor Guzman, and thank him,' said Pat, as she accompanied Cobham to the door. 'He was so kind. All James's clothes were

216

covered with blood, and he bought new ones for him; otherwise he couldn't have caught the plane.' She turned to Caudle, smiling fondly. 'His head's all right now; it always was as hard as oak, but you should see that wound in his arm. It's all black and blue all round.'

'Good-bye, Sergeant,' said Caudle firmly.

'Good-bye, sir. Have that arm seen by your doctor here. Those gunshot wounds are tricky.'

'It was a *knife*,' said Pat, anxious that he should get it right.

'Of course, so your husband said.' He met Caudle's eyes again. 'Well, sir, I must say, that *is* a story.' He shook hands. 'Good-bye, sir. Good-bye, Mrs Caudle. I expect you're glad to have him back safe.'

She had her arm round Caudle's waist. 'I won't let him go abroad again alone.' Lucky devil, thought Cobham, as he went out to his car.

Pat was looking at Caudle anxiously. 'But I didn't say anything wrong, did I?'

'No, darling, of course not. But you must remember to talk as little as possible to the fuzz. They can twist everything you say.'

Back at the Yard Cobham went in to see Garrard and made his report. 'When she said he was black and blue all round the wound, I thought, that sounds more like a bullet than a knife, although of course it could have been internal bleeding. So I tried it on. I said those gunshot wounds were tricky, and you should have seen him jump, sir. It sounds as if the SIS snooper's story was correct, and the other man winged him. He must have been with the ERP at the time, and they worked the escape.' He paused, frowning. 'But how, I just can't make out. There's something funny about that luggage story, and how was it he wasn't seen at the airport? Incidentally, it's true his hair's been cut short.'

'It sounds to be like a successful escape operation, cleverly planned, and if so they'd have had to disguise him. But it doesn't really matter. The main thing is that if we're right he was in a shooting affray with the SSN and shot one of their agents in self-defence. We don't have to tell the Argentines direct, but we'll have to let SIS know we think we can confirm their story. They can tell the SSN if they want to, but I doubt if they will. There seem to be no grounds for extradition.'

He thought for a moment. 'You did no harm in scaring Caudle, Robin. It got the result you wanted, and if he realises we don't believe a word of his story and shall be waiting for him to put a foot wrong, there's no harm in that either. He's a mild enough man, from the record, and I can only imagine Argentina went to his head.' (In this, Garrard was right.) 'Now he's at home, he'll pipe down.' (But there, for Garrard, he made a rare error of judgement.)

That evening Caudle was restive, and Pat watched him anxiously. 'Is your arm hurting a lot?'

'No, it's only itching now. I'll have to get Doctor Greenall to take the stitches out. I'll give him a ring tomorrow.'

'What's wrong, James?'

'Nothing.' He did not look at her.

She was silent. Then she said brightly, 'I'm getting used to your hair. But what a funny thing to do!'

'I told you. It was the hairdresser at the hotel. I felt I needed a trim, and while I was reading the paper he ran amok. You don't mind, do you? It'll soon grow.'

'That'll teach you not to let anyone cut it but me. But I'm beginning to like it. It suits you, James. It's more manly.' Another pause. 'You *are* worried about something, aren't you?'

'Oh do stop nagging, Pat. It's just—I suppose it's jet-lag.'

'What on earth's that?'

'I told you I was nearly twenty hours on that bloody plane. Even after shorter trips people often find it difficult to reorientate. Let's go to the George and play darts.'

'But your arm, darling—'

'I don't throw with my left hand, do I?' He knew he had spoken too sharply, and got up quickly to put his arm round her. 'It's lovely to be home, with you, and you know it.'

She turned her face and kissed him eagerly. 'I do love you so,' she whispered, and guilt hit him like a hammer blow.

He had always felt they should frequent the public bar of the George, and get to know the locals. But they couldn't afford to go often, and had made few friends. People didn't seem to want to know about his kind of politics. They wanted action now—one way or the other.

He brought back two pints of watery bitter to the table where Pat had found places. The ash-trays were overflowing, and the floor was littered. Other people were enjoying themselves, too busy to speak to the Caudles. James looked around with distaste, and a picture came into his mind of the fire-lit room at 'El Ranchito', and Manuela's eyes on his face. He drank up his pint quickly, and went back to the bar to get a short drink for Pat—port and lemon, which she adored—and a double whisky for himself.

'I suppose we can afford it for once,' she said, lowering her voice.

'Yes, of course we can. Listen, darling. I have to go and see Letty tomorrow, to tell her about the trip. I'll go by train.' He saw her looking at him wistfully.

'Do we really have some money to spare, even after my expensive holiday?'

'Yes.'

'Well, couldn't I come along with you. I'd love to see your rooms at St John's again. It's so long since—' She stopped, desperately afraid of a rebuff. 'It wouldn't cost any more, actually, if I drove you.'

He took one look at her flushed, worried little face and decided. 'Of course you can. I tell you what we'll do. We'll take a punt through the Backs.' He put his long hand over her small one. 'I'll see Letty in the morning, and then we'll buy things for lunch and picnic in the punt.'

'And watch the ducks sliding down that overflow at the weir? Oh do let's. I'll make sandwiches to take with us—'

'Of course not, we'll buy them in Cambridge.'

'No, we won't. It's too expensive, and anyway, mine are better.'

Letty greeted Caudle with an affectionate

kiss and gave Pat a peck on the cheek. Then she looked at James sternly. 'I don't think Patricia will be interested in what we have to talk about—'

He interrupted hastily. 'Of course not, Letty. All I'd like is for you to let Pat sit in the Fellows' Garden. She's brought her binoculars and can watch the birds.'

'Of course, my dear. Go out into the Court and you'll find the door on your left, clearly marked. If anyone asks what you're doing, say you're waiting for me.'

'Oh thank you, Aunt Letty.' Pat handed the parcel of sandwiches to Caudle. 'They'd get too hot in the sun.' Then she disappeared.

'What on earth's she talking about?'

'It's our lunch, Letty. I'm going to take her out in a punt for a picnic.'

'Pity. I thought we might've had lunch together. You spoil that girl. Never mind. Let's get to business. Tell me the whole story.' She sat down at her desk and Caudle settled himself on the window-seat, with his back to the light. He knew his face tended to give him away, and though he was anxious to give her a full account of those eventful five days, there wasn't going to be any mention of Manuela. Letty was too damned inquisitive, and she'd have had the whole sorry tale out of him if he gave her a chance.

She listened without interrupting, except for an astounded yelp when he told her of the shooting. When he finished she said, 'This man Santos is certainly competent, isn't he—and helpful. Took you to his flat, looked after you like a mother, and devised a very ingenious scheme for smuggling you out of the country. We owe him something, James. But for him you could be rotting in a Buenos Aires gaol. I think I ought to write to him, or would that be too risky?'

'Don't think of it,' said Caudle firmly. 'It'd be the last thing he'd want, however well you wrapped up your thanks. In any case, he'll be coming here in a week or two, if Mendoza decides to go ahead. But I doubt it, you know. As I said, when they plan what they call an expropriation they aim at grossing a million dollars by one coup.'

Letitia smiled. 'Oh, I think we could arrange that for them.'

'What *are* you talking about, Letty dear? We aren't in that sort of league. I think we ought to drop the whole idea.'

'Oh no. I've been thinking of what you said, James, that my fifty thou would get us nowhere. But half a million would give us a real opportunity, wouldn't it?' She saw his baffled look. 'Of course it would. Lodged in a Swiss numbered account and brought out in large cash dollops as required. Think what you could do for *The Banner* with that sort of lolly.'

'But how, for God's sake? What are you talking about?'

She waved her hand, distributing cigar ash on the carpet. 'It's just an idea,' she said airily. 'Something I worked out for a thriller—and took damned care not to tell anyone about the plot, of course. But it all hinges on when Santos and his boys could set up the job.' She rummaged in her handbag, and produced a diary. 'Let's see. It'd be Friday night, September 10th. If Santos surfaces soon that'd give him a few weeks to prepare. You won't be back at school by then, will you?'

'Of course I shall. But why that date?' He smiled suddenly, remembering something she had said when they had first discussed kidnapping operations, and slapped her well-padded shoulder. 'Is that when the unsuspecting Professor Clements comes to dine with you?'

'I'm not gunning for Gerry Clements any longer,' she said, with a sigh of satisfaction, like a large tabby cat after a saucer of cream. 'I reviewed his book on the Tragedies for the T.L.S. They let me have a page and a half, and I sent him up rotten.' (Her slang was always a weird mixture of ancient and modern.)

'Then who's your target now, and why that date?'

'It's when Sheikh Daoud bin Khalid gets his honorary degree from the gnarled hands of our Vice-Chancellor. That's on the eleventh, but he spends the previous night in the Judge's Set at Cranmer.'

Cranmer College is by no means the oldest of the Cambridge colleges, being an Elizabethan foundation, but it is the grandest, and used to have the privilege, not always appreciated, of entertaining the Circuit Judge on his visits to Cambridge for the Assizes. There is a beautiful set of rooms formerly available for the Judge and his clerk and butler, and now used for other guests of honour at the discretion of the Master, whose Lodge adjoins the Set.

'Why Cranmer?' asked Caudle, puzzled.

'Because that's the Sheikh's own College. I remember him well, since he was one of my pupils—an attractive youngster, lazy as hell, but plenty of brains and far too much money. He was the leader of a very rowdy staircase.'

'But you mean—*kidnap* Sheikh Daoud? He's as rich as Croesus; he'll have a bodyguard that'd fill the Great Court.'

'Exactly, James. They'll guard the Court entrance to the Set.'

'And there must be windows, at least, on Little Court; you've forgotten them.'

'I haven't. As you say, that's what they'll do. But there's another way of getting into the Set. I know. I've used it.' She saw the incredulous look on Caudle's face, and bridled. 'All right, I'll tell you. When I was an undergraduate another girl bet me a case of champagne I couldn't spend the night in Queen Victoria's bed, the one the Judge used when he was here. Well, I did.' She stopped, vaguely embarrassed.

'Go on, Letty. You're blushing.'

'It was a long time ago, James. He was the son of the Master, who was abroad at the time, and there was only one maid left in the Lodge to look after Desmond. So I worked on him, and he hid me. Then when the maid had gone to bed we opened the door that leads into the Judge's Set from the Lodge—the key was on the Lodge side, of course—and there we were.'

'In Queen Victoria's bed. You old devil!'

'I took a monogrammed pillow-slip to show the girl who dared me—she wouldn't have trusted my word, I suppose—and gave it back to Desmond next day.'

Caudle laughed. It was the first time he'd really felt like laughing since his return from Argentina. 'Oh, Letty dear, it's a wonderful plot for a story, but this is for real. There isn't any young man in the Lodge now. The Master's a bachelor of seventy-five.'

'And that's just as well. He gets in caterers to do his entertaining for him. There are only a couple of servants, and they're almost as old as he is. And you've missed one very important point.'

'What's that?'

'Old Blenkinsop isn't only Master of Cranmer; he's doing his stint as Vice-Chancellor of the University. And he'll be giving the reception and dinner-party for Sheikh Daoud in his Lodge. That's the night before the ceremony, as I said.'

Caudle stared at her. 'So what are you planning? You tip off Santos, he gets his thugs dressed up in black ties and invited to the reception, then out with their guns, mow down Daoud's mob, scatter any British cops, charge out into King's Parade with Daoud in their midst and roar away in their stolen escape-cars?'

'You've forgotten the communicating door. And anyway,' added Letitia, 'my thriller plots are a bit more sophisticated than that.'

'Oh Jesus!' said Caudle in despair. 'It isn't a story, Letty. I told you. This is real life, and I've just had a taste of it and don't want another.'

'It wouldn't be you doing the strong-arm stuff, dear boy, it'd be Santos and his men.'

'There'd be a blood bath, and you

know it, and we'd be responsible. What's happened to all our views on violence?'

'As I've worked it out, there wouldn't be any bloodshed.' She told him her plan, puffing quickly at her cigar, and scattering more ash.

Caudle smiled. 'It's very ingenious, just like your books, but it wouldn't work, and in any case Santos wouldn't buy it.'

'We'll see. I'll let you know when he arrives and we'll have a council of war. Now you'd better take your Patricia off to lunch. Enjoy your picnic.'

He was going to the door when the compulsive curiosity of the professional novelist got the better of her. She knew she ought not to remind him of the killing, but—'James.'

He stopped. 'Yes.'

'When you shot that man, what did you *feel?*'

He lifted his right hand and stared at it, frowning. 'I don't know. He was a brave man, and although he saw I was armed he took a chance. I don't know what I thought. For the first two days I struggled to take it in, but now it's a complete blank. I keep on trying to realise what I did, telling myself he was married, with children—that's what I read in the papers—but it's no good. I can't make myself even be sorry for them. I don't understand it at all.'

He was looking very distressed, his eyes on the floor, and Letty felt ashamed of herself. 'It was a reflex, James, can't you see? What your father trained you to do. See an enemy with a gun, and kill him. You were no more responsible for that action than one of Pavlov's salivating dogs.'

'What you're saying,' he muttered, 'is that I might do it again ...'


## CHAPTER SEVENTEEN

It was a fortnight afterwards when Sergeant Cobham brought a file of papers into Garrard's room at the Yard. It was entitled, 'Xavier LOPEZ @ Juan SANTOS @ Ramon GONZALEZ', and there was a summary sheet inside the cover, which the Chief Superintendent read through quickly. He put the file down.

'I see. So he's here, calling himself Gonzalez for a change—but the SSN put us wise to that—and he's staying, typically, at the Hilton. He's been observed consorting with exiled members of the MIR. What have they been up to recently?'

The MIR—*Movimiento de Izquierda*

*Revolucionario*—is an extremist Marxist movement, very active in Chile both before and during Allende's rule, which to MIR minds was not nearly radical enough. After the military *putsch* a large number of MIR members fled the country, most to Argentina but some, through the courtesy of Her Majesty's Government, to England, where they were accepted as political refugees, like many more moderate opponents of the military regime.

'They're digging themselves in, sir, and sticking together, but they've done no damage so far.'

'So what d'you think Santos—let's still call him that—is doing with them?'

'The ERP have a fairly close relationship with the MIR in Argentina, sir, and have given them financial aid. Perhaps he's arranging the same thing here.'

'Could be. Has he been seeing the local Trots again?'

'No, sir, only the MIR. Going the rounds. Their groups and settlements need money badly, and perhaps it's just that. The ERP have money oozing out of their ears, and they're always handing it out to their co-religionists—I mean fellow Marxists. All the same—'

'Well, Robin?'

'It'd be odd if they didn't want something in return, and I wonder what.'

'Yes, that's on the cards. Has Santos seen the Red Hen yet? Or Caudle?' He thought. 'Or talked to either on the phone?'

'No sign of that, sir. Incidentally, there's a girl with Santos this time, Manuela San Martin. And she's a real peach. No record.'

'Are they lovers?'

'There's no evidence, sir. She's staying at Claridge's, and seems to know people here. She was dining out last night at the White Tower, with a couple about her own age, early twenties. I didn't recognise the man, but he looked sort of top-drawer. Huntin' and shootin' type, I wouldn't wonder. Drives a Bentley. Her English is perfect, so it might be the other girl is an ex-school friend. Now, Santos goes for the birds in a big way, two different ones the last two nights,' sighed Cobham enviously.

Garrard was looking through the file. 'And they arrived four days ago, on different aircraft. Why do you conclude they're associated, then? I mean, if they don't go out together?'

'It's further back in the file, sir. On the visits to the ex-MIR people she went with him. She might be his secretary, I suppose. We could do with more like that around here, sir.'

'Restrain yourself, Sergeant. I agree it

looks as if Santos is worth watching. We don't want any of those MIR thugs to become operational, especially with ERP money behind them. Keep up the surveillance on identified MIR members, and watch Santos and the girl. Did you find out how Caudle got through the Argentine controls?'

'The SSN think he must have used a forged passport in the name of Frederic Mason, a man who doesn't exist, and got into the aircraft in disguise. At the British end he used his real passport, and since he was booked on the plane anyway he had no problem. The ERP must have arranged it; he couldn't possibly have done it by himself.'

'Yes. But of course the ERP couldn't risk him being caught. It doesn't necessarily mean they'll want to contact him here.' Garrard thought for a moment. 'But you'd better keep a close eye on him, too, Sergeant, at least until he starts teaching again.'

While this was happening Letitia Hennessy was looking at a letter she had received that morning, in a plain envelope addressed to her at St Mary's. It ran, 'Dear Doctor Hennessy, I am in England for a few weeks and should be glad to have a further talk with you at your convenience.

If this is agreeable to you please let me know when I may call on you in College. Yours sincerely, Ramon Gonzalez.'

She was asking herself how the hell she could reply, when the bloody fool hadn't given an address—when she remembered, and with a thrill of excitement took from its hiding-place behind a drawer in her disorderly desk the 'Parker' pen Caudle had given her. She twisted the two halves apart and extracted a red pill from its container. Then she made up the solution as she had been told, formed a swab from a toothpick and a pinch of cottonwool, and carefully applied the liquid.

Bright green letters suddenly appeared on the paper, in vertical lines: 'Please note my new name. I should like to elaborate the matters discussed with our mutual friend. Can you lunch with me at The Six Bells, Grantchester, on Thursday, 19th August at one o'clock? If so, would you kindly reserve a table in *your* name? I will ring you at your home to confirm, but please say just yes or no on the telephone, for security reasons. J.S.'

'Elaborate,' she said to herself scornfully, 'there's a Latinsim for you!' Or was it, though? She took down the A-M volume of the *Shorter Oxford English Dictionary* and looked the word up. No, by God! '... to work out in detail, 1611 ... to transmute into a developed product, 1607', but still evidently considered correct use by the S.O.E.D. Well, you could always learn!

Hennessy the don satisfied, Hennessy the revolutionary took over. She read the message again. Why couldn't he have invited her by telephone? Security, obviously; he'd made that clear in his last sentence. He thought *her* telephone might be tapped. Interesting! And why no mention of James? He ought to be there, too, and the ERP could pay for his luncheon out of their so-called expropriations.

When Juan rang that evening it was from a call-box. Letty was sitting in her cottage outside Clayhithe, reading a suspense novel by a rival crime writer, and gleefully finding much to criticise. The voice said, 'Am I speaking to Doctor Hennessy?'

'Yes, and thank you for your invitation. I'll be there.' She slapped the receiver down. The professional touch!

That short conversation was intercepted by Special Branch and marked 'Unknown caller/Letitia Hennessy'. Next morning the tape was played back to Detective Sergeant Robin Cobham. He listened, frowning. 'Have we got a voice print of Juan Santos alias Gonzalez?'

'Yes, Sarge. Those phone calls to the

IMG and WRP on his last visit.'

'Well, try and get one from this, too. It's very short but you might get some similarities.'

The DC came back later and laid two sets of photographs of zigzag lines on Cobham's desk. 'It's the same voice, Sarge. He always starts the same way. "Am I speaking to ...", and look at the comparison. Same peaks and all.'

Cobham rang Garrard and told him. 'They're up to something, sir. He didn't want to give away the rendezvous, so he wrote to her and rang later to confirm. And listen to the Red Hen's reply. That was no social call.' He switched on the tape recorder.

Garrard said, 'I agree with you. Just like on the telly. The terse reply, and slam down the phone. She couldn't have made it clearer she was up to something. But what on earth is it, Cobham? What have those two got in common? Her kind of revolution is all in the mind, while his is well-heeled thuggery. Keep after them, I don't like the smell of this.'

# CHAPTER EIGHTEEN

The following Thursday morning, as Caudle's Morris rattled along the A1, packed with holiday-makers driving north under the hot sun, there was one thing he was determined about. He and Letty must not get involved with Juan Santos. The man couldn't be trusted not to double-cross them. It was true, Caudle thought, that he owed Juan, as well as Manuela, a vote of thanks, since they'd saved him from a lot of potential nastiness with the Argentine police, but that was in their interests, too. They couldn't have been sure he would have kept silent under interrogation. But operational collaboration was another matter, and he wanted no part of it. Luckily, he felt sure Juan wouldn't touch Letty's hare-brained project with a barge-pole.

When she let him into her cottage at Clayhithe her first words were, 'I couldn't tell you more on the telephone, James, because Santos thinks they may have bugged my line. We're going to meet him at the Six Bells in Grantchester.'

'I guessed there was to be a meeting.

D'you know what he wants?'

'Our ideas for his ops, I hope. That was the understanding, wasn't it? And we've got a good one for him, haven't we? I've gone over it again from start to finish, and it's the cat's pyjamas.'

'Yes, but Letty, Juan couldn't put your precious plan into operation with only a few weeks' notice. It takes months of preparation. They proved that to me.'

'We'll see.' She went out with him and got into his car. He drove off. Letty said, 'Whatever's the matter with it—the Morris, I mean? Every time you do over thirty she makes a horrible noise.'

'A big-end's going, I'm afraid. I'll have to have it re-packed.'

'Sell the car and buy another, boy. We can afford it.'

'Nonsense! A new one'd cost—'

'Do as I say. Trade it in for a new Marina. Don't argue, James. Just do it, and I'll divvy up. We can't afford to risk anything going wrong when we're operational.'

'But we aren't going to be operational, for God's sake! Do let's get that clear, at least. We don't believe in violence. It's what distinguishes us from all the other Marxist groups.'

'Listen to who's talking. I'm not referring to your gun-slinging. You told me you actually offered operational help to Mendoza, though why on earth you exceeded your brief I can't imagine. What got into you, James?'

'I don't know. But we've got to get out of it now, and I'll take the rap.'

The table reserved for Doctor Hennessy was under an apple tree, laden with fruit, in the little orchard behind the inn. In the long grass bees buzzed lazily among the flowers, and the air was heavy with the scents of summer. A waiter pulled out chairs, whisked a napkin at some ambient wasps and retreated when told they would wait for their friends before ordering drinks. 'I warn you,' cautioned Caudle. 'These Argentines eat a lot.'

'He's paying. And there he is now. But who's the woman?' Letty was startled at the expression on Caudle's face. He was staring at the two who advanced across the turf, Juan in a pale grey mohair suit and the girl very elegant, in coral linen with heavy silver bracelets.

'I thought you said he was coming alone,' said Caudle huskily.

'He didn't say. But who *is* the girl?'

'She's one of them.' He got to his feet.

Manuela was smiling. 'Hullo, James. How nice to see you again.' Juan was bowing over Letitia's hand, with angry eyes on Caudle. Then he turned, and shook hands formally. 'I didn't want to trouble you to come here from London,' he said shortly.

'He's my chief assistant and adviser,' said Letty firmly. 'I hope you have no objection, Señor Santos?'

'Of course not; I'm delighted to see James again.' He didn't look it, and Letty wondered why. Caudle was still adjusting the chairs, his eyes on the girl's face. *Well*, thought Letty, her old eyes glinting, there's a turn-up for the book.

'This,' said Santos, 'is my fiancée, Manuela.'

The waiter came, and Santos suggested dry martinis; the others nodded. Caudle couldn't have spoken anyway. Turning to Santos, Letty thanked him for his kindness to Caudle in Buenos Aires, and for his clever manoeuvre to get him out of the country. 'And dealing with that wound,' she added. 'It was so good of you to put him up in your flat and nurse him so efficiently.'

Before the astonished Santos could reply Caudle broke in. 'Actually,' he said grimly, 'it was Manuela's flat. You must have misunderstood me.' There was an awkward pause. He'd never even mentioned the girl's existence, thought Letty.

The waiter arrived with the drinks and handed round the glasses, misty with cold, and put a plate of olives on the table. They sipped, and Letty noticed Manuela trying to catch Caudle's eye as she raised her glass. He sank half his Martini in a single gulp. The waiter handed out menus and said the smoked eel, locally caught, was a speciality, and that the chef recommended the duck with orange. Letty nodded abstractedly. Santos ordered a fillet steak for himself and the others asked for the duck. They all chose smoked eel as a first course. Without asking anyone Santos, after perusing the wine list, ordered three bottles of Niersteiner Domtal 1969 and asked for them to be brought in an ice bucket.

'Are you going to drink that with your steak?' asked Letty sharply.

'I am,' he replied blandly. 'Now, Doña Letizia, we all know what brings us together. I am instructed to say that though we are willing to consider any operational plans you may suggest, we shall require no help if we act on them. There is no question of asking your Group to have anything to do with planning or carrying out the actual operations. This is a matter for professionals and—with respect—you have no experience in the field. We shall use our own operatives.'

Letty and Caudle exchanged a glance of surreptitious relief.

'In consideration for any practical suggestions you can make in suggesting and researching for targets,' continued Juan, 'we can offer you a twenty per cent interest, but only when an operation stems directly from your sources and when it proves successful. I'm sure you'll agree that this is fair.'

Letty's eyes narrowed, and she looked at him thoughtfully over the rim of her glass. 'I do *not* agree it's fair, Señor Santos. The brainwork in devising an operation of this kind is a major part of its success and I have a very good operation all worked out for you. Even if you do the heavy work, I insist on thirty per cent.'

Santos had just removed an olive stone from his mouth. He looked at Letty smiling, and flicked the stone away on to the long grass. Letty pointed to some sheep sheltering in the shade of a tree not far away, watching them incuriously. 'Don't do that,' she said. 'One of them'll eat it and choke.'

'You seem to consume a lot of elderly mutton in this country,' he retorted. 'That'd be one for the pot. I don't bargain, Doña Letizia. Twenty per cent.'

Manuela put her brown hand on Juan's arm. 'She's quite right about the sheep,' she said reprovingly. 'Use the ash-tray.' Then she turned to Letty and smiled diplomatically. 'What do you think of our offer, Doctor Hennessy.'

'If he doesn't want a first-class plan, carefully worked out, then he's missing something. But if he does, O.K. Thirty per cent.'

Juan was smiling broadly. 'Let's hear this splendid plan, then. If it's so good that we can actually use it we'll say thirty per cent.' His smile, thought Caudle, was insufferably patronising.

He intervened. 'It's an ingenious idea,' he said, 'but requires very quick and delicate action. That might not be quite your line.'

'Your opinion in such a matter,' said Juan sarcastically, 'commands my instant respect.'

'I expect James means,' suggested Manuela, needling, 'that you'd want someone who was very quick with a gun, if anything went wrong.' He glared at her.

Letty broke in sharply. 'Stop wrangling. Do you want to hear my plan, or don't you?'

'Yes, please,' said Juan, with a slight bow.

'Very well. Have you heard of Sheikh Daoud bin Khalid?'

'No.'

'He is the Foreign Minister of the Ruler of Al Bakhra, a state in the Persian Gulf that has a yearly revenue of over two thousand million pounds from oil. Daoud is irreplaceable, I understand. The Ruler would pay a million pounds for his release at the drop of a hat.'

Juan was silent for a moment. 'A million. Yes, it might be worth it.' His eyes were on Letty's face. 'But how d'you suggest we kidnap this man. Will he be coming to England?'

She explained, and Juan laughed outright. 'My dear lady, it's an ingenious idea, I grant you, but you forget that an Arab potentate goes nowhere these days without a bodyguard. We considered something of the sort when we had a visit from one of them in Buenos Aires not long ago. It was impossible to get near him. He was never alone. His own guard and our secret police were tumbling over each other.'

'My dear Señor Santos, I am well aware of the obstacles, and the fact that our own Special Branch will also be on the job. But they'll guard the main entrance to the rooms where the Sheikh will be staying. They can hardly watch the internal door that communicates with the Vice-Chancellor's Lodge. And that,' she added, with a dramatic wave of her hand, 'is how your men will enter and leave the room where the Sheikh will be sleeping.'

'But the communicating door will surely

be locked on the Sheikh's side?'

'What will that matter, if your men are already inside it?'

'But there will be people—' Santos saw the waiter approaching. The man put down the ice bucket and set out the smoked eel, butter and a basket of toast. Then he poured a little wine into Juan's glass, waited for his approval and filled the others. Caudle tried his cautiously; it was a little too sweet for his taste and strongly scented, but still a very good wine.

When the waiter had gone Santos drew a deep breath. 'But how do they get in? The Sheikh might bolt the door on his side and go out into—what did you call it?—the main court and enter the Lodge through the official entrance. And even if my operatives could capture him, how would they leave without going through the court where all the guards will be? There's so much you haven't explained, Doña Letizia.'

'Taking your last point first, there's a side door from the Lodge into Cranmer Lane. As for the Sheikh's movements, they're all laid down.' She set down her fork and, still munching, bent down and took from her capacious handbag a folded paper, which she spread out. 'You see what it says. 6.45 pm: The Dean of Cranmer College will enter the Judge's Set through the communicating door at ground level, greet His Highness and bring him into the Lodge and up to the drawing-room, where the Vice-Chancellor will receive him and introduce his staff. 7 pm: The guests arrive. Their invitation cards will be checked by Special Branch officers at the main Lodge entrance in Great Court. 8.30 pm: The guests invited for the reception will leave, and the main door will be closed. Dinner will be served in the Queen Elizabeth room. 11 pm: The dinner guests will leave, and when the last has departed the Dean will escort His Highness to his rooms and leave him. His Highness will be asked to lock the communicating door on the inside. The Dean will then leave, and the main Lodge door will be closed for the night.' She handed the paper to Santos. 'They're obviously afraid of a bomb or something. I gather the Sheikh has enemies.'

Juan was obviously impressed, and he read through the list of orders, frowning. 'Who laid down these regulations?'

'The Special Branch man from the V.I.P Squad, who came down last week to discuss the security arrangements. He insisted that there should be a strict time-table that everybody must stick to, so that he could place the guards properly. He made several copies for the Dean, and I whipped one while he was explaining the time schedule to me. You see,' she added casually, 'I'm one of the dinner guests.'

Juan looked up sharply. *'You* are?'

'Of course. I was one of the Sheikh's tutors when he was an undergraduate here.'

Manuela was looking puzzled. 'But if the whole programme has been worked out in such detail, when is it to be? Not too soon, I hope?'

'Three weeks tomorrow,' said Caudle, smiling grimly. 'September 10th.'

Juan waited impatiently while the waiter changed the plates and served the main course. Manuela smiled at Caudle and asked about his arm. 'Have you had the stitches out?'

'Yes, of course,' he said gruffly. 'It's all right now.'

As soon as the waiter was out of earshot Juan broke out, 'It simply can't be done. It's quite a clever plan, Doctor Hennessy, but—'

Letty was dissecting her duck. Outraged, she laid down her knife and fork. *'Quite clever?* It's a dead ringer, young man. I've given you a sure-fire winner, on a plate, and you look down your nose at it. I've told you how to get in, get at your target, and get him out, all with risks so small as to be derisory.' She returned her attention to the duck, and continued more mildly. 'If

246

there's a snag I haven't thought of, please tell me. What are you worrying about?'

'You didn't give me a chance to explain, Doña Letizia,' protested Santos. 'It's the timing. Three weeks is far too short. We haven't got reliable operatives here yet, and there would be a great deal of research to do. We'd have to set up safe houses or flats, and what we call a people's prison to hold the Sheikh safely and in reasonable comfort. Then there's the whole question of the escape route, and the bargaining programme. It just couldn't be done in the time.'

'But you fixed up everything for me with quite extraordinary speed,' put in Caudle, mockingly.

'We were saving your skin,' said Juan harshly, 'and we were on our own ground. Here, it's completely different. I have some contacts, but I couldn't train men and plan everything in three weeks, and my own operatives won't be ready for two months yet. No, I'm afraid it's quite impossible. Hiring the houses, for one thing, without attracting attention. Buying or borrowing the escape cars—'

'Good Heavens, man, you don't need all that,' said Letty. 'Caravans.'

'Caravans?'

'Yes. You can hire them, without any questions asked, if you put down enough

247

cash as security, and next month they'll still be so thick on the roads that with an occasional change of numberplates—and surely you could fix *that*—you'd have the police knackered. Cross any county boundary, and as like as not you're in another police district. That's why they were so long in getting the kidnapper in the Lesley Whittle case. It's simple. And think of netting a million pounds—well, no, your share would be seven hundred thousand. But even that's more than a million dollars. It isn't peanuts, as a start for your operations.'

'I suppose,' remarked Caudle to Manuela, balefully, 'what's really lacking is guts, or as Juan would say, *cojones.*' That remark of Juan's back in Buenos Aires still rankled. He felt a foot pressing against his leg under the table and smiled at her, pleased with himself.

Letty threw him a look of astonishment. What had come over him? Manuela slapped his hand sharply. 'Stop it, James. It isn't that, is it, Juan?' The gentle pressure of her foot continued.

Juan had flushed deeply. Ignoring Caudle, he spoke to Letty, quietly and seriously. 'Even if we could arrange the escape route and the rest, it's the first part that is so difficult with untrained men. As I said, I can't rush over my own team because they still haven't enough English. You think it's a simple thing to do, just get into the house and extract the Sheikh. Your plan is intellectual, Doña Letizia. It isn't practical. A dozen things could go wrong. Suppose people *don't* do what they're supposed to do. Suppose your plan to unlock the door to the street—I imagine that's what you have in mind—doesn't work. Suppose your Special Branch think of that entrance, too, and place a guard there. I can't take such risks with a first operation. I'm sorry, but ...' He stopped, as a thought struck him. 'No, I won't turn your plan down out of hand. You talk about *cojones,* James. Now show us.'

'Not in front of ladies, surely,' murmured Caudle to Manuela, who stifled a giggle. 'What d'you mean exactly, Juan?'

'I mean,' continued Juan doggedly, '*you* do the first part, James. You're on the spot, this is your country. You have all the advantages, and we all know how smart you are with a gun if anything goes wrong. If you can get Sheikh Daoud to a rendezvous anywhere you like, but not less than ten miles from Cambridge, I will arrange the rest—the escape route, the prison, the negotiations, the collection and laundering of the money and its sharing out. Do that, and your cut will be forty per cent, four hundred thousand pounds if the ransom is a million.'

'I'm afraid that's quite beyond our powers,' said Letty sadly.

'No it isn't,' said Caudle suddenly.

'Don't be a fool, James,' said Letty sharply, and much alarmed.

Manuela said, 'It seems a practicable suggestion to me, but it'd need a lot of—' She looked at Caudle expectantly, her eyes dancing.

'I accept,' said Caudle. 'Don't worry, Letty, I can see how to do it. It's really just a question of nerve.'

Letty had retired for a few minutes, and Juan had taken the waiter on one side and was arguing about the bill. Manuela stood close to Caudle. She whispered, 'That was a splendid gesture, James. Juan will be mad. But can you really do it?'

'Is it true you're engaged?'

'No. Mendoza wouldn't allow it anyway.'

'I suppose you merely sleep with him,' said Caudle, in an agony of jealousy.

'Did I merely sleep with you?' She gently scratched the palm of his hand.

'Oh Manuela, don't, please.'

'Ring me at Claridge's tomorrow morning, early.'

'*No*, Manuela.'

'But ask for Miss San Martin. Don't forget. It's my real name.'

James accompanied them to the hired car and walked very slowly back to where Letty was sitting under the apple tree. He stood, looking at her defiantly.

'Well, knight-at-arms, stop palely loitering and explain what the hell you've got in mind. Apart from that girl. You don't have to explain; I can see why you never mentioned her before. I suppose it was she who nursed you so tenderly?'

'Yes.'

'And so, full of gratitude, you obliged her. Strewth! What fools men are!'

'You told me once I ought to have a passionate affair.'

'But not with a slinking Salome like that.'

'Shut up, Letty. It's over.'

'I've heard that before.' She snorted.

'Do you want to hear my plan, or not?'

'All right. But before you start—and for God's sake sit down, man—I hope you realise that it was she who precipitated this whole disaster. You came here today determined to have nothing to do with the ERP in any practical sense; now you've committed yourself, and me, to do all the hard part. And why? For that girl. She simply egged you on just for the fun of it, the heartless bitch.' He was turning

251

away, furious, when she shouted at him. 'Sit *down*, James. Now then, let's hear.'

When he had finished his explanation she said thoughtfully, 'It could work. It's very ingenious. My part's easy, but you'd be sticking your head in a noose. What happens if you're caught?'

'We have our story ready. Sheikh Daoud is the epitome of the worst aspects of capitalism. We have tried to abduct him, not with any thought of ransom, but to draw attention to our Group and what we stand for.'

'A violent gesture in a peaceful cause. The members won't like it.'

'It's only the cover story. That's a risk we must take.'

'And if Santos and his thugs don't turn up, as arranged, what then? I don't trust that lad.'

'Then we return Daoud in broad daylight to the front gate of Cranmer, and call a press conference.'

'And just bluff it out?'

'Why not? Who would believe that our Group, with its reputation for non-violence, could ever have had anything more sinister in mind?'

'H'm. That's clever, too. What are you going to tell Patricia?'

'Nothing. I'll have to get her safely out of the way before the action starts. She can go and stay with her sister. And Letty, she doesn't know anything about Manuela.'

'I should hope not. The poor little thing would curl up and die.' She lumbered to her feet, groaning. 'That duck's lying heavy on my tum. All right, James, if you're so sure of yourself, we'll do it. But keep away from that girl. Anyway, until after the coup. No, what am I saying? Altogether. She spells trouble for you, believe me, and she's made enough already. So lay off her. We're operational now, boyo.'

## CHAPTER NINETEEN

The conversation in the shabby bedroom of a Kensington hotel—'Families Catered For'—was in the slurred Spanish familiar to travellers in South America, rapid and harsh, with final s's elided. Miguel Cruz, as he had called himself since his arrival in England, was a man with dark ravaged features in which there was a liberal admixture of Araucanian Indian. Juan Santos was listening to him attentively, because Cruz was a dedicated professional revolutionary who had made his name known and feared in the *Movimiento de la Izquierda Revolucionaria* in southern Chile, where the MIR had proclaimed its own laws, even after Salvador Allende came to his short term of power.

Juan nodded approvingly. 'You are sure these men are reliable, and have no criminal record here?'

'Of course.' The dark eyes stared at him coldly. 'I decided when we came here that we must keep clean for the time being. We've had to pass up some excellent opportunities. My men are well trained, with experience of snatch operations in the homeland, and they speak tolerable English.'

'What about a people's prison?'

'The welfare people bought us a farm in Essex, and we have three families settled there, in a sort of co-operative. They are farmers, not revolutionaries, but they will do what we say and keep their mouths shut.' He smiled grimly. 'They know better than to talk out of turn. There is an empty cottage on the land, which we've agreed to repair. The roof needs attention, and in one room we'd have to put bars on the windows. Using our own men it would take less than a week.'

'And if the police are curious about the bars, the cover story?'

'It's a store. The co-operative buys in bulk, and it could be tempting for thieves. There is a deep well, if anything were to go wrong. Drop a body in and throw rubble on top. The farmers have an earthmover.'

'And safe houses, cars?'

'Safe flats, yes, among our people in the towns. But we'd have to pay them well. Some are settling down all too easily, but there are many others on the dole. Cars we'd pick up in the parking places; it's easy. But we'd need two more of our own, and I'd like one of them to be a self-drive caravan, if the snatch is to be in summer. You see—'

'I understand the advantages of caravans,' said Juan, recalling Letty's explanation.

'You do? Well, that's it. It's all a question of *plata.*'

'I can get you the money. But first, I'd like to inspect the co-operative. If I'm satisfied, I have a proposition.'

'Let me hear it.' The dark eyes glowed.

'I must first explain that it's unlikely to come off. If it does, you'd have to pick up the target, already blindfolded, at a place in the country, take him away, changing cars at least once, and lock him into your prison under armed guard.'

'You supplying the arms?'

'Of course.'

'But the bargaining and exchange?' growled the Chilean. 'That's our weak

255

point. We still haven't the background knowledge.'

'I would do that, from London, direct with the Government of the person concerned, who is a foreigner. I would warn that Government that if they allowed any publicity about the ransom demand we should dispose of the prisoner. Once they had paid the money into an account I would designate, he would be released. You and I would be in radio contact, and as soon as you got my instructions you would take the prisoner far enough away from your co-operative and leave him tied up, but able to free himself after your car had gone.'

'Would this operation be done in the name of the MIR or the ERP?'

'Neither. It would appear to be a simple criminal action. That is how you would prefer it?'

'Yes. It is too early for publicity. But you are asking us to take the main risk, Señor.'

'As I said, it may not come off. In fact, it is more than likely that those who are planning the actual snatch will not succeed. If so, you will have carried out a useful exercise, and I shall have paid all the expenses and left you with the cars, the radio equipment—and the weapons. But if the operation is successful, your share of the expropriation would be large.'

'How much?'

They haggled for some time, but in the end agreed and struck hands. Juan said, 'I think we may be able to do business on a regular basis, but it is for Mendoza to decide.'

'If we can show Mendoza that there are opportunities here worth the having, with our help, it is good. In any case, the exercise will help to keep the men's spirits up. They despair of returning to the homeland and renewing our work for the Cause.'

'And don't forget the money,' said Juan cynically.

There were two weeks of Caudle's school holiday left, and a great deal to do. He had told Pat about Letty's winning Premium Bond, and that the new car was for his official use as Secretary of the Group. She was so delighted with the Marina that she didn't question his explanation, nor when he added that to facilitate the distribution of *The Banner* Letty was also donating a small Ford van, which she was keeping at her barn at Clayhithe. He told her he would have to spend several days in Cambridge with Letty, working out the new arrangements and fitting up the van, and she reluctantly agreed. But when he said he would have to be away for a weekend from the tenth to the twelfth of September she rebelled.

'I think you're seeing too much of Aunt Letty,' she said stubbornly.

'But darling, it's all for the Group. You can't be jealous of Letty. She's nearly seventy.'

Where relations between men and women were concerned Pat's instinct was unfailing. 'That doesn't make any difference at all. She's trying to separate us.'

'Nonsense, Pat. I'm sorry, but I've got to go. Why don't you spend that weekend with Rosemary? She'd love to have you.'

Rosemary was Pat's sister. She had three very small children, and for Pat, who was childless, a chance to stay in that chaotic small house in North London and take her nieces for walks in the park, show them how to draw birds, change her nephew's nappies and undertake a lion's share of the interminable washing-up, was something to be looked forward to.

'You told me Fred was going to be away on a course,' pointed out Caudle. 'She'll be delighted. Give her a ring.'

And so it was arranged.

On Saturday, a week before the ceremony in Cambridge for Sheikh Daoud, Caudle went into central London as soon as the shops opened and made some purchases necessary for the kidnapping operation.

He paused, fighting a lost battle. There was a vital message to give to Juan but, he told himself, it would be bad security to go to the Hilton. Much better to do it through Manuela. He had stuck to his intention not to ring her, as she had asked, but his resolution had been weakening daily, and this was as good an excuse as any, just to see her for a moment alone. He set out for Claridge's.

At the reception desk he asked to speak to Miss San Martin. There was a pause, and he heard Juan's voice. For a moment Caudle couldn't get a word out. Then he gritted his teeth, tried to sound casual, and said, 'Ah, Mr Gonzalez, I thought you might be around.'

'Manuela's in the bathroom,' explained Juan suavely. 'What d'you want with her, Caudle?'

'It's you I want to talk to.'

'Then come up, my dear fellow. We'll both be glad to see you, but you'll have to excuse Manuela's *déshabillé.*'

'I'll wait for you in the foyer.'

Caudle put down the receiver. As he walked across to a chair, he found himself trembling. He didn't notice a girl in a corner of the foyer, who was smoothing her hair in front of a glass and watching his reflection.

Juan kept him waiting twenty minutes. At last he came out of the lift with—to Caudle's jaundiced eye—the air of a rutting stag.

Caudle stood up, and they moved into a reception room and sat down. The girl followed, casually, but could not get near enough to overhear.

Juan gave Caudle a complacent glance and said, 'I suppose you want to call it off.'

'No. It's on. I want to know how we shall recognise the pick-up car.'

'Ah, the car. Its make will be determined by circumstances, but the driver will greet you with the words, *"Viva la Revolucion!"*, to which you will reply, *"Revolucion o muerte!"* '

'How original! But then the prisoner will know they're Spaniards.'

'He will have to hear a good deal of Spanish in captivity; I can't help that. The two men in the car will be South Americans.'

'So you aren't going to risk your own precious skin?'

'On the word of a pair of amateurs? Why should I?' He took a look around, noticed the girl, who was hovering nearer, and continued in Spanish, lowering his voice, 'His Highness will be well taken care of. I shall do the ransoming, and ask for a million, as agreed.'

'And as agreed, our share will be—'

'Four hundred thousand.' Juan waved his hand airily, as if it were a bagatelle. 'Now tell me the details of the rendezvous.' He listened while Caudle described the exact time and place. Then he said, grinning, 'I wish you luck, Caudle. You'll need it.' Watching the other's departing back he sighed with satisfaction. He'd get caught, he said to himself, and even if he should blab he wouldn't be able to prove anything at all.

Caudle's mood was black as he went out into Brook Street. He had had scruples, rather than fear, about what he and Letty planned to do, but they had vanished. He would show that fornicating bastard who was an amateur, and who wasn't.

The Special Branch girl went to a call-box and made her report.

# CHAPTER TWENTY

The reception was to have been an entirely Cambridge affair, but a few days before it was held Sheikh Daoud let it be known that he would like the Al Bakhra Ambassador and a senior officer of Middle

Eastern Department of the Foreign and Commonwealth Office to be invited, and the Vice-Chancellor, who hated to have plans altered, had grudgingly agreed.

The dinner that followed the reception, however, was much more intimate, and apart from a few of Daoud's friends from his Cambridge days was restricted to Cranmer College fellows and their wives and two of Daoud's former tutors, of whom Letty was one. They sat down to dinner at two mahogany tables, one headed by the Vice-Chancellor and the other by the Dean. The old Sheffield plate and silver candlesticks, brought from the safe on the ground floor, shone in the light of the candles.

Daoud was on the Vice-Chancellor's right. He seemed to be a little preoccupied. Old Blenkinsop turned to his guest of honour. 'I hope the food's going to be all right,' he whispered deprecatingly. 'It's what the caterers call their "Director's Special", I'm told, and God knows what that means. But I've had some good wine decanted.' An awful thought struck him. The Sheikh was a Muslim. 'Good Heavens, we forgot. Do you—er—drink wine?' He remembered having seen the Sheikh served with orange juice at the reception.

Daoud smiled. 'At private functions like

this, Vice-Chancellor, I allow myself a little wine.' He rolled the Moselle around his tongue. 'In perfect condition, sir. You still have the best cellar in Cambridge, if this is a sample.' He spread caviar on a piece of toast.

'Wait till you try the claret. I'm sorry your Ambassador and that fellow from the F.O had to leave so quickly. They both had telephone calls from London, and came up to make their excuses one after the other.' His voice betrayed his curiosity. 'No trouble, I hope?'

The Sheikh turned dark expressionless eyes on his host. 'A little, I fear. I felt the Ambassador should return at once to his post, and he agreed.' His manner did not invite further questioning.

The meal wound its slow way through six courses, and the Vice-Chancellor made a speech, mellow with nostalgia, to which Sheikh Daoud replied shortly, saying all the right things with grace and humour. Then Mrs Beddowes, the Dean's wife, caught Letty's eye and the ladies were ushered out into the great drawing-room. The men re-grouped themselves at the Vice-Chancellor's table to drink vintage port from the Cranmer cellars.

While the coffee was being served in the drawing-room Mrs Beddowes said, 'They'll take half an hour over their port, if I know the old boy, so we've plenty of time. There's a loo on this floor next to the Master's bedroom, and a cloakroom downstairs. Letty, you know the house, would you—?'

'Can't wait,' said Letty. 'Who's for the cloakroom?'

Three women volunteered, and they trooped down the staircase in their long dresses and waited their turns in the hall, chatting. Letty chose to be last. When the other women had climbed the stairs to the drawing-room she went quickly to a door at the rear of the hall leading to the servants' quarters, and opened it cautiously.

As she had expected, there was no one about; the servants were still upstairs, helping the caterers to clear up in the servery and keeping a sharp eye on the silver. The Lodge had been built for a large staff, and the vast kitchen, now hopelessly uneconomical to run, had been replaced by a new and shiny one, in what had been the scullery. Beyond the kitchens, the service staircase and the servants' parlour, was a passage with bedrooms on one side. A door at the end led to Cranmer Lane. Letty tried the room next to it. It was full of ancient furniture. This'd be the place, she thought, her heart thumping with excitement. This would make her plan possible. She unbolted the street door and turned the key. Caudle slipped in, bringing with him a gust of fresh air.

Letty re-locked and bolted the door. She whispered, 'Wait here, and if I don't come back for you shut yourself in this room.' She pointed. 'But watch your step. It's stacked with junk.'

She went back into the hall. The entrance door was still closed and there was no one to be seen. She ran back to the passage and fetched Caudle. The oak door communicating with the Judge's Set was under the curve of the staircase, and a moment later they were inside. It was quite dark.

Caudle was wearing a grey overall over his dark sweater and jeans. In the pockets were a pair of gloves, a torch, a fisherman's woollen cap and a pair of dark glasses. Cautiously, he flashed the torch, avoiding the curtained windows. They were in a small anteroom. The door to the bedroom was ajar, and another led to a housemaid's pantry, with shelves around the walls and a low lead sink, scarred by generations of slop-buckets. He felt for Letty's hand, drew her closer, and whispered, 'O.K, I can manage. But for God's sake, *be there!*'

She pressed his hand and walked back to the staircase, shivering. The whole thing had ceased to be a lark. Perhaps she was getting too old. She remembered that other time when she had been in the Set, clutching Desmond's hand and trying not to panic as he pulled her into that great bedroom, and towards that great bed. That too, had been a moment when the lark had ended. Desmond had been clumsy, and she hadn't helped.

Caudle shone his torch on the inside of the bedroom door. There was a key, which he removed, but no bolts. He flashed the torch at the bed. The light glistened on the monogram of Queen Victoria, welded into the brass curlicues of the bedhead. The bedclothes had been turned back, with black silk pyjamas laid out, and a pair of ostrich-skin slippers lay on the faded rug. A suit for wearing next day and a silk shirt, tie and socks were arranged on a dumb valet. A door led to a bathroom and another to the entrance hall, beyond which, he found, were the sitting-room and the rooms for the Judge's clerk and butler. All windows were heavily shuttered.

He retreated to the housemaid's pantry, closed the door and settled down for a long period of waiting.

About the same time, in a furnished room in Bayswater, Miguel Cruz was giving final instructions to two dark stocky men, with broad shoulders. He had a map of the London Underground spread on the table, and pointed to stations as he mentioned them. He spoke in Spanish.

'You'll leave here on foot, and on your way to Queensway Station watch out for a tail, but don't make it obvious. If there is one, slip him.' The men nodded. 'In the station buy tickets to High Barnet—where I'm pointing. But you're not going as far as that. You'll go by Central Line to Tottenham Court Station—here it is—and change to the Northern Line. By this time you must have made quite sure that you've shaken off your pursuers, if there're any still on your track. Now, two stations before High Barnet you will get out. This is it, Woodside Park. Paco will be waiting for you in the Austin outside the station. He will hand over the keys and you, Jesús, will drive. Everything you need for the job will be in the boot—guns, hoods, rope, sticking plaster and radio. Paco will leave you, and will report to me by telephone. Is all this understood?'

The two men nodded again. They did not waste words.

'*Muy bien!* You will then drive to Cambridge, park the car and pick up another as you rehearsed it yesterday. Then drive to the rendezvous, making sure you arrive exactly on time, even if you have to stop for ten minutes in a lay-by on the way. If the prisoner is not handed over to you, after the correct exchange passwords, do not delay. Drive on and return in five minutes. If the snatch team still fails to deliver him drive on without waiting and meet me at the rendezvous in Chelmsford. On the way call me on the radio and report either "Yes" or "No". If you have received the prisoner he will be transferred to the caravan in Chelmsford and you will take the stolen car away and ditch it. I will get in touch with you in any case, and you will not come to this place again.' Cruz stretched himself. 'Let us show our Argentine friends that we know how a snatch should be made.' He switched off the light. 'I will leave first. Wait five minutes.'

The two men grinned, saluted with clenched fists, and waited while Cruz left the hotel. From the window of the darkened room they saw him go out into the street, and saw also a man detach himself from the shadows of an entrance on the opposite side, and follow. They smiled. The tail wouldn't be on Cruz's heels for long. He was an expert in shaking off pursuit.

The men had joined the ladies in the grey and gold drawing-room, but it was obvious that the evening was to end soon. Promptly at eleven o'clock the Vice-Chancellor rather ostentatiously drew a gold half-hunter from his black waistcoat and consulted it. Mrs Beddowes gave the signal and the exodus began.

Letty, in her turn, shook hands with Sheikh Daoud, who said politely, 'I'm so sorry I haven't had much chance to talk to you, Doctor Hennessy. You're part of my cherished Cambridge memories.'

I'm part of your immediate future, too, thought Letty, but aloud, 'Some of them, Sheikh, might be better forgotten.' For a moment his dark eyes twinkled.

She went down the magnificent staircase, across the Great Court, lit only by the stars, since the moon was new, and out through Tower Gate to her small M.G. The guards had been clearly visible, both at the gate and patrolling in front of the Judge's Set. Letty smiled.

She drove fast through the empty streets and out into the country, where her cottage, near Clayhithe, was set in a quiet lane. The old barn beside it served as a garage. She left the M.G on the gravel, let herself in and changed into a grey overall, similar to the one worn by Caudle, over slacks and an old bush shirt. Standing in front of the bathroom mirror she carefully made other changes in her appearance. Then she walked round to the barn. Inside were two vehicles, Caudle's old Morris, now stripped of its number-plates, and a brand-new Ford van, with a name printed in large white letters on its red sides.

On one of Caudle's recent visits he had brought with him a tin of white acrylic paint and a roll of red Fablon, very similar in colour to the new van. With the doors of the barn closed against curious neighbours, they had gone to work. The result was impressive; even in daylight it was difficult to see that the Fablon strips with their painted letters were very easily removable. Letty had also stencilled the new numbers on the plates taken from the Morris, and Caudle, using a power-tool and metal screw-bolts, had attached them over the existing ones. The screws were only hand-tight, and he could remove the plates in half a minute.

Letty backed the van out and got down to take a careful look around. There was complete silence, except for the call of a night-bird, and she closed the barn-doors, locked them, and drove out into the lane. She was now wearing a flat grey cap, with a glazed visor, and a short red beard.

For Caudle the wait seemed endless. Early on in his vigil he had made an incursion into the bedroom and other parts of the Set, and had verified that there was no one in any of the rooms. It was as Letty had expected. The Master's old manservant had acted as valet for the Sheikh's one night in the Set.

Caudle had softly shot the bolts on the door to the Court, and that had been a tricky task, because he could hear two men outside talking in Arabic. In the anteroom he could hear nothing, because two doors separated him from the servants' quarters, where the caterers were still no doubt carrying away their gear, and there was no sound yet from upstairs. When the luminous hands of his watch told him it was eleven o'clock he waited impatiently for the first sounds of the departing guests—and then he heard them, the chattering, the thanks-for-a-lovely-evening, the sound of the great door being opened and, finally, closed.

Almost ten minutes afterwards he heard steps descending the staircase and approaching the communicating door. And voices. He ran silently into his pantry and shut himself in, locking the door.

'... so glad you enjoyed it, Your Highness.' The sound of the door opening. 'Let me just see that you have everything you want.'

'There's no need, my dear Dean, but thank you. Oh, there is just one thing ... There may be a call for me from London.

The gate-porter will put it through?'

'I'll warn him as I go out. We don't want him waking the Master, do we?'

The Sheikh laughed politely. 'No indeed. I only hope I hear the bell; it's in the parlour, and I expect to sleep soundly after that really excellent wine.'

The Dean's voice again. 'Wait. May I go into your bedroom for a moment?'

'Of course.'

The Dean, more faintly: 'I thought so. There's an outlet by the bed. We had that installed last year, when the Duke was here. I'll transfer the set from the parlour.'

The voices died away. Then they came back. The Dean was saying, 'The servants will have finished tidying up and will be in bed by now, but if you should want anything during the night just press this bell. Their bedrooms are on this floor, and they've been warned to be on call.'

The Sheikh laughed. 'I shouldn't dream of disturbing them.' He spoke almost curtly, and Caudle sensed that the man was anxious to get rid of his solicitous friend. But the Dean was determined to see that everything was as it should be.

'I think Randall's laid your things out properly. Now, he'll bring you in a cup of tea at eight o'clock. You're sure that's all you'll want?'

'Yes, thank you, Dean. My chauffeur will be calling for me at half-past. I'll bid you goodnight.'

'Just a moment. Keys. There's one for your bedroom door—no, that's funny; it must have fallen out. I'll just—'

'No, please don't bother, my dear fellow. If I did want to lock myself in I could use the key in the door to the Lodge, but I don't think that's necessary. Goodnight, Dean, and thank you for arranging everything so carefully.'

'Goodnight, Your Highness.'

The oak door closed with a thud, and a moment afterwards the one leading to the bedroom was pushed shut with an impatient foot. Stealing out of his hiding-place, Caudle could hear the tinkle of the telephone. He crept nearer the bedroom door.

The Sheikh was having some difficulty with the sleepy night-porter. 'It's the Al Bakhra Embassy, Porter, and I assure you there *will* be somebody there. Ask to speak to the duty officer, and say it's Sheikh Daoud, in Cambridge, who wants him ... Sheikh *D-a-o-u-d* ... Or tell him its his Foreign Minister.' A long pause ... Then a flood of words in Arabic, and it was clear that Daoud was issuing peremptory orders. It was fourteen minutes to twelve. Still a long time to wait.

At ten minutes to one Caudle put on his dark glasses and gloves and took the toy gun from his pocket. It was a cleverly made facsimile of a Smith and Wesson 9mm, impossible to spot as a fake unless you picked it up. It felt awkward in his hand, used as he was to the weight of the real thing. He took a deep breath, walked silently to the bedroom door and opened it.

The light by the bed was on, but the dark glasses prevented Caudle's eyes from being dazzled. A man in black silk pyjamas was lying in the great bed propped up on the pillows. He had a memo pad in his hand and was dropping the gold pencil to reach under the sheet when Caudle instinctively raised the gun. The hand came back slowly, a diamond ring flashing on the third finger. The Sheikh sat up, staring at Caudle expressionlessly. He said nothing.

'Please get out of bed,' said Caudle, his voice trembling slightly. He coughed, and added more firmly, 'I want you to get dressed. You're coming with me.'

The Sheikh said in his deep, guttural voice, 'I refuse.'

'Don't do that. I don't want to use force. Please be sensible.'

'You're an educated man. What on earth

do you want? Is this a student lark?'

Caudle used the formula agreed with Letty. 'It's just a propaganda exercise, and we have no intention of hurting you, provided you do what we say. You'll be released very shortly if all goes well.'

'You represent a political movement. Which?'

'No further talking. Get dressed.'

Daoud got out of bed and walked towards the wardrobe. 'Stop,' said Caudle sharply. There might be another gun there. 'Your suit is laid out for you on that chair.' Still pointing the gun he slid his hands over the jacket and trousers. The pockets were empty.

While the Sheikh pulled on his trousers Caudle moved to the bed and felt under the sheet. The cold metal was reassuring. It was a Colt automatic, and he quickly thrust the facsimile gun into the pocket of his overall and hefted the Colt in his hand. Suddenly, he was quite calm and in command. He glanced at his watch. Five minutes to go. 'We shall make you as comfortable as possible,' he said encouragingly. 'But don't call out, at any time. That would be fatal—literally.'

The Sheikh nodded. He had seen Caudle's thumb moving toward the safety-catch.

The telephone by the bed rang sharply.

Caudle hesitated. He saw a slight smile on Daoud's saturnine face. 'That will be the Embassy, I expect. Do you want me to answer it?'

Caudle said nothing, but bent down and jerked the telephone plug from its socket. The bell stopped. 'Finish dressing, please.' The Sheikh tied his shoe laces and stood up. With the gun in his back he went out into the anteroom. Caudle took the key of the communicating door from the lock and when the Sheikh and he had passed through locked it on the Lodge side, slipping the key into his pocket. He showed the way to the servants' quarters with a flick of his torch. There was absolute silence as they went down the passage past the servants' bedrooms and Caudle pushed the other man gently forward until they came to the street door. He listened, heard the throb of the van's engine, slid back the bolts and turned the key, which he removed from the lock. The door swung open, and with the gun pressing into the Sheikh's side he felt behind him and re-locked the door.

The red van was by the kerb, with the words 'Johnson & Wright, Caterers' in big white letters on its side. The rear doors were open.

'Get in,' ordered Caudle in a whisper, jabbing sharply with the gun muzzle. The

276

Sheikh obeyed, climbing awkwardly over the sill, and Caudle followed, pulled the doors to and twisted the locking-handle. There were two inflated air mattresses on the floor, and a little light came in through the small window behind the driver's seat. The Sheikh settled himself down philosophically as the van moved off.

Caudle glanced ahead through the little window—and his heart almost stopped beating. A policeman was walking down the street towards the van, flashing his torch on the doors opposite.

Letty kept her head. She slowed down and stopped the van beside the constable. Taking the half-smoked cheroot from her bearded lips she said in a gruff voice, 'We're the last lot, matc. No more now. The bleedin' party's over.'

He flicked his torch at her face and the peaked cap, checked the name on the side of the van, and nodded. 'Goodnight, then.' Passing on, he came to the back door of the Lodge, tested the handle, and went on his way, whistling.

During the last of Caudle's visits he had driven Letty along the roads near Cambridge and they had planned the rendezvous carefully. Juan had said it must be at least ten miles from the city, and eleven miles out, where the old Newmarket road had been left to form a blind spur by a massive, built-up roundabout, they had found what they wanted. It was near enough to risk having no change of cars, which would have been awkward to arrange, and the rendezvous would be screened from the adjacent main road.

At this time of night the normally busy Newmarket road was deserted. After a stretch of open country they came to beech woods, with their branches arching overhead to form a tunnel, the foliage flickering in the shimmer of the van's headlights.

A large sign for a roundabout was coming up on the left, its outlets marked clockwise: 'Race Course' ... 'Newmarket' ... 'Stetchworth and Woodington' ... and finally, facing back to point almost parallel with the road they were driving along, 'Harlow and London'. Letty slowed down. Just beyond the sign the old road veered off to the left, marked with the red, white and blue T-signal showing that there was no through-way.

Letty turned into the spur and ran the van down to where the road was blocked by the embankment of the roundabout, and there was room to turn. This she did, and brought the van back half way to the mouth of the cul-de-sac. A few lights from the Egerton Racing Stable twinkled through the trees, but for the rest, silence and darkness. On the other side, beyond a narrow belt of beeches, a low rail fence and a dense screen of hawthorns and elders bordered the highway.

Caudle opened the rear doors and jumped down, still with the automatic in his hand. 'I'm afraid I can't ask you to stretch your legs,' he said to the Sheikh, politely, 'but it won't be long now.'

'I'm quite comfortable, thank you.'

*'Hurry,'* whispered Letty. 'I'll take the gun.' She was standing behind one of the rear doors, not wishing to let Daoud see her silhouette against the starlight.

'How much longer?' asked Caudle.

'Just about ten minutes,' whispered Letty.

He took off his gloves, and with his nails found the edge of the Fablon sheet stuck on the van's side. He raised it a little, replaced his gloves and slowly stripped off the Fablon lengthwise, revealing the blank red paint underneath. Then he did the same for the other side and unscrewed the false number-plates, which he handed to Letty. Finally, he rolled up the two lengths of sticky plastic and crossing the line of beeches climbed the fence and thrust them deep into a bramble thicket. Screened by the bushes he was able to see the road clearly. A couple of paces would take him to the verge, and when the Santos car turned into the cul-de-sac he could run back to the van in a moment. He waited.

Letty took a quick look round the edge of the door. Sheikh Daoud was sitting cross-legged on his mattress, silent. This was becoming a little uncanny, thought Letty. It was so much easier to deal with a fictional character, she realised, than one of flesh and blood. But they'd be shot of him soon.

Suddenly he spoke. 'Whom are we waiting for?'

Good lad, thought Letty. He remembers his grammar. In her gruff voice with the pseudo-Cambridgeshire accent, she said, 'This is a delivery van, isn't it? And that's what we're doing, mate. Delivering you to friends who'll take care of you, and arrange the ransom.'

'Ransom?' The Sheikh's voice was sharp. 'Your colleague said this was a publicity stunt.'

'He was having you on, son. This is a snatch, all right.'

Daoud swore briefly, in Arabic, then relapsed into his thoughts.

Caudle heard the sound of a car, distant, but clearly audible in the quiet night. His pulse quickened; this must be the one.

But it was approaching far too fast. He ran through the screen of bushes on to the verge, with some idea of signalling it to slow down, but the car roared past the turning and swept by in a rush of swirling air just as he switched on his torch, and saw two grim, swarthy faces staring ahead. The driver slowed down for the roundabout, and with tyres screeching swung round three-quarters of the circle and out into the London road. Caudle's heart sank. If this was the car the stupid buggers had missed the entrance to the turning. But something else was wrong.

Another car, travelling at high speed, was almost on him as he leapt back into cover. Light flooded the road as a Jaguar, blue lamp twirling, the high wail of the siren sinking to a moan, tore by. The driver must have seen the lights of the other car through the trees, because he skidded into the roundabout right-handed and shot away down the road to London.

The tail lights of the Granada were far ahead down the straight stretch of road as the Panda tore after them. 'We'll box them in where this road joins the duel carriageway at Six Mile Bottom,' said the driver tautly. 'Tell 'em, Joe.' The man beside him lifted his radio.

Caudle ran back to the van and whispered to Letty. 'The cops are after our friends, I'm afraid.' He took back the gun and glanced in at the Sheikh, who still seemed lost in meditation. 'It must have been them. I hope to God they get away.'

'Not a chance,' said Letty, involuntarily raising her voice and speaking normally. 'The bloody fools! All the cops in the area will have been warned by radio, and if they give this lot the slip they won't get far.' She looked at her watch. 'We'll have to call it off, James.'

'What a pity!' remarked the Sheikh, coming out of his trance. 'I'd much rather you didn't.'

There was a startled silence. Then Letty said, 'Don't you *want* to be released?'

'Actually, no. Have you a safe place you can take me to?'

Letty had come out from behind her door, and was peering at Caudle. But he had no ideas either, and the silence was complete.

'Then I have a suggestion,' said Sheikh Daoud, from the darkness of the van. 'I have a house in Bedfordshire, near Old Warden. I bought it six months ago, through an intermediary, partly to have a retreat in which to enjoy the English countryside, and partly as a sort of hide-out, in case things went wrong. It's also a very good investment.'

'And things *have* gone wrong for you?' said Letty, curiously.

'They have indeed. At this very moment I fear they may be going very badly. I will explain later, but I think it might be best to get away from here, don't you? If your fast-driving friends get caught, and reveal where they were to meet you, the police may be here at any moment.' He saw them hesitating, and added, 'It's a long drive, I know, but I have an English caretaker at the house and some good Scotch whisky. I shall be delighted to offer you—er—one for the road before you return to Cambridge. No one would know, I assure you.'

'But this is nonsense,' broke in Caudle angrily. 'We'd be putting ourselves in your hands.'

'You're there already,' retorted the Sheikh, his tone hardening. 'Your voice was unmistakable, Doctor Hennessy, in spite of your phony sex-change.'

With the sound of tearing calico the red beard came away, and Letty tossed it, with her cap, into the van. 'All right,' she said unhappily. 'We'll drive you to your house, but you'll have to take over the navigation when we get near to it.'

# CHAPTER TWENTY-ONE

The two Chileans in the Granada had studied the map carefully, and knew that their only chance to shake their followers—and it was a slim one—was by doubling back to the complex of roads near Harlow.

At the start, their part of the operation had appeared to be going smoothly. Arriving in Cambridge they had left the Austin near an open-air car-park selected earlier, during the recce made the previous day, and went to it on foot, carrying their kidnapping gear in a suitcase. It was half-past twelve, and the custodian had long since departed. For some time they stayed in the shadow of a wall while a courting couple took advantage of the back seat of their car. As soon as they left the Chileans inspected the cars parked near the exit, and chose a Ford Granada. Jesús had two large bunches of Ford keys, divided into those for door and ignition. He shone a torch through the window. No Krooklok or chain, *gracias a Dios!* He crouched down and inserted the keys one by one. The other man kept watch, holding the suitcases.

Seven minutes later the engine sprang into life. The second man ran to the car, threw in the bag and sprang in. It was sheer bad luck that the owner, who had attended dinner at Cranmer, had stayed on, talking to a fellow-don who slept in college. He arrived to see his car being driven away, without lights. Swearing, he ran after it as it turned into the street—and almost felled a policeman, who was going into the car-park for a surreptitious smoke. Stammering in his haste, the academic gave the number and description of the car. The constable pulled out his personal radio and called his base.

All the Cambridge Panda cars were alerted, and one of them spotted the car on the Newmarket road and gave chase. By the time the Chileans shot past the rendezvous where they should have taken delivery of the Sheikh other cars were converging on the area, and one of them got to Six Mile Bottom in time to set up a barrier.

When the line of yellow cones appeared across the road ahead, with a blue lamp flashing behind, Jesús tried to get by along the verge. He failed. The Granada ploughed through the thick grass, skidding, and overturned in the ditch. Although Jesús was pinned against his steering wheel and unable to move, his friend managed to scramble out, with the bag in his hand. But he had struck his knee, and fell as a constable ran up.

The Chilean was dazed and in pain, but he had pulled out the Browning from his jacket and had his finger on the trigger when the constable fell on top of him. The shot went wide. In the Granada, Jesús was trying desperately to extricate his gun as another constable reached in through the window and paralysed his arm with an expert blow from his truncheon.

When the suitcase was opened they found the transceiver, and a number of things that could only have one explanation.

It had taken time for the Al Bakhra Embassy to convince the night-porter at Cranmer that something was wrong with the telephone. The old man had to awaken the under-porter so that he could investigate. But the guards at the entrance to the Judge's Set said His Highness had not emerged, and when they tried the door it was bolted. The under-porter remembered the communicating door, and awoke the servants in the Lodge. They were unable to get into the Lodge either, since the key was in Caudle's pocket, and concluded that the Sheikh was fast asleep and had left the telephone disconnected.

Before going back to bed the manservant thought he ought to check the street door, and it was only when he found it locked, with bolts drawn and the key missing, that the alarm was raised.

By the time the CID officers arrived the Special Branch guards, ignoring the protests of their Arab colleagues, were banging on the windows of the Sheikh's bedroom, without response. They broke in—but no Sheikh.

The constable patrolling Cranmer Lane was summoned by radio, and he told of the little red van. The manager of the catering firm, roused from his bed, querulously declared that his men had only used one van, and it was a big one ...

About this time the red van was crossing the county border into Bedfordshire.

Miguel Cruz was sitting in his caravan, parked in a country lane near Chelmsford, when the signal from the two Chileans came through on the transceiver. It should have been either yes or no. But it wasn't. The man in the Granada muttered hastily, *'Policia atrás'*, and switched off.

Cruz swore. They'd bungled it, and to make matters worse had broken his rule and spoken in Spanish. He waited for a further explanatory message from the little radio, hoping against hope that on this vital operation, to which so much of importance for the future was attached, his men might have got away and still made contact. But there was silence.

He made his call to the Hilton from a public box in Chelmsford. This was the emergency arrangement, for use if the radio link could not be employed, since he suspected that by this time the frequencies used by his two compatriots might be blown. When the exchange operator replied Cruz asked to be put through to room 906. Juan was asleep, but he grabbed the receiver quickly, fearing trouble. 'Who is it?' he asked.

'Is that room 806?' came Cruz's guttural voice.

Juan froze. '903' would have meant that all was well, and that the Sheikh was safely in custody; '909', that just as Juan had half expected Letty and Caudle had not turned up at the rendezvous. But '806' was a different matter; that indicated police involvement.

'Did you say "806"?' he asked.

'Yes, sir. I'm sorry. Have I got it wrong?'

'You have indeed,' said Santos in an icy voice, and rang off.

He poured himself a stiff whisky, and thought furiously. Cruz was at liberty, which meant the cops had got on to the two men in the escape car. Perhaps they had followed the English couple, and captured the lot of them, including the prisoner.

He swore. The Chileans could be trusted not to talk, but if that old woman panicked she might say anything. He could only find out the true facts by contacting Miguel, but it would be hours before the man could change cars and make his way back to Kensington. There was nothing to be done for the time being, and Juan knew he could always deny complicity. There couldn't be the smallest concrete proof of his involvement.

They had avoided Cambridge and followed minor roads to Royston. On the other side of the M1, Letty stopped the van, opened the rear doors and spoke to the Sheikh. 'We're approaching a village called Broom. It isn't far from Old Warden. Hop in the front, Sheikh; it's up to you now.'

'Let me look at the map ... I see. You take this little white road and the house is here, beyond the lake. I'll show you when we get nearer.'

A few miles further on they saw the dark glimmer of the lake and turned into a narrow road running through parkland, with great stands of trees, dimly seen. They skirted a long wall which rose to frame tall, wrought-iron gates, and it was here that Daoud told Letty to stop.

He got down stiffly and tugged at a chain. A bell rang loudly, and after two further tugs a tall, heavily-build man came out of the high-gabled lodge inside the gates. He was wearing pyjamas and a dressing-gown. 'Who is it, then?' he called out angrily. The small van didn't impress him.

'Mr Orlandi, the new owner. You must be Simpson.'

'I've not been told to expect you, sir.' Simpson was clearly puzzled by the van. 'Are you all right, sir?'

'Of course. My car was involved in an accident when I was driving north. These kind people offered me a lift.'

'But your chauffeur, sir? Is he—?'

'He's unhurt and is staying with the car. I'll sleep here for the night and he can pick me up tomorrow. Come, open up, please. And you'd better bring some whisky up to the house. Did the case arrive?'

'Yes, sir. I'll open it right away.'

'Good. And ask Mrs Simpson to make some sandwiches, please, and bring those, too. We're hungry.'

Shaking his head, the man swung the gates open. 'Orlandi', wondered Letty. So Daoud hadn't only bought the house through a go-between, but under a false name. It really was designed as a hide-out, as he'd said.

The large grey stone house lay back in the trees at the end of a quarter of a mile of drive. As the van turned into the gravel sweep the headlights showed a wide Victorian façade with turrets of heavily-ornamented stone.

The Sheikh took some keys from his pocket, walked up the broad steps and unlocked the front door. Letty opened the rear of the van to allow Caudle to get out, and they followed. As they went in Daoud found a switch, and light shone on a cluster of great animals' heads, gazing glassy-eyed at the intruders. On the black and white tiled floor lay a twelve-foot tiger skin, its massive head and bared fangs even more forbidding than its stuffed companions.

The Sheikh was as much taken aback as his guests. 'I bought the house with its contents from the late owner's family,' he explained, 'but I didn't quite expect—Let's see if we can find somewhere a little more welcoming.' He opened a mahogany door and led them into a panelled room, heavily furnished, with buttoned leather chairs and dark oil paintings.

'I think we've struck lucky,' said the Sheikh, pointing to a cabinet with a tantalus and a tray of glasses on top of it.

They had left the doors open behind them, and now there was the sound of tyres on gravel and Simpson appeared. He had pulled on trousers and a dark mackintosh, and carried a tray of sandwiches and plates, a bottle of malt whisky and a siphon. 'There's other drinks in that cabinet, sir, but Mr Bayliss said this was your favourite.' He held up the bottle of Glenlivet, and the Sheikh nodded. 'I'll just get you some water, sir, if the other gentleman would like it.' Caudle's appearance had come as a surprise to him.

'Thank you, Simpson; then we'll serve ourselves. Just see that a bed is made up and that there's hot water, and then you can go. Be ready in half an hour to see this lady and gentleman out.'

They settled themselves comfortably, with powerful shots of malt whisky and water in the heavy cut-glass tumblers. 'I can't quite see you relaxing in this setting,' observed Letty, curious.

'On the contrary, dear lady, I think my agent Mr Baylisss has done me very well. We Arabs don't really like the modern, glass-sided buildings we are forced to erect everywhere. We prefer dark rooms and old, comfortable furniture. This house seems quite perfect for a retreat; it is the typical dwelling of the English country gentlemen whom I so much admire, for they know how to live. You must understand that I love the countryside of England, with the rain, and the grass so fresh and green and'—he smiled—'all the sand tidily concentrated on the beaches. So different from Al Bakhra.'

Letty's heart warmed to this man, and she smiled kindly. Sheikh Daoud looked at her familiar face. 'I do so wish,' he said wistfully, 'I had seen you in that beard. It was too dark to perceive anything but your outline. What are you going to do with the beard and the uniform? Shall I tell Simpson to bury them in the garden?'

Before Letty, completely at her ease and now on her second glass of whisky, could reply Caudle said, 'No thank you, Sheikh. We'll take them with us and dispose of them somewhere.' After all, it was the only evidence, apart from the Sheikh's word, that connected them directly with the kidnapping. Caudle was feeling deflated. The great adventure was degenerating into farce. But there was still the comforting weight of the gun in his pocket.

Letty said, 'I think you promised us an explanation, Sheikh.'

'Well, it's all rather complicated. I heard at the reception tonight that the Ruler of my country, His Highness Sheikh Habib, had been made prisoner by his eldest son. Sheikh Ahmed, the usurper, is a violent young man, who has many equally violent friends in the Palace Guard, and I suppose he made use of them. The army—we have a battalion and a squadron of armoured cars—is on manoeuvres in the desert. Sheikh Ahmed dislikes me intensely, partly because with the Ruler's full approval I have limited the output of our oil wells, which are not inexhaustible, in accordance with a long-term plan for the development of the country. The oil company which has the franchise dislikes me equally, and for the same reason, and may also be involved in the insurrection. I don't know yet. Ahmed has another reason for regarding me as his enemy, since I have more than once warned the Ruler against his intrigues, and Ahmed suspects me of trying to get his younger brother declared heir to the Divan. As you may guess, my position is not merely that of Foreign Minister.'

He saw his listeners were giving him rapt attention, and continued, 'Later tonight I heard from the Embassy that the usurper has already sent emissaries in his own jet aircraft to England to demand my instant return. This is disquieting news, since I could have been summoned home by telegram, and I rather fear that Ahmed, sooner than have me alive in Al Bakhra, would prefer me to meet with a fatal accident here. The Ambassador insisted that I should return to London immediately. I think he was ringing me again when James—I'm sorry, I don't know your other name—cut him off. In any case, he told me there was no question of giving me asylum in his Embassy. I don't know whether he is on Ahmed's side, or just afraid for his own skin, but in either case I shall see that he is dismissed the moment the Ruler Sheikh Habib returns to power. Everything depends on how the army commanders will react, but I believe they are completely loyal to the Ruler. Now you see why I need time, and a secure hiding-place.' He took a silk handkerchief from the breast pocket of his suit and dabbed gently at his face.

'It's a great disappointment,' said Letty, 'but if you are in such danger we must help you. I saw the agitated whispering at the reception between your Ambassador and the F.O man. So that's what it was about.'

'So now,' said Caudle bitterly, 'we have the job of protecting a top-class capitalist from his just deserts. We are a *revolutionary* movement, Sheikh Daoud. We needed that money for our campaign.'

'Ah,' said Daoud, smiling, 'the ransom. How much was it to be?'

'Our share would have been four

hundred thousand pounds; the others would have taken the remainder of the million.'

'A million pounds? I see your point. Sheikh Habib would certainly have paid that amount for my ransom. But not Ahmed, believe me. He'd simply have had your throats cut. But I wonder—Are you a violent movement?'

'No,' said Letty firmly. 'We are entirely against violence as a form of revolution, or indeed for any purpose.'

'I'm glad,' said the Sheikh drily, 'that you have corrected my impression. May I have my pistol back, please?'

Caudle hesitated. He had got used to that gun. But what good would the damned thing be, except to incriminate him if he were caught? He handed it over with a sigh.

Daoud took it and tossed it on to a sofa. 'Thank you. Now, I'm all in favour of non-violent revolutionary movements. They are an excellent opiate for the people; they help to sublimate feelings which might otherwise find expression in more dangerous ways. So,' he continued, smilingly ignoring the outraged faces of his guests, 'provided you both keep faith with me, and don't let anyone—anyone at all, even the police—know where I am, and provided also, of course, that all goes well

296

with me, I shall be pleased to contribute a hundred thousand pounds to your funds.'

'We don't want your tainted money,' said Caudle fiercely.

'Oh yes we do,' said Letty, taking the last of the pâté sandwiches.

'Have it as you will. And now, unless you would like some more refreshment, I suggest you ought to be on your way.'

They were both very tired, and took turns driving the van. They lost their way at once, and were further delayed when they had to wake up a garage owner to get petrol. It was nearly six in the morning when they reached Clayhithe and put the van away in the barn. They quite forgot that in the rear lay a bundle of overalls, with the beard, the cap, the facsimile gun, and two forged number-plates.

## CHAPTER TWENTY-TWO

At half-past eight Juan woke to hear a peremptory knocking on his bedroom door. He put on a dressing-gown and unlocked it.

A young man in his late twenties stood on the threshold, dressed in a neat flannel suit with a club tie. He produced an identity card which read, 'Detective Sergeant R. Cobham, Metropolitan Police', and asked politely, 'Are you Señor Ramon Gonzalez, sir?'

'I am. What do you want?'

'May I come in, sir?'

'Can't you wait until I've dressed?'

'I think you may like to know what I have to say first, sir, in case you want to put on a warmer suit.'

Juan stared; he did not like the sound of that remark. 'In weather like this?' he said, gesturing at the open window and the blazing hot sunlight outside.

'It'll be early spring in Buenos Aires, won't it, sir? Could be very chilly.'

Juan sat down heavily in an armchair. 'Are you threatening me, Sergeant?'

'Oh no, sir. We just think it's time your stay in England came to an end.'

'Do you, indeed? I shall get in touch with my Embassy as soon as—'

Cobham interrupted. 'We've been in touch with them already, sir. As far as they are concerned, the sooner you leave the better. There's a plane at ten forty-five. You and Miss San Martin will just have nice time to pack your bags and catch it. We'll see that you get through the controls quickly.'

'Who is this lady?'

'You ought to know that, sir,' said Cobham reproachfully, 'seeing you've spent the night in her room at Claridge's several times in the past few weeks. And she accompanied you on some of your visits to Chilean immigrants, didn't she? Former members of the MIR, if I'm right, sir.'

'I didn't know people in this country weren't allowed to discuss their political views, even if they were revolutionary.'

'No, sir. It's when they try to put them into effect that we don't like it.'

'And what have I done, exactly?'

'Your real name, sir, is Xavier Lopez Suarez. You entered the country three months ago with a forged passport in the name of Juan Santos, and four weeks ago as Ramon Gonzalez. The fingerprints in both passports are identical with your own. Now, that's an offence, sir, entering the U.K under false pretences, but we aren't pushing it this time, only if you ever attempt to return to this country under whatever alias. The Argentine Embassy were rather hoping we'd prosecute you, but they don't really mind, as long as you leave today. The Security Service in Buenos Aires—the SSN, isn't it?—is anxious to have a word with you, I gather.'

Juan winced. 'And you're hand in glove with them, I've no doubt. All right. I'll get packed.'

'That's what Miss San Martin is doing already, sir, with a woman detective constable to—er—help her.' Cobham wandered round the room, pulling out drawers and glancing through their contents. Santos made no attempt to stop him; he knew there was nothing to find, except the transceiver, and that looked like any small, battery-operated radio set.

Cobham picked it up and smiled. 'Japanese,' he said, 'and very clever camouflage. We had a lecture about them on my W/T course. Where's the little hole—ah, there it is. You stick a pin in, and the whole of the back of the set comes away, and there's your transmitter. I wonder why he didn't call you on this,' he said slowly, turning to watch Juan's face.

It was a nasty jolt, but Juan's face was impassive. 'I haven't the least idea what you're talking about,' he said contemptuously.

'You received a phone call at three-thirty this morning. It came from a call-box. What was it about?'

'It was someone who wanted a different room.'

'Then it's curious, isn't it, sir, that he didn't ring back to the exchange and ask for the right one?'

Juan stifled a yawn. 'I really couldn't say

300

what the imbecile would or would not do, Sergeant.'

'No, sir. The thing that struck us as odd was that this call came to you only a short time after two men were picked up by the Cambridge police with a stolen car and various articles which showed criminal intent. Like handcuffs, sir, and a rope, hoods for disguise, wide sticking plaster for preventing the victim from calling for help, and a couple of guns to keep people like me away. We don't like that sort of thing here, sir. It looks as if the two Chileans—perhaps you met them on one of your visits to the ex-MIR men—were planning a kidnap. And that, again, is odd.'

'Please stop talking in riddles, Sergeant,' snapped Juan. Now, with luck, he might learn something of what had actually happened.

'They couldn't have been planning to kidnap Sheikh Daoud, because he'd been snatched already.'

'Sheikh Daoud? The Al Bakhra Foreign Minister? You mean to say he's been kidnapped? I haven't seen the papers yet. I suppose the gang was captured, too?'

'No, sir,' said Cobham, puzzled. Could Santos really be in total ignorance of last night's affair at Cranmer College? 'They got clean away, with their victim. There's no trace of Sheikh Daoud.'

He saw the look of stupefaction on Juan's face, and taking a folded newspaper from his pocket dropped it into the man's lap. 'Read all about it, sir, while I finish looking round your room.'

Juan was flabbergasted. So they had *done* it, those two amateurs. They'd actually snatched the Sheikh, and when the Chileans didn't turn up, they'd got him away somewhere on their own. And just at the time he and Manuela would be on their way back to the doubtful welcome of the SSN, Hennessy and Caulde would be asking for a million pounds ransom, and keeping the lot. For Juan Santos it was utter defeat, and had to be avenged.

When Cobham finished his search, ostentatiously pocketing two small bottles of what looked like pills but were in fact secret writing material, Juan said to him, 'It's a pity. I ought to see Doctor Hennessy to say good-bye, but I suppose she's disappeared, too.'

He received no reply, and looking up at Cobham's face met a glance of such savage contempt that he hastily turned away.

Caudle slept until nearly four o'clock in the afternoon of that eventful day, and awoke to hear Letty moving about downstairs. He took a shower, shaved and dressed, while she toasted tea-cakes and later served them with honey and Earl Grey tea in the room facing the garden. They talked, a little sadly, about their adventure, but with undisguised relief at its outcome.

At five o'clock Letty switched on the television and shaded the windows so that they could see the screen clearly. There was a news clip of Sheikh Daoud, wearing Arab robes, arriving in England two days previously, and being greeted by his Ambassador and the Foreign Office man who had been at the reception. The announcer said, 'There is something of a mystery about Sheikh Daoud's disappearance last night after the dinner given in his honour by the Vice-Chancellor of Cambridge University. It is feared that he has been kidnapped, but there has so far been no attempt to demand a ransom, unless it has been made direct to the Al Bakhra Government. Two Chilean immigrants, who were found to be driving a stolen car in suspicious circumstances, are helping the Cambridge CID in their enquiries.

'This matter,' continued the announcer, 'is made even more significant by the fact, recorded in our earlier bulletins, of the seizure of power in Al Bakhra by Sheikh Ahmed, son of the former Ruler, who is being held under house arrest.' (A clip of shots of Al Bakhra City and of the two Sheikhs, father and son, at a public function.) 'It is singularly unfortunate that Sheikh Daoud should have disappeared from the very college in Cambridge where he studied as a young man and where, this morning, he was to have received an honorary Doctorate of Laws.' (A still photograph of the Lodge at Cranmer, taken from the Great Court.)

Letty was delighted. 'To think,' she said, as she finished her second tea-cake, 'that you and I, James, are the only ones who know.'

There was a knock on the door.

There had been a conference at CID headquarters in Cambridge earlier that afternoon.

The Detective Chief Inspector in charge, a portly figure whose collar, and indeed all his clothes, appeared a little too tight, was saying, 'As I see it, Sergeant, this is a straightforward local CID matter, and nothing to do with Special Branch. An important foreigner has been kidnapped. Two Chileans stole a car and when caught by my men were found to be armed and in possession of the typical accessories of a professional kidnapper. If they weren't involved in the Sheikh's disappearance it's a remarkable coincidence.'

Cobham, the man from the Met, was at his most diplomatic. 'I fully agree, sir. But the protection of VIPs is a Special Branch responsibility, and I thought—'

'I don't care what you thought, Sergeant. It's no longer a question of protection, but of criminal action, and that is my concern.'

'I see, sir. But may I make this point? A known member of the Argentine ERP, a guerrilla movement, has been in England for the past month and in contact with former members of the Chilean MIR.' He saw the C.I throw up his eyes, and added hastily, 'Another guerrilla movement, sir, and one to which the two men you captured belonged. We felt sure they were hatching up some scheme together, and so it's proved.'

'Then why wasn't I warned?' asked the C.I truculently.

'We had no idea the activity would be in this area, sir, nor indeed that it could happen so soon. They must have heard of Sheikh Daoud's presence in Cambridge and acted fast. Now, the Argentine, Xavier Lopez Suarez, wasn't directly involved in the kidnapping, since he spent the night at his hotel in London, the Hilton.'

'Good God! Is that the sort of place they frequent?'

'They have the money, sir, and to spare.

305

But this man has also been in touch with Doctor Hennessy, of St Mary's, and before he left this morning for Buenos Aires, at our request, he hinted strongly that Doctor Hennessy was involved in the kidnapping. However strange this may seem, it is a fact that Doctor Hennessy is well known for her revolutionary views and we might conclude that there was a political motive behind the kidnapping.'

'That's a very big assumption, Cobham, based on a hint from some foreigner who was anxious to push the blame on to somebody else. We believe that Doctor Hennessy, who is a distinguished scholar, is quite harmless, and that was why I refused your Branch's request to put her under surveillance.'

'Just one question, sir. Was she at the dinner-party at Cranmer College last night?'

The Chief Inspector ran his stubby forefinger down a list that lay on his desk. 'She was, but—'

'Could she have gone down to the ground floor during the course of the evening—but late, after the caterers had gone—and unlocked the door into Cranmer Lane? You'll agree, sir, that this would explain the most puzzling part of the Sheikh's disappearance.'

'I don't know. We can find out. But this

is pure speculation.'

'And the other question, sir, is whether she spent last night at her cottage in Clayhithe. If she didn't, there might be a *prima facie* case for further enquiries.'

'H'm. And the man Caudle, whom you mentioned earlier?'

'I've been in touch with your staff about him, sir. His car was parked in Cambridge last night and hasn't been moved since. There is no trace of Caudle. Perhaps it is he who is guarding the missing Sheikh.'

'Well, Sergeant. Let's leave it like this. Caudle is your affair, since he comes from the Met area. Enquiries about Doctor Hennessy are a different matter. In spite of her revolutionary ideas—she's known here as the Red Hen'—he gave a short bark of laughter—'she is an important figure in Cambridge, and I don't want the whole University up in arms, accusing me of persecuting her. What I will do, though, is to send Detective Sergeant Roberts here to see if she's at home and have a discreet word with her about her movements.' He looked at Cobham fiercely. 'Will that satisfy you, Sergeant?'

'Thank you, sir,' said Cobham. Inwardly, he cursed the fat man on the other side of the desk. The job of interviewing Letty was one he'd wished to keep for himself. It would need tact and charm, and he reckoned he had both. Still, Roberts was a good chap. He'd talk to him.

Letty said, 'See who that is, James dear.'

A young man was standing on the step. 'Good afternoon, sir. May I ask, is Doctor Hennessy at home?'

'Yes. Whom shall I say?'

'Detective Sergeant Roberts, sir, Cambridge CID. I'd just like a few words with the lady, if I may.'

Caudle left him standing and went back into the room. 'It's the CID,' he whispered anxiously.

'Well, show him in ... Would you like some tea?' she asked as the young man came into the room.

He glanced at the tea table. 'You've just finished, haven't you? Don't bother then, please.'

'It's no trouble. The kettle's still hot.' She went into the kitchen.

'May I ask your name, sir?' the Sergeant enquired politely.

'James Caudle. I'm staying with Doctor Hennessy.'

'And you stayed here last night, sir, I suppose?'

'Of course. Why not?'

'You didn't attend the reception at Cranmer College, sir?'

'Of course not. I'm not a don.' What

was it they'd decided to say? Oh yes. 'Doctor Hennessy picked me up in the town after the dinner.'

'That's rather odd, sir, isn't it?'

'No, it isn't,' retorted Caudle sharply. 'And I don't see the reason for these questions.'

Letty came in with the teapot and a fresh cup and saucer. 'You're not trying to bully poor Mr Caudle, are you?' she asked in a voice like a friendly dragon.

'Indeed not, madam. Just wanted to get things straight.' He took the cup and sipped thankfully. But the difficult part was coming. 'You see, madam, we're just trying to check the movements of the guests at last night's dinner at Cranmer College. I take it you went straight home after the party was over?'

'No. I picked up Mr Caudle outside "The Grapes", where he'd been since closing time, and brought him here. I really don't know why I should be answering these questions. You'll be asking to search the house next.'

Roberts put down the cup, empty, and got to his feet with alacrity. 'Well, that's very kind of you, madam. I'd like to have a peep. It's just routine, you know. Is this the way upstairs?'

James was about to stop him when he caught Letty's eye. 'Show him the bedrooms, James. I shouldn't like him to think we're having a dirty weekend.'

Roberts looked into Letty's room, which had clothes scattered all over it, and hastily withdrew. He went into the guest room, and saw the bed still unmade and a pair of pyjamas lying on the floor, where they had been thrown.

'I'm supposed to make my own bed,' explained Caudle, with a stiff smile, 'but I do that when I get into it.' Thank God, he thought, the fisherman's cap wasn't visible. He must have put it in a drawer. It was only then that he remembered the tell-tale bundle in the rear of the van ...

The Sergeant took a slow look round the rest of the upstairs floor and went down to the garden room. He knew something was wrong, but not how to put his finger on it.

He said to Letty, 'Thank you very much, madam. Now, if I could just have a look at your garage—I expect it's in that barn I saw outside.'

'Of course it is. But you'll only find my MG and the van there.'

James Caudle's veins seemed to be freezing. Agitatedly, as the man went out of the door into the garden, he tried to signal to her, shaping a bundle with his hands. She returned his look, baffled.

The Sergeant was already striding down the path to the barn as they caught up with him. 'What van is that?' he asked mildly. But his pulse was quickening.

'It's for delivering our newspaper, *The Banner*,' explained Letty. 'To save postage. I only bought it last week, and it's a beauty. Over 40 mpg. Come along, I'll show you. The barn isn't locked.'

James thought, she can't stop him peering into the back. He dug his fingers sharply into Letty's ribs. The indignant look she turned on him, behind the Sergeant's back, changed to horror as she remembered.

Roberts was opening the barn doors wide. Facing him was the little MG, and behind it the red van. At least they had thought of keeping the van out of sight when they had returned in the early morning.

The Sergeant had one idea firmly in mind. With the doors open there was plenty of light, and when he idly stroked the sides of the van his fingers left marks in the dust of the journey. It couldn't possibly have been re-sprayed or over-painted. The surface was as smooth as silk.

Letty said, 'I really think we've spent enough time on your routine enquiries, Sergeant. Now we won't keep you.'

Roberts hesitated. The Chief Inspector had refused a search warrant. If he asked her to open the rear of the van it would mean driving out the MG first, and the lady might not take this too well. The C.I had said she wasn't to be pushed. He closed the doors.

As they walked back to the cottage he said, 'I don't suppose, Doctor Hennessy, you have any ideas about how Sheikh Daoud was kidnapped last night? It's a complete puzzle. Almost looks like an inside job.'

Letty was so relieved that she could scarcely speak for a moment. Then she said, 'I don't think he was kidnapped at all. There hasn't been any ransom note, or whatever you call it, has there?'

'No.' Roberts turned and looked at her puckish, lined face expectantly.

'I think he just walked out of the rooms he was occupying, opened the outside door, prudently locked it on the outside, in case some thief might come along, and just went off on his own. We all saw at the reception that he'd received some very disquieting news, and of course we know now what it was. Perhaps he wanted to think over his position quietly. I'm sure he'll turn up somewhere soon.'

'Thank you, madam. That's a very interesting idea. I must tell the C.I. Good-bye, Doctor Hennessy, Mr Caudle. And thank you both.'

'It's only your duty, Sergeant, we know

that,' said Letty. 'And remember, Sheikh Daoud was the one person who could have opened that outside door from inside. I'm sure you can rule out the servants. They're utterly trustworthy. And as for the caterers, who must have used that door to take away their gear, I should've thought you could exclude them, too. Jackson and Wright are a very old and reliable firm.'

'I'm sure you're right, madam. Well, I'll be off, then. I suppose you're returning to London tonight, sir?'

Caudle was too preoccupied to reply for a moment. 'Tonight? No, I'm staying here.'

'I was thinking of your car, sir,' said Roberts gently.

'Good Lord, I'd forgotten it. You couldn't give me a lift into the town, could you?' He added, 'You see, I left it in Cambridge.'

'Sorry, sir, but I'm going the other way. But I'd move it as soon as you can. There's always a danger of some kid picking it up for a joy-ride.'

'I'll run you in, James,' said Letty. 'We'd better do it now.'

The Sergeant got into his car, drove a little way down the road in the opposite direction to the city, and turned into a lane, where he stopped. That business with Caudle's car smelled to Heaven. Why wait in a pub to be picked up? Why not drive to Clayhithe and stay in the cottage until she turned up? Surely she could have given him a key. He walked back to the entrance of the lane and peered round the corner. It was nearly a quarter of an hour before he saw the MG emerge and set off towards Cambridge. And she'd said 'at once'.

Roberts spoke into his personal radio. 'Is Sergeant Cobham still there?'

'Yes, Sarge,' said the desk officer. 'He's waiting for you to come back.'

'Tell him I'll be a little time yet, and say Caudle's gone into town with Hennessy to pick up his Austin. Then he says he'll be coming back to Clayhithe, but it might be worth checking. Got it?'

'O.K, Sarge.'

Roberts drove quickly back to the cottage. It was a lonely road and there was no one about. He'd just remembered something else, something Hennessy had included in her imaginative explanation for Daoud's disappearance, that struck a wrong note. She'd suggested that Daoud might have locked the Cranmer Lane door on the outside to prevent a thief entering. But there had been no mention of the fact that the door had been found locked, either in the press or any broadcast. It was a typical CID gambit, to conceal a piece of evidence in case someone gave himself away. And it appeared to have worked.

The barn door was locked, but the window at the side was old and badly fitting, and Roberts forced back the catch with the blade of his knife and climbed in. It was a big risk, because if he were caught the C.I would give him hell for breaking not just the letter but the spirit of his instructions, but he knew something was wrong, and the van might provide the clue. What's more, he thought, he'd show that cocky Robin Cobham that he didn't have *all* the ideas.

The van was unlocked, and he released the handbrake and pushed it forward a couple of feet. He switched on his torch, but the interior of the van was bare. Then a glint of shiny metal caught his eye. He brought the light closer. There, on the inside wall, right down near the floor, someone had scratched letters in the paint. DAOUD.

## CHAPTER TWENTY-THREE

On the seven-thirty news from BBC 2 there was a brief mention of the abortive search for the missing Sheikh and pictures of the two senior army officers from Al

Bakhra who had flown in to accompany him home. They had refused to be interviewed. The announcer added, 'After the bloodless palace revolution, in which the Ruler was deposed by his son Sheikh Ahmed, the people of Al Bakhra seem to be adjusting quickly to the new regime. Ian Sinclair reports.' There was a shot of an earnest-looking young man in a sweat-stained open shirt, standing by the entrance to a building roofed with smooth white domes. Dark-robed figures were passing as he spoke. 'In this sun-scorched city life has returned to normal.' There was a loud crackle of gun-fire. Sinclair looked round apprehensively, and mopped his streaming forehead. 'The sound you may have heard is a few jubilant soldiers, just back from the desert, firing salutes in the air, as is their custom. The army leaders are solidly in support of Sheikh Ahmed, who seized power yesterday in a dramatic coup. He is a popular figure in this small, incredibly rich State, and his progressive views on the use of the oil revenues contrast with those of his father, who is still under house arrest at his villa on the coast.'

'Poor Daoud,' observed Letty.

Caudle said, 'I expect he's got enough money stashed away abroad to keep him in comfort for the rest of his life.'

'But he must feel that all he's worked for

has gone for good. Ahmed will run those wells dry in no time.' Letty put down her glass of whisky. 'It's a bit early, but I'm hungry. I'd better get some grub.' As she stood up a thought struck her. 'You know, James, I can't help feeling sorry for Santos. After all, he did try to help us. If the Ruler gets back into power—and I don't suppose that BBC man knows what's really happening—we ought to offer Juan half the hundred thou.'

'Oh nonsense, Letty. Don't waste sympathy on Santos.' His thoughts flew back to that humiliating scene in the foyer of Claridge's, with Juan crowing his sexual triumph—and Manuela in her room, half naked as Juan had left her. Caudle glowered. 'Don't ring him, Letty. It's bad security anyway.'

'Oh I can wrap it up.' She went to the telephone, looked up the number of the Hilton, and dialled. Caudle heard someone answer, and she asked for Mr Gonzalez. She listened to the distant voice and said, 'Thank you,' putting down the receiver. 'That's funny; he's gone. Left this morning for Heathrow. He must have been scared those chaps they caught would tell on him, I suppose. Well, that solves that problem. What about eggs and bacon?'

'Splendid. I'm ravenous.' So Manuela would be alone now.

It was a quarter to nine, and they were sitting over coffee, chatting happily, with goodwill towards all men. 'I don't think those army thugs they sent over will have caught up with Daoud,' said Letty, 'but we'd better listen to the nine o'clock news. I'm beginning to get a kick out of this, James. Here we are, safe as houses, while everyone else is standing on his head.' She drew contentedly on her cigar. 'And we can find out what's happening by turning a switch.'

Caudle heard the noise of a car drawing up at the gate, and looking out of the window saw two men getting out of a black Wolsely. 'One of them's that sergeant,' he said urgently, 'and good Lord! The other's the fellow who came to see me in London. Well, we're in the clear. They won't find that bundle in a hurry.'

Letty joined him, watching the two neatly-dressed young men as they came up the flagged garden path. She sensed something ominous in their approach.

When they came in Roberts spoke, and this time with confidence. He now had the support of his C.I. 'I'm sorry to trouble you again, madam, but would you be kind enough to let Sergeant Cobham and me look at your garage?'

'Not unless you have a search warrant, young man. I know my rights as a citizen.'

He produced the warrant and let her read it. 'I must warn you both,' he said sternly, 'that you don't have to answer any questions at this stage, but that if you do your answers may be taken down in writing and used as evidence.' He had a notebook and pencil in his hand.

'All right. But you won't find anything—whatever it is you're looking for.' She took the garage key from her bag. 'We'll go with you.'

Caudle's Austin was parked on the drive. She opened the barn doors wide and exposed the MG, with the van behind it.

'Now, madam,' said Roberts, 'if you'd please run the MG out into the light, and then the van, we can see them properly, can't we? Perhaps Mr Caudle would shift his car forward to make room.'

When this had been done the two officers made a pretence of examining the MG and found nothing of interest. Then they opened the doors at the rear of the van.

'It's quite empty,' said Letty, smiling.

There was still enough daylight to show up the small letters scratched in the paint. Roberts affected surprise. 'What's this, madam?' He took out a torch and leaned into the van. 'It's a word—D-A-O-U-D. How did that get there, I wonder?'

'Perhaps,' put in Cobham, 'the Sheikh

had a diamond ring.'

Caudle was about to speak when Letty stopped him. Her face had flushed darkly. 'I have no idea,' she said coldly.

'And you, Mr Caudle?'

'I'm afraid I can't help you.'

'Then let's try something else,' said Cobham, whose wandering gaze had stopped at Caudle's shoes. 'That's mud, isn't it, sir. And we've had a dry spell lately. Where did you pick that up? It's on your shoes, too, madam.'

They remained silent, and very unhappy.

It took the two Sergeants only a short time to find the muddy patch under the stand-pipe beside the compost heap. A fork had been thrown down near it, and Roberts picked it up and ran his finger down the tines. They were sticky. He took the fork in his hand and gently probed the top layer of kitchen waste and grass cuttings, then more deeply, until he found something solid. Gingerly, he exposed the bundle of overalls and unwrapped it. Cobham retrieved the objects inside the bundle one by one, and laid them out on the path: a flat cap with a visor, two old, repainted number-plates, a pair of dark glasses—and a gun.

Roberts made a dive for it, hooked his pencil through the trigger guard—and only then found that it weighed almost nothing.

'The murder weapon,' commented Letty sarcastically.

Cobham smiled. 'I wonder what happened to the beard. Ah, there it is.' He had spotted the bedraggled scrap of russet hair among some potato peelings, and disentangled it fastidiously. Letty felt as if she had been stripped to her foundation garments in the middle of St Mary's dining hall. She pressed her lips together. Caudle put his arm round her shoulders.

Cobham seemed to have assumed charge. 'Let's go inside and sit down, shall we? Then we can talk it over and give you all the time you want to think up the answers,' he said, smiling. He was a decent sort, thought Letty. For a copper.

The two police officers refused the whisky Caudle offered. He and Letty drank quickly.

'Now, Doctor Hennessy,' said Cobham. 'Let's have the truth, if you please. What exactly happened last night?'

'Your friend said we didn't have to answer if we chose. Well, we do so choose.' It was a tongue-twister, but she got it out.

'Mr Caudle?'

'That is my position, too.'

'It's your part in this affair, sir, that I'm very anxious to get clear. We know that Doctor Hennessy disguised herself, drove a van—falsely purporting to belong to the caterers' firm—into Cranmer Lane at one o'clock this morning, stopped at the back entrance to the Lodge and left again, presumably with Sheikh Daoud inside it. Where were you?'

'Well—'

'Don't answer, James.'

'You drove your own car to Cambridge last night, but didn't come here. So where were you if not in that van?'

'I was in The Grapes, drinking beer until closing time. Then Doctor Hennessy picked me up.'

'No, sir. No one answering to your description was in The Grapes at closing time. Now, we know from statements made by other lady guests that Doctor Hennessy was, for a few minutes, on the ground floor of the Lodge and probably alone, since the caterers and the servants were busy upstairs at that time. She went downstairs with the other ladies, all with the same—er—object in view, but she was the last to return to the drawing-room. She could therefore have unlocked the outside door. But what would be the point of that? The same door was used extensively later in the evening by the caterers before they left. I think she opened that door to let you in. It wasn't until long after the dinner-party had ended that Doctor

Hennessy returned with the van. During that time you must have been concealed in the Sheikh's rooms, and you accompanied him when he left in the van, probably,' added Cobham smiling, 'with that phony gun at his back.'

Letty broke in before Caudle could say anything. 'You've got it all wrong, Sergeant,' she said calmly. 'Sheikh Daoud is not being held under duress. He is quite free to do as he likes.'

'That was just a theory of yours, madam,' said Roberts. 'You offered me that as a fanciful solution.'

'It is true, young man,' said Letty fiercely. 'You have my word.'

'Then what,' asked Roberts pointedly, 'was the point of the gun?'

That stumped her, and Cobham came back into the act. 'Before you answer, madam, I'd better inform you that your connection with Xavier Lopez Suarez alias Juan Santos alias Ramon Gonzalez is known to us.'

'What d'you mean—us?'

'The Special Branch of Scotland Yard, madam,' said Cobham impressively. 'We are convinced that this man, together with his accomplice Manuela San Martin, planned to carry out a kidnapping last night, with the help of some Chilean immigrants who are in custody. At our request Lopez and San Martin have already left for the Argentine, but before he left he was ungallant enough to suggest that you, Doctor Hennessy, were also involved.'

Letty drew a deep breath, and exploded. 'The dirty little double-crosser!'

'I couldn't agree with you more, madam. Now may we have your explanation?'

'The Sheikh wasn't just afraid of being kidnapped,' she said slowly. 'He was in fear for his life. There were two thugs after him.'

Cobham exchanged a puzzled look with Roberts, who said, 'Now, madam, let's see if we can put this together. You mean that the Sheikh knew he was in danger of being assassinated by the two Chilean terrorists we caught, and asked you to help him get away to a safe place?'

Letty smiled; she was much relieved. 'It seems a possible explanation, doesn't it?'

'It does not,' said Cobham loudly. 'The news of the coup in Al Bakhra came during the reception last night. You stayed for the dinner that followed, and left the College after eleven o'clock. At one o'clock you were seen leaving the Cranmer Lane entrance. If Sheikh Daoud only asked for your help during the reception or dinner how could you have returned here, disguised yourself—and the van—repainted the false registration plates and got back to

Cranmer Lane, all in two hours?'

'I can move quickly when I want to,' snapped Letty defiantly.

'And why should the Sheikh have signed his name on that van?' put in Roberts. 'Incidentally, if you were going to help him, why didn't you suggest he should simply wait until everyone was in bed, walk out by the back door and go to the police? For that matter, why didn't he just call in the security guards in the first place? We'd have looked after him.'

Letty looked concerned. Caudle said, 'That's for you to find out. We're not saying any more.'

'All right,' said Cobham. 'But there's one person who can—or cannot—confirm your improbable story.'

'It isn't my story,' protested Letty. 'You've made the whole thing up yourselves.'

'Then tell us the truth.'

'No.'

'Mr Caudle?'

'No.'

'Then we shall have to ask that other person.'

'Who's that?' asked Letty apprehensively.

'Sheikh Daoud. Who else? Let's go and see him right away, shall we?'

Caudle and Letty looked at each other in anguish. Then she firmly shook her head.

'It's his secret. We can't betray it.'

'So you know where he is?'

'Of course we do. We took him there. But we won't tell you. In a day or two he'll come out of hiding, and you'll be sorry you ever suspected us.'

'I wonder, madam,' said Roberts. 'You still haven't explained that gun.' He stood up. 'Doctor Letitia Hennessy, James Caudle, I am arresting you both on suspicion of having taken Sheikh Daoud bin Khalid under duress to an unknown destination for an illegal purpose. You have already been cautioned. You will come with me to Cambridge Central Police Station, and I think you would be wise to bring with you what you need for at least one night.'

The telephone rang. Roberts stopped Letty from answering it and picked up the receiver. 'Detective Sergeant Roberts here ... O.K, Fred, put him through ... Yes, sir. I was about to report that Sergeant Cobham and I have found conclusive evidence that Hennessy and Caudle were involved in last night's kidnapping, and ... But that's impossible, sir. I've already *arrested* them.' A long pause. 'Yes, sir, quite conclusive, the disguise, forged number-plates, and a *gun,* sir. Well, it's a facsimile automatic, sir, Smith and Wesson, but ... I'm sorry, sir. All right. If that's what you want, sir.'

Roberts put down the receiver and turned round, mopping his face. Cobham looked at him questioningly, but his colleague was intent on one thing only, to get out of Letty's earshot. He signed to Cobham and they went towards the door. 'Please sit there for a minute, would you?' he called over his shoulder.

They sat waiting in silence, glumly at first, but gradually relaxing. James realised that Manuela had left, that she was by now somewhere over the Atlantic, and that she wouldn't be coming back. As long as she'd been within reach, in spite of his resolve, she had been a challenge, an exciting, disturbing lure from an alien world. He suddenly felt a longing for the familiar things and the shelter of a known environment—his small house, with its books and hi-fi, and the winery in the cellar, and Pat's loving, anxious face—which he might next see from behind bars. Even teaching and armchair revolution had *some* things to offer. One had to get oneself into perspective.

For a few moments Letty saw herself in a hard, relentless light—an old woman who wasn't as clever as she thought, shown up as a blundering amateur as soon as the professionals appeared on the scene. But then her natural optimism returned. How her colleagues in the Crime Writers

Association would envy her if she were sent down for three months! How about that for inside experience, just what the best thrillers were made of, and what publicity for her books! What a chance, too, to write the next story without any distractions! If the beak gave her six months, even better; she'd have a thriller and half the book on Lawrence Stern under her belt when they opened the gates. She might even let her hair revert to its basic white; who knows, it might turn out to be a really becoming silver by this time.

The two Sergeants came back, looking wary but almost friendly, like Tweedledum and Tweedledee, thought Letty. Roberts said, 'We think it only fair to inform you, madam, Mr Caudle, that Sheikh Daoud is at liberty and has made a statement to the police. I withdraw the charge of kidnapping and apologise for having made it. But there are certain matters the Chief Constable, *himself*, would like to discuss with you both tomorrow morning in his office at ten o'clock precisely.' He could see Letty starting to protest, and hastily dropped his official manner. 'For God's sake, madam, do as he asks. It is in your own interest. He's the top man, you understand, so don't make the mistake of giving him any lip. I'm sorry, but you'll see what I mean. It's sound advice I'm giving you.'

Caudle caught Letty's rebellious eye and held it. 'Thank you, Sergeant,' he said politely. 'We'll both be there.'

As they went out Cobham tried to get in the last word. 'I must borrow one of your thrillers from the library, madam,' he said, with a hint of sarcasm. 'I'm sure that as a *writer* on crime you're a real expert.'

Letty smiled at him sweetly. 'I don't suppose you'd solve one of my mysteries any quicker than you've solved this one. If at all.'

Blast her! It was too true, thought Cobham, and he'd fairly asked for it. He hadn't a clue what had really happened, and from what Roberts had told him he wasn't going to be given a chance of finding out. But he turned and smiled at her. She was a gutsy old dragon. As for Caudle, as far as anyone could know for certain, he'd done damn-all except swan around in the background, looking guilty.

They waited impatiently for the ITN bulletin at ten o'clock. The announcer said there had been further developments in the Al Bakhra situation. 'We know now why Sheikh Daoud found it convenient to disappear so dramatically last night. He was afraid that the Al Bakhra Ambassador in London, a firm supporter of the deposed Sheikh Habib, might prevent him by force from returning to his country. As soon as he heard through friends that His Excellency had flown to voluntary exile in Switzerland he made contact with Brigadier Malik and Colonel Abboud, who had arrived in the new Ruler's personal Trident to see him safely to Al Bakhra. They drove to his home in Bedfordshire, where he had taken refuge, and went with him to Cambridge. There he called on the Chief Constable and gave a full explanation of his movements. Over to Douglas Markham at Gatwick.'

'But those were the two he was trying to avoid,' cried Letty, very agitated. 'They've tricked him somehow.'

The face of Sheikh Daoud, wearing Arab robes and headdress, smiled at them from the screen. Behind him was the Trident, bearing on its nose the green device of Al Bakhra, in which a date palm, an oil rig and the crescent of Islam were cunningly combined. The ITN reporter was speaking to him.

'Would Your Highness tell us the story of the so-called kidnapping?'

'I have already made a statement to the police in Cambridge, but will repeat the main points. First, I apologised to the Chief Constable for having caused so much trouble. I admitted that I had acted precipitately. When I heard last night that my friend Sheikh Ahmed had deposed his father I was overjoyed, but I knew that my Ambassador was obstinately loyal to the former Ruler—he had made that clear at the reception so kindly given for me by the Vice-Chancellor—and I had other enemies in this country who might try to prevent me from returning to Al Bakhra. I needed time.'

'You were in personal danger, Your Highness?'

'I went in fear for my life. That is no exaggeration. There are some quarters in which the progressive plans that His Highness Sheikh Ahmed and I have worked out for the benefit of our country are strongly disliked. I will say no more than that.'

'Such as the American-owned Al Bakhra Oil Company, Sheikh?' asked the reporter eagerly.

'My dear fellow, you can hardly expect me to say yes to such a question. The nationalisation of our oil industry is a matter that the new Ruler will have to consider, like so many others.'

'But how exactly, Your Highness, did you succeed in going to ground so that your enemies could not reach you?'

'Through good friends who came to my help in the nick of time. To them I have a debt to discharge'—the Sheikh's bland glance seemed to fix for a moment on the TV camera—'and I have therefore obtained the Chief Constable's agreement to withhold their names and his assurance that even if they are suspected of any—er—friendly contravention of your laws no action will be taken against them. I wish I could do more.'

Daoud turned and walked towards the steps of the aircraft, where an Arab officer in tropical uniform was standing stiffly at the salute.

Caudle switched off the set and stared at Letty. He was half angry, half tempted to laugh.

She was fairly seething. 'He *conned* us, James. All he wanted to do was sit on the fence until he was sure his pal Ahmed was firmly in the saddle. And you heard what he said about discharging his debt to us. He reckons he's discharged it already. He said there was nothing more he could do. A hundred thou gone for a Burton! And no chance of the fuzz putting us in clink, and all the lovely publicity.' She sighed, and looked across at him affectionately. 'Back to cultivating our bloody gardens, James, for both of us.'

The publishers hope that this book has given you enjoyable reading. Large Print Books are especially designed to be as easy to see and hold as possible. If you wish a complete list of our books, please ask at your local library or write directly to: Dales Large Print Books, Long Preston, North Yorkshire, BD23 4ND, England.

This Large Print Book for the Partially sighted, who cannot read normal print, is published under the auspices of

**THE ULVERSCROFT FOUNDATION**

---

## THE ULVERSCROFT FOUNDATION

. . . we hope that you have enjoyed this Large Print Book. Please think for a moment about those people who have worse eyesight problems than you . . . and are unable to even read or enjoy Large Print, without great difficulty.

You can help them by sending a donation, large or small to:

**The Ulverscroft Foundation,
1, The Green, Bradgate Road,
Anstey, Leicestershire, LE7 7FU,
England.**
or request a copy of our brochure for more details.

The Foundation will use all your help to assist those people who are handicapped by various sight problems and need special attention.

Thank you very much for your help.